M̲ᴀᴋꜱɪM

LAS VEGAS PETROV BRATVA

NICOLE CYPHER

ALSO BY NICOLE CYPHER

This list was compiled at the time of publishing. For a comprehensive list, check out Nicole's website

Gruco Crime Family Series:

HIS PROMISE

HIS PET

HIS PRIZE

HIS PUPPET

HIS PROPERTY

HIS PASSEROTTA

Las Vegas Petrov Bratva:

MAKSIM

ALIK

VITALY

LUKA

ARSENI

NIKITA

Liberating Deceit:

CAGING LIBERTY

TAMING LIBERTY

CLAIMING LIBERTY

The Darker Places Series:

DESIRED

DEPLORABLE

DETHRONED

DEMOLISHED

JULIUS

Soulless Kings MC:

FENDER

JOKER

Standalone Novels:

UNHINGED

VICIOUS KNIGHT - Newsletter exclusive

FREE NEWSLETTER EXCLUSIVE

Vicious Knight

Everyone has secrets...

What do you do to the person who learns yours?

I'll tell you what I did. I went after her.

I **wrecked** her credibility.

I **destroyed** her friendships.

I **ruined** her reputation.

And she responded in the most foolish way possible. She fought back.

My last name might be Knight, but she's the furthest thing from being rescued.

This book contains scenes and situations that may be triggering for some. Reader discretion is advised.

1

ELIRA

I'm still wearing the dress.

It's no longer the bright white that stuck out so vividly among the others on the rack, calling to me like it was my destiny to wear it. I knew it would fit perfectly even before I tried it on, just had that feeling.

I've always known I had an average body, *too* average even, but the dress somehow accentuated curves I don't have, flattering me in ways that have never made me feel so beautiful.

Now, wearing the same dress, I've never felt so ugly.

Whimpering pulls my attention to the corner of the cargo space, but I don't allow my eyes to linger on the girl. She's having a private moment, one all of us have had at one time or multiple since we've been in this space.

There were a lot more moments in the beginning. Most of us have run out of tears by now, but every time the back doors open to the cargo truck, the shaking intensifies. That hasn't happened in what feels like hours, the rumbling of the truck constant, so it must be coming soon.

I wish I knew where we were. Or where we're going. Or knew this country at all.

James, my fiancé and the whole reason I agreed to make the illegal trek to America, lives in New York State, which must be hundreds of kilometres away.

Which means he can't save me. Nobody can save me. Nobody even knows me.

The woman next to me chants words to herself that I don't understand, but I think the language is Russian. Everyone has been too frightened to speak, so even the foreign words sound like a courageous bit of comfort.

"Do you speak English?" I ask. I don't bother asking if she speaks Albanian.

"*Shh*," someone hisses.

The Russian woman doesn't answer. Instead, she quiets, the universal *shh* one thing we all understand.

It's dark in here, only slivers of light shining in through cracks in the exterior, but when the door opens, we've caught glimpses of each other. We're a melting pot of kidnapped girls. It makes me wonder if our kidnappers simply camped along the Mexico-US border, waiting for international girls, vulnerable and alone, to snatch.

Or maybe they weren't at the border like I was. Maybe they snatched these girls from an airport. Maybe they have all kinds of ways of stealing freedom.

It's a sick sort of irony for this to happen in America when Americans seem to have such warped opinions of my country. My people welcome foreigners with open arms, not … this.

My throat hurts as my heart pangs. My dress, *the* dress, sticks to my skin with sweat and filth, mocking me, reminding me what a stupid girl I am to ever think I should leave Albania. That there could ever be a better life for me somewhere else. Somewhere like here.

What. A. Fool.

The rumble of the truck eases as we slow, pulling my eyes open. I wrap my arms tightly around my knees and stare at the cargo door, waiting for the inevitable.

Will it be my turn?

Will I be chosen this time?

Do I *want* to be?

I'm not sure. I'm terrified, already my hands are trembling before I even hear their voices, but I think breathing in the smell of urine and fear, drowning in the unknown, must be worse than the fate on the other side of that door.

Or not. Either way, I'll find out. If it isn't my turn now, it will be soon.

The hoarse voice of the driver floats into the cargo space just before he bangs three times on the door. The sound is so jarring that I flinch, scooting inches away.

My mother's voice enters my head, and I use it to drown out the sound of the metal door grinding open, basking the dark space in blinding light.

Be a good girl, Elira. You know what men want.

She told me this at the airport when she thought she was sending me off to a better life as a betrothed woman. Even so, there was nervousness in her eyes that didn't feel like it belonged in a fairy-tale ending. She must've known even happiness comes at a cost.

You know what men want.

Except I don't know what these men want. Not really, not beyond the obvious. I don't know anything, and that scares me worse than the guns they carry.

Even squinting, I can only make out a man's silhouette as he climbs into the cargo space, the light behind him too bright for my sensitive eyes. His hand lifts to cover his nose as he coughs.

"Jesus Christ, how long have you had this load?"

The driver cackles at the new man's repulsion for us. We're nothing to him. Less than nothing to him. Our filth is somehow more of a burden for him than it is for us.

"About a day and a half. Only three stops left."

The new man shakes his head. Slowly, my eyes adjust. I can see his thick eyebrows and the blue of his shirt.

"*Up*," he growls. I don't know if he's talking to me, but I stand, my spine rigid.

The Russian woman stands as well, and as he steps up to each of us, I have to look away. He has an evil in his eyes that I didn't hear in his voice, and now I can say with certainty that I don't want to be chosen. I want to live in this cargo space until I die.

He grasps my jaw, roughly jerking my head up to look at him, and my breath stutters, but I don't cry out like I want to. I can feel how wide my eyes are and imagine how weak I must look to him, how vulnerable. I wonder how much he likes it.

He looks down at my dress, *the* dress, and he must not see the magic it did for me because his lip curls, and he lets go of my jaw, moving on to the Russian girl.

I slowly lower to the floor, not making a sound in case it reminds him I exist, and when he makes his choice, I hate myself for being so relieved it isn't me.

* * *

HOURS PASS.

I don't know how many. Time is impossible to measure in the thinning space, but by the time the door opens again, it's dark outside. Last time the door opened to reveal the night sky, it let in a cool breeze, so I cross my arms in anticipation. No breeze comes. It's just as hot as it was before.

4

Something is different this time. I can sense it without pinpointing exactly what it is, and I think the others can too.

We're on edge. There's only one stop after this, so the time for wondering who will be next is over. It's all our turn now. The four of us make up the last pick of the litter, the unwanted ones, and I can only imagine this isn't a good place to be.

When the sliding door is fully opened, the driver stands with his hand hovering in the air. Two other shadows are perched on either side of him, and when a flashlight he's holding clicks on, the little I see of the men disappears as I duck my head. The beam glides over us, blinding our sensitive eyes one by one.

"*Out.*"

Tension squeezes my shoulder blades, but I don't move. I won't be the first to obey the command, not when I don't know what's waiting for us.

The driver growls before banging the flashlight against the side of the truck, startling every one of us who've become accustomed to the silence. "*Out.*" He's louder this time. More insistent, and it occurs to me that I don't know the number of women in here who speak English, if any. I also don't know how long until the driver becomes violent.

The smell of urine gets stronger as a girl starts to cry, and I throw a glance that way, not knowing what I hope to convey but wishing I had said something sooner. That we would've acted like we were in this together instead of hoping ill fate to fall on each other to spare ourselves.

I stand, straightening *the* dress for reasons I'm unsure of, then slowly make my way out of the truck. The driver grows impatient with me, his hand waving in another universal *hurry up* gesture.

As I climb off the truck, I lock eyes with a man I wish I

5

hadn't, making that mistake the second time today. He smiles ever so slightly, but it isn't a kind smile. There's no warmth, no welcoming.

The driver yanks me by my arm, throwing me between the two men, then he roughly pulls on the two girls who've chosen to follow me. He has to go inside the cargo space to retrieve the other girl, and I busy myself taking in my surroundings as a distractor from the screams.

I can feel eyes on me, but I don't look the man's way. Instead, I look out at … dirt. More dirt than I've ever seen in my life. It stretches more kilometres than I can count, and if I didn't know better, I'd say it led to the edge of the Earth. The strange theories about the Earth being flat must have come from people who live here.

Where are we? Mars?

I search for trees, for water, for any signs of life, but there's nothing. There looks to be hills in the distance, but even those look barren, no green in sight. It makes sense, I guess, when I think of how weird the air feels. I've never been outside of Albania, but I've heard the air is more humid there than most places. This is the opposite. There isn't any moisture here to spare for the plants, let alone for the air.

"In a line," Driver snaps after shoving the last girl onto the dirt.

"Do they all speak English?" the man who smiled at me asks. I can still feel his eyes on me. Instead of looking at his face, I stare at his bright red shoes, moving when Driver shoves me into another girl to manually form the line himself. I don't know if I should pretend I don't speak English or not, I just get the sense that I shouldn't stand out. Not to these men.

"Hablo Anglés?" he asks, clapping his hands in front of the woman he brought out of the truck. He not only butchered the pronunciation of that sentence, but he is also speaking Spanish to a Filipina woman. I've never seen a man this ignorant.

She nods and cries when he slaps the side of her head.

"Yes," she says.

He moves to the next, and when he gets to me, I hesitate. I don't know why. I don't know why I think it matters, it just feels like it does. Like I should keep everything hidden that I possibly can.

"*Nuk flas anglisht.*"

"What?" Driver's eyebrows bunch as if he thinks he didn't hear me correctly.

I shake my head like I don't understand. "*Nuk flas anglisht.*"

When he slaps the side of my head, I cringe and raise my hands. "*Nuk flas anglisht! Nuk flas anglisht!*"

Driver takes a step back to address the two new men. "All but that one."

"Is she a virgin?" the man who smiled at me asks. I don't see him point or look to see where his eyes land, but I know he's referring to me.

My skin crawls hearing that question, little bugs worming their way beneath the surface. I can hear my mother's voice again.

Be a good girl, Elira. You know what men want.

"Can't exactly ask, now can we?"

"You didn't check for a hymen?" He sounds disappointed. I can hear the frown in his voice.

"She's fresh off the boat, my guy. She hasn't been checked for shit."

"What about you?" the other man asks, grasping the Filipina's chin.

I don't see or hear how she responds because when a

warm finger snakes beneath one strap of my dress, I jolt upright, my head snapping to face my unwelcome admirer.

He glides his finger up and down, sending the bugs beneath my skin squirming, and it takes all my willpower not to scream or try to run. We're already out in what must be the middle of a desert. It would be too easy to kill me if they wanted to.

His finger moves to my mouth next, and instead of recoiling, I close my eyes and hold my breath while letting him brush my chapped bottom lip. When he stops, I open my eyes.

"Hmmm." His lips twist to one side like he's thinking while his eyes trail me. He looks like I'm a menu and he's trying to decide what he wants to eat. "My boss might be a little ticked, but I think you'll make a nice addition to his collection."

He smiles at me, revealing a slightly chipped front tooth that would be endearing if he wasn't a monster.

"I think you'll be a nice addition to *my* collection," he says, his voice quieter as he tucks my hair behind my ear.

I don't recoil, nor do I respond to words I'm not supposed to understand. I don't know why he says them. Maybe to scare me, maybe to hear himself speak.

"How much?" he asks the driver who's been speaking with the other man. He turns his head my way while I bow mine. Blood rushes past my ears.

This is it.

This is the next step. The *first* step, really.

I am about to be this man's whore. This man's boss's whore.

When my eyes sting, I close them, telling myself it may not be that bad. That in a way, I was coming here prepared to be someone's whore, even if it was under the guise of marriage.

8

It could be okay. It could be… It could be…

It could be worse than death.

"Thirty thousand."

My heart pangs as the man speaks with the finality of a judge slamming a gavel.

"Sold."

2

ELIRA

*O*nce again, my world is bathed in darkness, only now the rumble of the truck is a distant memory I long for. Music plays so loud wherever we are that I squint, seeing nothing through the black bag my buyer has put over my head.

He cut the bindings around my wrists when he hauled me out of the trunk of his car, so I have one arm wrapped around my stomach while he holds the other, guiding me.

Is this a party?

Where are we?

I almost ask, but I can't. I don't think he'd tell me anyway.

Will he be angry when he finds out I lied about not speaking English?

Should I ever tell the truth?

How much will he reveal in front of me if he thinks I won't understand?

So many questions. *Too* many. I try to focus on what I do know, on learning the man next to me. He's ... evil. How could he not be?

Do I know anything else?

I think for a moment, my mind spinning, searching for information that may be important. All I can think of is for a guy who can afford to buy women, it's strange that he can't afford a good dentist.

My foot hits something, and I gasp.

"Up," he commands over the music, tugging on my arm.

I cautiously toe the metal thing that I hit, but I have little time to figure out what it is before Chipped-tooth drags me off the floor. My feet seek to ground me and find the metal piece. Finally, it registers that we're at a staircase.

Communication would really come in handy right now.

His touch made me recoil when he first grabbed me, but now I find myself leaning into him, begging him for guidance.

When my toe collides with metal, I cry out and try to pause, but he doesn't let me. It isn't until we reach flat ground a few moments later that I whimper my relief, pulling away from Chipped-tooth to create as much distance as his grasp will allow once again.

He knocks three times on a door we must be standing in front of, but it doesn't open, and he doesn't knock again. We stand silently, the music still loud but distant while I count back from forty in my head for the sake of slowing my mind.

Eleven, ten, nine, eight, seven...

"Come in," a voice calls after what feels like an unusual amount of time.

A knob twists and the door creaks open right before Chipped-tooth shoves me forward, my hands flying in front of me to catch empty space. I manage to right myself, standing hunched with my arms crossed over my chest, itching to remove the bag.

I don't have to wait long. Chipped-tooth rips it off my head, revealing three men staring at me. Two stand on either side of a desk that the third man sits at, his feet propped on top as he leans back in his chair with a cane balanced on his lap that he seems too young to have.

Do you remember when I said I shouldn't have made eye contact with those men? That I could see evil?

This man... One nanosecond of eye contact has me lowering my head to the floor, hoping my hair will double as an invisibility cloak.

It takes less time for me to figure out that this is Chipped-tooth's boss than it did for me to figure out the staircase.

He reeks of malicious authority. This room reeks of it. Now that the bag is off my head, it's like I can smell it throughout the whole building, along with the stench of the truck that I seemed to have carried with me.

I don't dare look at the boss, but I do peek at the man on his left. By the way his nose is wrinkled, I'd say he's noticed my stench as well. Or he's just disgusted with me.

I almost look away, but a scar running across his neck catches my attention, and it's hard to command my eyes from it.

Did someone try to cut his throat?

Who are these people?

"Pakhan Nikita," Chipped-tooth says, and I can't be sure, but I think he does some sort of weird bow. "I hope I'm not interrupting?"

Nobody answers. Chipped-tooth waits maybe five seconds before going on.

"I thought you might want to see your new girl." He bunches the back of my dress and uses it to propel me forward. I gasp, stumbling before catching myself on the edge of the desk. "She's fresh from overseas. I don't know what country, but I think there's a chance she could be a virgin. I thought you'd appreciate the first taste."

The first taste.

The first.

The first of many.

I bite the inside of my cheek to keep from crying and stare down at the smooth mahogany. My hands threaten to shake, so I grip the desk tighter, not standing up, not even moving. If I move, I might try to run, as stupid as that'd be. I don't know if I'd be able to help myself.

"The first taste…" Nikita says, his voice even. He laughs, but I don't get the sense that he's amused. "The first taste of what? Crusted pussy? I could smell her as soon as you walked into the building. Is this what you'd like me to taste?"

"No, sir." Chipped-tooth sounds nervous, and I look behind me to see him raising his hands, a chuckle coming up his throat like he's trying to play this off. If I could sink into a hole in the earth, I would. "I will clean her up first, of course."

"I don't want you to clean her up, Anton. I want you to be smart." He taps his head to emphasize his words. "I want you to *know* not to bring me dirty girls. I want you to not waste my money on dirty bitches you buy out of the back of a fucking *semi*." He seemed relatively calm before, but now his face darkens, casting a storm cloud over the room.

He drags one foot off his desk, then the other before slowly standing to limp his way around it, not bothering to use the cane. As soon as I see which direction he chooses, I go in the opposite, nearly bumping into the only man left I haven't studied.

I gape at him now, wide-eyed as I wait to see if he'll lash out for me being so close, but he doesn't look at me. His arms are crossed over his broad chest while he watches his boss, his blue eyes serious, his strong jaw set. His neatly cut blond hair and gray slacks would make him look like a businessman if it weren't for the bulging muscles that protest through the white fabric of his shirt or the firm look on his face that could hardly be considered charming. Even lacking the scar across his neck like the other man, he looks just as deadly. I consider moving away from him, but away from him means closer to the boss, so I stay put while watching what happens next.

"You *think* she could be a virgin. You don't know what country she's from. Do you know what that tells me, Anton?"

Anton's Adam's apple bobs as he swallows. He shakes his head.

"That tells me she could just as easily be someone else's used up whore. That frustrates me, Anton, it really does, but what frustrates me even more is that you came to me lacking information that you could've gotten if you'd just. Asked. The. Cunt." He smiles, but there's nothing friendly about it. When he looks at me, I duck. "What country are you from, *darling?*"

The way he says darling somehow sounds more offensive than cunt.

Should I answer?

The idea of lying to this man feels very different from lying to Anton. It feels dangerous. It feels *stupid*.

I'm just about to open my mouth when Anton speaks for me.

"She doesn't speak English, sir."

As Nikita's eyes close, the energy in the room turns deadly. Anton messed up. Badly. Badly enough that right now I'd rather be me than him, which is really saying something.

A slow, insidious breath blows past Nikita's lips, and when he opens his eyes, he looks this way. I freeze. My instinct is to look down, but our eyes don't meet. He's looking above me.

"Maksim, you're a young, single man. You're quite accustomed to fucking whores, yes?"

There's a pause as the question hangs in the air, then finally, "Occasionally, yes."

"Would you like to fuck the used-up, grimy cunt of a bitch who doesn't understand your language well enough for you to relay how you like your dick sucked?"

"No, sir."

Nikita nods once like he agrees. "Me neither."

He turns back to Anton in a swift movement that confuses me for a moment, and I squint, watching Anton's black shirt get wet with something. His eyes go wide, and he looks down like he's just as confused and surprised as I am.

My eyes find the short blade poking from Nikita's grip just before he jams it into Anton's gut, again and again.

I cover my hand over my mouth as I scream, backing into Maksim only to jolt forward. My eyes instinctively find the door, but I think Maksim can sense it because he lays a hand on my shoulder and guides me backward.

Nikita doesn't stop stabbing. Blood pours from Anton's mouth that he never had a chance to plead from, and his eyes are dead, but Nikita holds him up by his shirt, seesawing the knife into him like an absolute fucking psychopath.

I bite my cheek so hard I taste blood and force my eyes to close but then open them immediately afterward. This is not a sight I want to see, but closing my eyes on a man like this is terrifying. I couldn't look at him when I first walked in here, but now I need to see him at all times just to make sure he's out of reach.

This man is my owner.

This man.

I wish I'd been chosen by the one before. Or any of the men before.

I wish I'd never left Albania.

I press my palm against my mouth when I sob, trying to quiet myself, but it's uncontrollable. It isn't just my hands shaking, it's my entire body. My heart alternates between beating fast and stopping altogether, unable to choose between the two.

When Nikita finally lets go of Anton's shirt, his corpse crumples in a heap on the ground, his head turned my way so those dead eyes can stare at me. There's no evil in them anymore. There's nothing.

Nikita tosses the knife onto the floor, next to a puddle of blood staining the carpet, and as soon as he turns around, I back myself into Maksim. I can't help it. Maksim could have a knife that's bigger, deadlier. He could be just as disgusted with me.

But it seems impossible that any man could be as bad as Nikita.

Instead of granting me any sort of sanctuary, Maksim's hand slips from my shoulder, and he walks around me to a closet, his gait calm and confident, no sign that he has any reservations about what just happened.

I check out the guy with the scar on his neck. He's leaning against a wall with a foot propped against it, his posture relaxed.

Neither man cares about what just happened.

Neither care about what will happen to me.

What *will* happen to me?

I back against the wall and sit on the carpet, pulling my knees to my chest like I did in the cargo space, trying to make myself invisible now more than ever.

Maksim brings a roll of plastic out of a closet and spreads it out on the floor before proceeding to roll the body onto it, wrapping it up like a burrito. It's the most sterile, unfeeling thing I've ever seen anyone do. Like flossing teeth or setting a cruise control.

The guy with the scar leaves, and although I don't know anything about him, I wish he'd stay just so there's one more person to hold Nikita's attention who isn't me.

Nikita stands facing away from Maksim and cracks his neck. I keep waiting for him to remember that I'm here. Keep thinking that I'm next.

My eyes move to the big roll of plastic. There's still plenty left. They keep it in that closet just for occasions like this.

I want to puke.

My eyes dart to the door when it opens, revealing Scar's return along with two other men, one carrying a bucket. Water sloshes out of it when he sets it on the floor next to the blood.

Bucket Guy crouches and pulls a sponge from the soapy water but stops when Nikita makes a disapproving, humming sound.

"Let the girl make herself useful."

Bucket Guy exchanges a look with the other new man, and together they pick up the plastic-wrapped body and exit the room.

I stay where I am, pretending I don't know what he wants me to do. The smell of blood is taking over the smell of the truck, and the thought of the man's insides being on my hands makes my nausea twice as bad.

I swallow down bile, closing my eyes.

And it's a mistake because I was right, closing my eyes on Nikita is a bad idea.

His hand is in my hair, yanking before I have a chance to register his closeness, and I whimper as he hauls me to the blood stain. My hands sink into red goo when he drops me, and finally, the nausea wins. I turn my head to the side and dry heave, nothing in my stomach to come out.

Nikita kicks my leg, not hard but not a nudge, just enough to make it clear to the non-English-speaking foreign girl that he won't put up with me messing around. I wipe saliva onto my shoulder, tasting dirt and salt, and pick up the sponge to get to work on the carpet.

My lungs burn from excursion as I vigorously scrub and try not to cry out. Not out of remorse or sadness, but out of fear. Pure, horrible fear that I didn't realize deserved a voice.

They talk while I'm scrubbing like I'm not even here. Like nothing has happened. Something about a deal happening tomorrow night at an airstrip. They switch back and forth between speaking English and what I'm growing more and more confident is Russian. I know a little Greek, a smidge Italian, nearly no Russian, but I'm pretty sure 'blyad' means whore, and it's been said several times now.

The water has turned a bright red color that reminds me of the late Anton's shoes, and every time I dip the sponge, I question if I'm doing more harm than good. It needs to be refreshed, but I'll scrub this entire carpet red before I open my mouth.

"This bitch is taking too long," Nikita says, sounding bored. "I'm going home. When she's finished, you both can do the same." I feel him draw near, so I scrub harder, fighting the instinct to freeze.

"What do you want us to do with her?" Scar, or *Roman* as I've come to learn, asks.

Nikita pauses behind me, and now I can't fight my instinct to freeze. Even my lungs quit working. Not my heart, though. It beats fast and hard, pulsing in my temples.

"Maksim, you've been a good boy, lately... You keep her." Nikita's cane presses against my ass that's perched in the air while I bend over the blood, and he shoves me so I fall forward, knocking me into the bucket so watered-down blood sloshes onto my face and chest.

My lungs tighten

as the cocktail drips from my hair, my shaking sending the drops flying. I stay perfectly still and don't dare get up while he's behind me.

"I'm sure she cleans up fine," Nikita says. "And who knows, maybe Anton was right about her being a virgin."

He uses his cane to lift my dress up my thighs, making my teeth sink into my bottom lip to keep myself from screaming. "I'd have her tested first."

There's a pause before Maksim replies. "Thank you, sir." He still sounds sterile.

I'm not even a nice *gift* let alone 'product.' I don't know that I'm capable of feeling like less of a human being than I am in this moment.

Nikita removes his cane, allowing my dress to fall, and when he leaves, I let my lip go free and sit up, facing away from the two men.

I know I should get to cleaning right away, but I take just a moment. Just a moment to feel truly, terribly sorry for myself.

This is so much worse than any nightmare I ever could've imagined.

Someone behind me laughs.

I hunch forward as my muscles tense, bloodied water seeping from the sponge as I squeeze.

"Don't," Maksim scowls before Roman has said anything. Roman must've been the one to laugh. *Because Maksim getting stuck with me is so funny.*

But I'm... I'm *only* Maksim's?

I'm not a prostitute for others as well?

"I didn't say anything," Roman replies.

I allow a few more seconds to pass before I push the sponge into the carpet, smearing the blood my senses have become accustomed to. I'm one with it now.

"Out of curiosity..." Roman's tone is full of humor. "Are you flattered or insulted?"

Instead of answering, Maksim starts this way, so I pick up my pace, scrubbing at the blood with as much intensity as I had when Nikita was in the room. I don't know why I ever let up.

When he walks past me, I peek up at his huge form. I registered that he was tall before, but now that his size actually matters, his broad shoulders seem to expand. Muscles ripple through a white shirt with every step, and they're so expansive that the shirt doesn't start to slacken until midway down his back, cutting off diagonally to hint at the V-shape formed by hours spent in a gym. Or worse, a ring.

This man is dangerous. He lacks Nikita's aura but compensates with strength and size. He wouldn't need a knife to kill me, probably wouldn't even think to use a weapon beyond those bare hands.

I lower my eyes and scrub the carpet harder.

He returns from the closet carrying something, but I don't look to see what it is until he sets it down beside me. It's a large plastic bottle with no label. I look up at him, waiting for him to tell me what it is, to give me some kind of instruction, but it occurs to me that he won't because he doesn't think I'd understand him. Obviously, he wants me to use the stuff on the carpet.

He picks up the bucket of water and leaves while I unscrew the cap to the mystery bottle that isn't a mystery for long. I put my nose to it, but it really isn't necessary. The ammonia smell is so strong, I turn my head away and slap the cap back on the bottle.

Roman laughs behind me, and before I can think about it, I toss a glare his way.

His eyebrows raise as a smile blooms, making me aware of the look I'm giving him. I snap my head forward and pray he doesn't hurt me for that.

Can he hurt me?

Is he allowed?

Would he have to get Maksim's permission?

How does this work?

My shoulders hunch as Maksim returns, fresh bucket of water in hand, and when he sets it in front of me, I get to work, pouring a small amount of ammonia in before soaking up the blood. It works so much better.

"I think I like your girl," Roman tells Maksim. "Or as Nikita calls her, your *used-up, grimy cunt of a bitch who doesn't understand your language well enough for you to relay how you like your dick sucked.*"

"Are you trying to set me off?" Maksim asks with a hint of anger.

Roman laughs. "Come on, it's a funny punishment, and you know it. It could be worse."

"You understand the problem this causes for me." Now Maksim sounds serious. *Really* serious. I am very obviously a burden for him.

Is it too much to hope that he'll simply let me go?

"Just don't take her home," Roman suggests. "Keep her at Hugh's. Or my place." That last part sounds like a joke. I *hope* he's joking. But I don't know who Hugh is.

Why can't he just let me go? I'm an illegal immigrant in this country, and these people obviously have a lot of money. They probably *own* the police, so I won't be going to them for help. I'll head straight to New York to find James, then I'll figure out a way home. Fuck America.

"And look like I'm rejecting a gift from the Pakhan? He's punishing me for having a meager relationship with a Gruco. The last thing to do when he believes my loyalty to the Bratva is compromised is reject him personally." I peek over my shoulder to see Maksim wave his hand dismissively. "You're right, it's a punishment. Not the first, not the last. I will handle it."

"You could just kill her," Roman suggests, making my

spine stiffen. I should look away, but I can't. Not until I see Maksim's reaction. "Say she tried to run."

Maksim rubs his thumb over his chin as his eyes drift to me. When they find mine, I don't look away. Don't move. We stare into each other's eyes, me quietly panicking, him weighing Roman's words, thinking I understand none of them.

He's going to kill me.

Slowly, I face forward and will my heart to slow, trying to calm the panic. I close my eyes and scrub leisurely, just enough to keep them from yelling at me while I think.

Where did that knife go?

Opening my eyes, I glance around but don't see it. Did Maksim pick it up when he took care of the body?

He must have.

Does he still have it on him?

Maybe. If he doesn't, he probably has some kind of weapon.

Could I get to it? Could I get to anything?

I reposition myself so I can see the men while I clean. First, I check out Maksim, searching for a gun holster more out of fear than preparation. I don't actually know how to use a gun. When I don't find anything, I move on to the room, and it doesn't take long before I spot the knife Nikita used on the desk.

My eyes lock onto it, garnering all my attention to the point that my movements seize. I have to force myself to look away.

If he's going to kill me, I have no other choice.

I have to kill him first.

3

MAKSIM

I do not enjoy killing the innocent.

I am not a sadist. I do not think of myself as cruel. I don't kick dogs, I don't leave babies to cry, I don't even turn off my porch light on Halloween. I buy full-size candy bars to leave in a bowl even when I know they'll be grabbed by the same two or three kids.

I am not inherently a bad man. I am a man who does bad things when times call for it. Times like tonight.

The Albanian girl sits with her hands tucked beneath her in the passenger seat of my car. I know that she's Albanian because before we left the warehouse, I showed her a map so she could point to her home country, far, far away from here. I pity her, I really do. I don't know how she wound up here or why, but it's a long way to travel just to die in the desert.

We're thirty miles away from the nearest sign of civilization, but I keep going a few more miles. There's a hilly spot I have in mind that reminds me of what the Mexican border looks like, at least in the dark, and I'm guessing she crossed from Mexico to get here. She was in a truck for a day, at least, so she must've been on the far end of the border.

When I see the familiar turn, I take it and drive the two miles in until we're close to the hill. Then I put the car in park. The girl doesn't look at me, but her breaths are fast and shallow. She's terrified. She has been since the moment I saw her, but I think she can guess what's about to happen. Still, she doesn't cry or beg. I haven't heard her speak a peep of Albanian yet.

"Relax," I coo, placing my hand on her shoulder. She jumps, her head whipping toward me, her eyes wide.

I smile and hold up my free hand while massaging her shoulder with the other. "It's okay. I'm not going to hurt you."

I'm a bastard, I know.

Pulling my hand away, I shut off my car and climb out of the vehicle, letting my smile fall as I take a long breath.

I walk around and carefully open the passenger door, extending my hand for the girl to take. None of my movements are hurried or rough. Everything about this must be suspicious, but I let none of my intentions show in my actions.

You could see it as cruel, but I don't want her to know what hit her. I want her to die with hope, not fear. Not looking down a barrel, but at salvation that only exists in her head.

It's either cruel or merciful. I'm really not sure which.

She lets the suspicion show in her furrowed brow as her eyes dart over my face before carefully, she takes my hand to let me help her out of the car. I pull out my phone and bring up Google translator so I can type a message in her language.

Just over that hill is the Mexican border. There's a man on the other side waiting to take you home.

I scan the translated text then turn my phone around so she can see. Her eyes eagerly dance between me and the screen. Several seconds go by without her responding, like she either doesn't understand or doesn't know how to process it.

I'm leaning toward thinking it's the former when her body flings into mine, her arms wrapping around my midsection.

"Faleminderit," she cries, and although I don't speak the language, I know it means *thank you*. She sobs against my chest, squeezing me tightly while guilt knocks on my conscience.

Okay, *now* I regret the merciful tactic. I should've just killed her. This feels more cruel than anything.

A sharp pain stabs my side, making my arms wrapped around the girl tense and my thoughts vanish.

I look down at the blade in her hand, dripping with blood, and before I have a chance to respond, she thrusts it into my side a second time.

My mouth opens, but sound doesn't come out because she pulls it out and does it again, then a fourth time, her quick movements reminding me of Nikita, and finally it occurs to me that I should let her the fuck go to get the little devil off me.

"Fuck," I yell, shoving her backward. She falls, but so do I. One knee hits the ground while I touch the five fucking stab wounds seeping blood. The blade is short—Nikita enjoys slow deaths—so the cuts aren't *that* deep, but bleeding out is a possibility.

Fucking *cunt*.

I don't get out my gun. Not yet. I have dealt with so many people, no number comes to mind, so I fully predict that this bitch will try to run away.

Imagine my surprise when she comes at me. *Again*.

"Stop!" I yell, catching her wrist when she goes to stab my neck. The knife drops as I squeeze, but I let her go when she kicks relentlessly until I'm on the ground, shielding my face with my hands. *"Jesus Christ."* I go for my gun, but she screams like a fucking gladiator and kicks me in my face, bloodying my nose.

I grab her ankle when she goes to do it a second time and viciously yank so she falls flat on her back on the hard desert earth.

"Stop," I repeat, climbing on top of her and pinning her wrists above her head while capturing her legs between mine. "No more."

She spits in my face, making me whip my head to the side while her saliva trickles down my chin. "Fuck you, you fucking American pig."

A growl barrels up my chest as I grip her throat and squeeze with fury. It's dark out, but in the moonlight, I watch her face turn red, watch her struggle for breath.

It could've been easier than this. Different. Less pain. Less fighting. But maybe she wanted it this way. A warrior's death.

It's how I'd want to go out.

A sick sort of respect passes through me as I'm choking the life out of this woman. This woman who speaks English, who heard my conversation with Roman, who knew I was taking her out here to kill her. Who had the spine to take the knife and the fucking *balls* to use it on me.

What a goddamn woman.

Something stabs my chest, not a knife this time, and I look down to see my gun in the girl's hand.

I laugh. "You have to cock it, baby."

She struggles for breath, clawing at me with one hand while holding the gun with the other. I debate securing her hands, but I don't. She's almost out.

Or at least I thought so.

My gun crashes against my head—another way you can use it, I guess—and I roll off the girl, grunting with pain. I

26

press my hand to my temple while my side pulses with sharp aches.

The girl's gasping fills my ears, and a second later, my gun cocks.

I glare at her as her trembling hands point my gun at me. I don't doubt for a second that she could pull that trigger. I've doubted too many fucking times now, I won't do it again.

But I can see the safety on.

She doesn't know it, but she's fucked. If I don't get on the road soon, I'll be fucked too.

My phone fell on the ground in the struggle, and she seeks it out now. Who exactly is she planning on calling?

I point beside my car's tire. "My phone's right there."

Her eyes train on me. "Get it."

"Why?"

"Because if you don't, I'll kill you."

I huff. "What were you trying to do before?"

"What were *you* trying to do before?" The accusation is clear in her eyes even if it wasn't in her voice. "We're not at the border. There isn't some man on the other side of that hill waiting to take me home."

"Yeah, you got me there, princess."

"Do I look like a princess?" she yells, *screams*, nearly manically as the gun shakes. She's been through hell. All nine circles.

"You need me," I say, my tone more serious. "You have no license, no passport, no money. You know no one. You can't go to the police because they'll bring you straight to the Bratva, so where exactly are you going to go? Do you know what state you're in? Do you even know how to drive a car?"

"The phone," is all she says, holding out her hand. I feel like the roles have reversed. I could take that gun right out of her hand and put a bullet in her head, but her stone-cold face is just so ... I don't know. Hot.

27

I need to see where she's going with this.

I pick up my phone, unlock it, then hold it out. When she goes to take it, I tug it back. "First, tell me who you're going to call."

"Give me the phone."

"Not yet."

Her lips thin, then, after a moment, they crack with a tremble. "My mother," she says, her voice breaking. "I just want to tell her I'm okay. I promised to call…"

Ah.

She wants to call Mommy… Not quite a survivalist move, but I do feel my chest tighten with pity.

"I don't want to kill you if I don't have to," she says like she's scared. It's another 'give me the phone or else' threat, but she manages to make it sound sweet.

She's holding the gun, but I doubt she has much faith in her ability to survive. I was telling the truth, and she knows it. She needs me.

I'm not planning on actually letting her make a call. There would be no real consequences for it because what the hell could her Albanian mother possibly do even if she told her she'd been kidnapped? But still. It seems like a bad idea.

The girl, a moment ago sweet and patient-seeming, snatches the phone from my grasp while I'm still considering how far I'm willing to go to humor her, and she quickly backs up several steps, no sign of slowing down.

"That's far enough," I snap.

The sad, scared little girl she showed me disappears as she crouches, chucking my phone to the ground.

What the fuck?

She rears the gun over her shoulder, and all at once, I get what she's about to do.

"Don't!"

I've hobbled two steps toward her, my hand holding my

side, before she slams the butt of the gun down to shatter the phone's screen.

"What the hell is wrong with you?" I bark, stopping when she stands while aiming the gun at me. I would kill her now if I genuinely didn't want to know.

Her shoulders square, her hands steadier than before. She really does think she's in control. "Now you need me too."

What?

The question must be written in my expression because she goes on. "We drove a long time to get here. How confident are you that you'll make it to a hospital before passing out?"

"Very."

She tilts her head to the side. "Then you're a fool."

I laugh, but the pain at my side is at the forefront of my mind. I've had many, many injuries, and she's right. I had every intention of calling someone for help. I can't drive like this. Not the whole way.

I need her. Right now, it looks like I need her more than she needs me.

Or not.

"I can get to a phone in thirty miles. I could kill you in less than ten seconds. The punctures aren't that deep; I have time."

"How can you kill me if I have the gun?" she asks, her voice full of authority.

I'm quiet for several seconds while I stare her down. "You're right. You'd better go ahead and kill me first while you have the chance." I take a step toward her, only for her to take a step back.

"Stop."

I continue creeping her way.

"Stop or I'll shoot!" she yells, growing panicky. She either agrees that she needs me, or she's lost the nerve to end a life.

I don't respond, nor do I slow my pace. I want to see if she'll do it, if she'll pull the trigger.

Her face pinches with anger as she points the gun just to the right of my head and clicks, trying to fire off a warning shot. Her eyes widen as soon as the click sounds, and she backpedals, horrified that her metal friend failed her.

"No!" she screams when I chase her down, securing her in my arms and squeezing until she stops thrashing. The gun falls on the dirt, adding to the dust cloud she's creating.

"*Enough,*" I growl in her ear. "Stop fighting."

"Please," she cries, thick tears streaming down her rosy cheeks. "*Te lutem mos me vrit.*"

"*Ya ne govoryu albanskiy.*" *I don't speak Albanian.* I say it in my native tongue just to be a smartass.

"Please don't kill me."

My hold on her slackens as she crumbles in my arms, whispering things in her language I don't think are intended for me anyway. Before I realize what I'm doing, my hand rubs over her back to soothe her.

I have many more reasons to kill her now than I did when I parked my car. My side is bloody, my nose is bloody, my head is bruised. My ego hurts most of all.

But I don't think I'll kill her. Not now that she's useful.

It was probably a bad idea to begin with, trying to get out of Nikita's cruel game. If I don't allow him to punish me now, he'll find something worse.

"I'm assuming you do, in fact, know how to drive?"

"Yes," she replies meekly.

I pull away from her and rip my shirt over my head, then I inspect my wounds for a moment before pressing the cloth to the holes seeping blood.

"Do you know how to use a GPS?"

She nods, hope brewing in her irises, a pretty golden brown I'm just noticing.

"Good."

She just stares at me, perplexed, waiting for me to go on. I don't blame her. There are so many unknowns for her, the biggest one being if she's going to keep breathing for long. Her head must be ready to explode.

I can't answer her questions. I have too many of my own.

Blowing out a breath, I hold out my hand as a sort of truce that I hope she understands. A sort of, *let's not kill each other for now*, agreement.

She hesitantly takes my hand and allows me to shake once before I let go. "I'm Maksim," I say, nodding to signal it's her turn.

She crosses her arms over her chest as if the desert heat has any kind of chill in the summertime. Finally, she speaks.

"Elira."

4

ELIRA

The blond-haired devil passed out fifteen minutes ago.

Every now and then, I look over to make sure he's breathing, and he is, steadily. Sometimes I'm relieved. Sometimes I'm disappointed. Sometimes I wonder why I haven't pushed him out of the car and driven somewhere safe.

But I know the answer. There *isn't* anywhere safe. These people, they could find me, they could find *James*, and then it'll be his body in the ground along with mine. The only way to keep him safe is to not call, but without help... They would find me before the sun came up. And if I let Maksim die, I'm terrified of what my death would look like.

I've gone over it a thousand times in my head. My best chance of survival is keeping Maksim alive and praying he has a forgiving side. I at least need to get him to safety before I run.

Right?

I'm still so unsure.

Maksim grunts, snapping my spine straight as I'm pulled

from my thoughts. I look beside me at his closed eyes, clenched with pain.

I stare out the windshield, following the GPS's directions as well as I can. The roads are confusing, and I have to follow close behind cars just to make sure I'm in appropriate lanes, but I do okay. I rarely drive back home, but the weeks that my father came to visit us when I was a child, he always had a car.

When I was thirteen, the last time I saw him, he stayed with us for an entire month. It was the longest I'd ever seen him in a single stretch of time, and in it, he taught me how to drive. He told me about America, his home country, and the traffic in Chicago.

For a minute, I pretend that's where I am. That it's my dad's car that I'm following close to, that he'll look in his rearview mirror, see me through the windshield, and recognize the daughter he forgot about over a decade ago.

A horn blares behind me, making my shoulders hunch as I lift my hands in an apologetic wave. I don't know what I'm apologizing for, but I turn the car to get away from the angry driver and let the GPS reroute.

The GPS doesn't take us to Maksim's house.

I'm assuming. If this is his house, he doesn't mind guests. *Lots* of guests.

I slow the car to a crawl as we pull up to an open, iron gate that people walk through while laughing and hanging on each other like they're drunk. They're piling into one of many cars on the street when I turn my attention to the front of the house.

Music is so loud, there's no way the police haven't been called at least once, but it doesn't seem to discourage the two guys running across the roof of the two-story, red brick home.

When they jump from the roof, I gasp and slam my foot

on the brake. I put the car in park and fling the door open, angling myself outside to hear what I think will be screams of terror but wind up being cheers.

What is going on?

I climb back in the car and nudge a sleeping Maksim. "We're here," I whisper. Why I'm whispering, I don't know. "*Maksim.*"

Movement up ahead draws my attention, and my breath catches when I see a man bounding through a gate, his arms spread out wide in a welcoming gesture as a grin stretches his lips. When I say *man*, what I really mean is *giant*. Goliath himself.

Did I say Maksim is big?

I take it back.

"Dobro pozhalovat' drug," the man calls, his voice cheerful, but his hands lower when he sees me. I sink in the seat.

"Maksim?" He walks quickly to the passenger door and yanks it open. Maksim's hand limply covers his wound with the cloth that's soaked with blood.

The man gasps, his eyes going wide as he yanks the shirt away to reveal the stab wounds.

Something feels like it catches in my throat. I try to breathe, but no air passes, so I put my hands on the steering wheel and try not to panic.

"*Zinovy!*" the man screams.

Breathe. Just breathe.

I manage to wheeze.

"What happened?" he asks me. I can see him inspecting Maksim's injuries in my periphery. "Zinovy!" he screams again. I don't look at him, but I can feel it when his impatience flings my way. "What happened?!"

A man appears from the backyard, running this way.

I still don't have it in me to speak. I'm having trouble breathing as it is, there's little I can do to form words.

I can put the car into reverse. I can get the *hell* out of here. That's what I can do.

Maksim stirs but doesn't open his eyes when the man shakes him. "Maksim, wake up."

"What happened?" the runner who must be Zinovy asks. I don't look at him either. I just wait for them to lug Maksim's body out of the car, and as soon as they do, I shove the car in reverse and let off the brake, my foot sliding to the gas pedal.

"Stop!" the large man yells, but I don't listen. I slam on the pedal, and the car jolts as I wiggle the wheel, trying to get control. I speed past the gate only to crash into a car parked on a curb.

My blood running hot, I go to put the car into drive but recoil as the windshield shatters from a bullet. I scream, raising my hands while tucking my head into my shoulder to announce my surrender.

Seconds later, a different man appears and drags me from the car while I struggle half-heartedly, still conflicted about what to do. One part of me says run, the other part says stop, and I can't seem to make up my mind.

When we get inside, I'm taken upstairs to the same bedroom they took Maksim to. He's laying on the mattress while Zinovy, a skinny guy with full-sleeve tattoos on both arms, works on him with antiseptic.

The big one stands over them, looking even more massive than he did outside. His bushy eyebrows are furrowed as he stares at Maksim, acne scars covering his troubled face.

He turns to me when he must realize I'm here, and I cower from his angry glare.

"Why did you run?"

Great question.

I don't answer. My instinct to not know English suddenly kicks back in, and I just stare, pushing my bottom lip out to look as pathetically innocent as a wounded dog.

They don't think *I* did this to Maksim. No sane person would believe that. Look at me. Look at him. I'm just a stupid girl. He's a big, strong man. A *killer*.

They won't know I did this until he wakes up and tells them. I move my eyes to Maksim, praying he won't wake up.

Maybe I should've stabbed him one more time.

"Hey." The giant takes one long stride to me and grabs me by the back of my neck, jerking my head up to look at him. "Answer my fucking question."

"Jesus, Hugh, she's *scared*." Zinovy looks up from tending to Maksim. "Give the girl a break."

"Stay out of this," Hugh snaps over his shoulder.

Zinovy holds up his hands. "I'm just saying. She saved Maksim's life by bringing him here. The least you could do is not be an asshole."

"I'm not being an asshole."

"I mean…" He shrugs and grabs a bottle of vodka. "*Prosti menya brat.*"

Maksim's face twists as vodka pours over his wound, and his mouth opens in a bellow. "Fuuck," he growls, opening his eyes.

"There he is," Zinovy cackles.

Maksim falls back, his arm covering his eyes as Zinovy works on the punctures.

"That's right, *Sleeping Beauty*. Back to bed."

Hugh's attention moves to me once again.

I shake my head before he can ask me another question. "Nuk flas anglisht."

His head tilts backward with a sigh, and he gives it a shake before addressing the guy with the gun behind me. "Can you get her to clean up? She smells worse than your mother's cunt."

His chest hits my back as he laughs. "Go fuck yourself."

A sense of shame washes over me, but the idea of soap

and water on my body is pleasant enough that I forgive the crass comment.

This house feels similar to the warehouse Anton took me to in that there are a bunch of Russian guys, but if there's a hierarchy here, I wouldn't know what it is. They feel relaxed with each other.

The man with the gun takes my arm and leads me from the room. Hugh calls behind us, "Put her in the basement when you're done."

The *basement*.

That doesn't sound like a place you put a girl who just saved your friend's life. If that's how they'll treat me thinking I'm Maksim's savior, I can only imagine how they'll treat me when he tells them what really happened.

5

MAKSIM

I wake up in Hugh's guest room—the one I've designated for myself after many drunken nights —with Hugh asleep in a chair next to the bed. His head hangs over his crossed arms, and a gun dangles from his hand like he's braced for an intruder.

I look toward the door, bracing myself as well, not quite sure of what to expect.

Last night plays fresh in my mind, and the first thing I see is the girl. Elira.

Where is she now?

Is she ... dead?

Would I be disappointed if she was?

I look down at the bandages wrapped around my torso and try to recall the last thing I remember. The drive here, I think. Elira's hunched shoulders as she leaned inches from the wheel, her eyes wide scanning Las Vegas's streets.

I wondered what she thought of all the lights, but I didn't ask. It seemed like a weird question, given what had just taken place. Plus, I think she was just afraid. Afraid of driving. Afraid of Vegas. Afraid of *me*.

Is she dead?

My lips sink with a frown, but I straighten them as I clear my throat.

Hugh jumps awake, his arms unfolding so his gun points at the door. When his eyes meet mine, he sighs and lowers the weapon.

"Who are we expecting?" I ask him, digging my palms into the mattress to sit up.

He leans back in the chair and huffs. "You show up with five stab wounds, a bruised temple and bashed face, and you have the nerve to ask *me* who we're expecting?"

Oh my God.

I nearly laugh. Nearly. Not quite. I'm a little too confused to fully feel the humor in him thinking the person who did this to me is a danger.

They don't know Elira did it.

Is it because she didn't tell them or because they killed her before she got the chance?

Or did she manage to get away? Would I still be alive if she had?

"Ah, so I guess the girl didn't tell you what happened," I say coolly, although I'm on the edge of my seat.

Why the fuck did I let Roman make me think killing this girl would solve my problems? If she's dead, what punishment will Nikita give me? What games must I play next?

"The girl who doesn't speak English?" Hugh asks, his dark orbs barely visible through slits. "Maksim, buddy, I feel like you've thrown me into a mystery novel. What the fuck happened? Who's the girl? Who did this to you?"

The girl who *doesn't* speak English.

Doesn't. Present tense. She's not dead. And she's gone back to pretending she doesn't speak English.

Now, I do laugh, earning myself a glare from Hugh.

I open my mouth, ready to tell him everything, but I stop

myself. Hugh is a soldier who works closest to me, close enough you could call him my right-hand man. He's also my best friend. He's my brother. I trust him with my life. He has my loyalty, and I know I have his.

But he's Bratva, and loyalty to the Bratva comes before loyalty to any one man. If Nikita asks Hugh what happened, I'd rather not put my brother in a position to lie on my behalf.

"Put your gun away and *relax*. I got into it with a few rowdy guys, but it's all right."

"What. Happened?"

I cringe as I sit up straight and watch my bandage to make sure it doesn't turn red. "That girl who brought me here... She's a whore from Albania. Nikita 'gifted' her to me last night. I must not have tied her up well because she got free and ran from my place. By the time I found her, she'd already caught the attention of a few guys who had her in an alley." I gesture over my shoulder. "Sneaky bastard came up behind me with a knife."

This story sounds so much more manly than what actually happened.

"Why didn't you call me?" Hugh's face pinches with disapproval. "You could've bled out."

"They smashed my phone."

He looks off for a moment while combing his goatee. "Did you take care of the bodies?"

I blow out a breath and wipe my hand over my forehead. I don't have to fake embarrassment. Elira kicking my ass is plenty shameful. "Well, that's the thing. They ran off after they hit me over the head."

Hugh's jaw clenches.

Now I'm going to have to find three douchebags who deserve to die just to make this story work.

"I'd like to get this taken care of before Nikita is made aware."

Hugh nods and stands like he thinks I mean right this second. "You got it."

"I'll let you know when I find the names. Just hang tight for now."

Tucking his gun in his waistband, he looks toward the door. I can tell by his glazing eyes that he's already forming a game plan. Normally, I love it. Today, I wish he'd chill.

"So where's the girl?" I ask, wiping a smudge of dirt off my bicep. I need a shower, but I'll check in on the little assassin first.

He blinks away whatever he was thinking about and looks at me. "In the basement... If you're expecting her to be grateful for you coming to her rescue, don't be. She's still a major flight risk. You owe Felix a new fender, and you're going to have to get yourself a new windshield."

I rear back. "What?"

Hugh laughs. "She freaked and backed into his car. Ricky shot at her to get her to stop."

He *shot* at her?

"But she wasn't hit?"

Hugh's brows bunch as he shakes his head. "No, of course not. It just scared her."

Good.

We let a couple of seconds go by while commotion starts downstairs. It sounds like Zinovy and his girlfriend going back and forth, followed by a plate shattering. It's always lively in this house.

"Listen, can I keep the girl here for a little while?" I ask, dragging Hugh's eyes to me. "It shouldn't be long. I'm just not sure what I'll do with her yet."

His eyes shine with pity before he blinks it away and nods. "Of course... I take it Anya doesn't know about her?"

I narrow my eyes and don't humor that with a response.

"Right." He rubs the back of his neck, then pulls out his phone. "I guess you'd better call Anya, huh? She's probably worried since they smashed your phone."

I catch the cell in one hand and thank Hugh before he leaves.

My little sister was supposed to spend the night at her friend's house—her 'friend' being a douchebag named Trevor who she slyly put in her contacts as 'Hailey' with four heart emojis—so it's unlikely she's noticed my absence, but I shoot her a quick text anyway.

Phone broke. Will have a new one this afternoon. Everything okay? -Mak

She responds in less than a minute with nothing but a thumbs up emoji, which is … annoying, but expected.

I toss the phone on the bed and head to the basement.

6

ELIRA

I'm already out of sight when the basement door opens.

I hold the metal bar I spent what felt like hours unscrewing from the pull-out bed tightly in my hand, closing my eyes and pressing my back against the side of the couch.

My heels scrape against concrete floor as I drag my feet closer to my rear, making myself as small as I can. There are little options to hide in this basement, so it won't be long until I'm found, but I still want to surprise my captor.

Someone hums, heavy feet planting off the last step into the basement.

Have they come to kill me?

Take me somewhere else?

Is Maksim awake? Did he tell them what happened?

"Are you hiding, Elira?"

My grip on the bar loosens at the sound of Maksim's voice, but I don't let go. He doesn't sound angry. Last night, when he gave me the keys to his car, he didn't sound angry then either. He sounded as if he wanted to call a truce. As if we could somehow put this behind us, and I wanted to believe him. I would be less skeptical if he hadn't spoken so softly when he took me out to the middle of nowhere to kill me.

"I'm not going to hurt you," Maksim says, his voice calm. Even. "You held up your end of the bargain saving my life. What kind of man would I be if I hurt you now?"

I tried to end *your life.*

He isn't stupid. He hasn't forgotten that part.

His footsteps start this way, making my grip on the bar tighten. I won't use it. Not unless I have to. But I feel a lot safer with it than without it right now.

He doesn't look the slightest bit surprised when he sees me, deep blue eyes locking onto mine. He stops just out of my reach, holding a plate of food that makes my mouth water the instant I register it.

Food.

My stomach gnaws. My head spins.

How long has it been since I've eaten?

Too long. I could go longer if he wasn't holding it in his hand.

"This again?" He nods to the bar held firmly in my grasp while a slight smirk lifts his lips. "I thought we were going to be friends."

Friends.

He doesn't mean that. I don't know what his endgame is for me, but if he was my friend, he would let me go.

When I say nothing, his smirk falls. Letting out a sigh, he lowers himself to the floor to sit a metre away. He extends a free hand while holding the plate slightly back with the other, giving a silent offer to exchange.

I hesitantly place the bar in his hand before taking the plate. My stomach gnaws some more, coming alive for the first time in probably a day and a half. I expect the aroma of the...waffles?...to blow up my senses, but it doesn't come, and

I don't wait for the smell to hit me. I pick up one of the small, oddly colored waffles and shove it in my mouth.

Maksim watches while I eat like a piranha, barely tasting, which is a good thing because I'm not sure these are waffles. They taste bland, and … I don't know, not good, but I don't suppose they give their prisoners the good food.

"Are you thirsty?" Maksim asks me when I only have one bite left.

No, I'm not, but I nod anyway in hopes that he'll give me a cup or something I can keep. I figured out how to get cold water in the laundry machine soon after they threw me down here, and that was after I'd hydrated in the shower. I've pretty much covered my bases in terms of hydration.

He pulls a plastic bottle of orange juice from the gray sweatpants hanging low on his hips and hands it to me.

I take slow sips, savoring the sweet liquid, and keep my eyes in front of me. Maksim looks better today. Too good for a man who almost died last night, the bandage around his naked torso reminding me of vengeance he must want.

The sound of metal crashing against concrete makes me flinch, and I jerk up to see that Maksim has tossed my bar across the room.

"You're cute, Elira," he says, tugging my eyes his way to look at him in my periphery. "I respect your fight. I even find it sexy."

I cringe at that, but he either doesn't notice or doesn't care.

That's what I am to him. A game. A fool.

Is he forgetting I almost won?

I should've learned how to fire a gun.

"But that's enough," he goes on. "No more fighting. My friends have been kind enough to allow you to stay here while I figure out a more permanent situation for you. If you choose to be the foreign girl who speaks no English and stays locked up in the basement, so be it. I will come once a day to bring you food until my boss no longer remembers you."

Finally, I turn to him. "What happens then?"

He shrugs, barely waiting before he replies like it's obvious, like there's no need to think it through. "Then I let you go."

I stare at him, showing nothing on my face. I show nothing because I feel nothing. I don't believe this man even for a second.

"You speak as if I have some choice *other* than to be kept in this basement," I say, brushing aside his lie to get back to what he was saying.

He nods. "You do." My arms press into my sides as he scoots toward me. "Can I be honest with you, Elira?"

I hate the way he says my name. It sounds dirty.

"I'm not sure you're capable of honesty, *Maksim*, but you can try."

He rears back like he's surprised, but then his face relaxes with an amused grin. "I'm not nearly as bad as you think."

I think you're a snake.

But … there *is* worse.

Nikita flashes into my mind, making me shiver. I don't know either man well, but I know Maksim is better than Nikita. He seemed better than Roman as well. And better than Anton.

Maybe Maksim is as good as it gets.

I don't know if he senses my sudden unease or if he was planning on touching me all along, but one hand smooths over my shoulder while the other caresses my cheek, guiding me to look at him. A minute ago, I would've wanted to slug him. Right with the reminder of Nikita at the front of my mind, it doesn't feel so bad.

"The truth is, I actually do need you." He speaks like he's admitting it to himself as much as he is me. He sighs. "It was rash of me to react the way I did last night. If my boss found out, he'd take it as disrespect. For the foreseeable future, I need you to be my living, breathing, *preferably obedient* whore."

I jerk my arm, but his soft touch on my shoulder turns firm as he holds me still.

"That does not have to be as horrendous as it sounds. It does not have to involve locked doors and restraints. If you're as smart as you are scrappy, it could mean your own apartment, your own car. Schooling if you want, a job, whatever it is you came here for in the first place, you could have it."

This, more than anything, boils my blood.

My ears heat, and my hands curl into fists.

For days I felt fear. More of it than any person should feel in a lifetime. I've felt fleeting sadness, sort of woah-is-me moments of weakness, and little anger. The people put me here are vile, but their intentions were honest, their purpose was honest, their lack of remorse was honest. They are more monsters beneath my bed than they are villains in my mind.

But this... This is *sick*. This is counterfeit. Insulting to my intelligence as well as my pride.

Am I to be *thankful* for this *generosity*?

"I did not come here to be someone's *whore*," I sneer, my teeth flashing like fangs. "I came here to be someone's *wife*."

Maksim's hand slips off my shoulder as he gives me a puzzled look, as if the idea of marriage could never occur to him. I don't suppose it could. A man like him is capable of many things, but love isn't one of them.

"You can't be serious."

He doesn't say it like it's a question, but I can tell he wants me to explain myself. I don't. I should have never opened my mouth about it in the first place. The less he knows about

James, the better. Right now, Maksim has no leverage. If he threatens James, he'll have all of it.

"Sweetheart..." Maksim clears his throat, readying himself like he's about to explain something beyond obvious. "Are you a mail-order bride?"

I narrow my eyes. "No."

"No?"

Don't say anything.

My jaw clenches while I glare.

"Okay, but you came here to get married?"

Silence.

"Have you *met* your fiancé?"

The way he says it, like I'm the punchline of some joke, makes me want to rip his head off. I can't help it. I speak.

"*Yes.*"

"Uh-huh." He nods like I've somehow only further proved some point he's trying to make. "How many times have you seen each other?"

Why?

"When you met, was it via Skype?"

I scoff. "I wouldn't consider that *meeting.*"

"Sure, sure. Was he a tourist in your country, then?"

Yes. So?

I need to stop answering his questions. Stop speaking.

But it's hard because he sounds... He sounds like he knows something I don't, and there's a knot forming in my stomach that I need to go away, which won't happen until he's finished.

"There are only so many ways for people to meet, Maksim. Eventually, you're going to get it right."

"How long was it before he proposed?" he asks. "It was *fast*, right? Probably on that trip."

My narrowed eyes soften.

How does he know that?

He shakes his finger, squinting like he's contemplating something. "I'll take a few more guesses, and you tell me how close I am. You're not from a city. He found you dirt poor in a gutter, probably in a village somewhere."

The knot tightens.

"The first time you met, you told him how much you always wanted to go to the States."

No.

That wasn't until the third night when I talked about my father. I've always wanted to know where the other half of me comes from, and I told him this.

He told me I was the most beautiful woman he'd ever seen in his life. That the short time we'd been together could never be long enough. That he wanted to show me my roots, to show me a new life, a *better* life with high-paying work that would be more than enough to support my mother and three sisters back home.

He wanted to help me, all in exchange for my love. He was handsome and charming and everything I dreamed a man would be.

He proposed. I said yes. That night, I gave him my virginity.

We were supposed to wait for my visa, but months passed, and he grew impatient. He asked me to fly to Mexico where all we'd have to do is pay to help me cross the border, which they did. I willingly climbed into that truck, not knowing it was the worst mistake I'd ever make.

We asked the wrong people for help. I'm paying for it.

"I was going to marry for love," I lie. I'd never admit the truth out loud. "Not for the visa."

"It doesn't matter what you were going to marry him for. He was never going to marry you."

What?

49

"He's a trafficker, Elira. It's pitiful you haven't figured that out on your own by now."

There was humor in Maksim's voice when he started this, but it's gone. He sounds serious.

I look away, choosing instead to stare at my knees. I'm wearing the dress again. *The* dress. It looks more like the one I picked out in the store now that I've washed it, but it suddenly feels dirtier than it did yesterday.

I close my eyes so I don't have to see it. "You're wrong."

"Even having zero clue who this guy is, I know with absolute certainty that I'm right."

My eyes burst open, my head snapping up to face him. "You're *wrong*!"

I hate him.

I've never hated another human being so much in my life.

Maksim raises his hands up before slowly standing, picking up the plate as he does. "You believe whatever you need to keep your sanity. But think about your situation and make your moves carefully." He points above us. "My friends are kind. Knock on the door, promise to be a good girl, and they'll let you out... But hurt someone or try to take off again, and I will throw you in a dried-up fucking well where you will live for the remainder of your excruciatingly long life... Sound fair?"

Tears sting my eyes, so my vision blurs. I stare at the tattoo on the right side of his chest, written in Russian so I wouldn't understand it even if I could see clearly.

I believe him. The man is a snake, a liar, a manipulator, but I believe that he'd punish me for acting out. As much as I want him to be wrong, to be vicious and cruel and vile, the way he pegged James is so on the mark. What he says makes sense. Enough sense for me to believe him about my fiancé too.

And I hate him for it.

I want to scream. I want to take a knife and carve my hatred over that tattoo.

But instead, I nod, letting a tear slip from my eye.

"Good."

And then he leaves. Like a harsh parent, he leaves me to sit in my shame, to be tormented by my thoughts.

Fear turns to anger.

Sadness turns to anger.

And eventually, I get sick of the basement. I go upstairs and knock on the door.

7

MAKSIM

*T*hree hours. Three phone calls.

That's what it took to track down Elira's supposed fiancé. It sounds like a lot of time invested, but two of those hours were merely waiting on a call back from the head of a trafficking ring the late Anton got a few of our whores—Elira included—from.

I don't know why I went out of my way to find him. The heartbreak on her face this morning when I told her what she should've already known was unnecessary on its own, but *proving* it... What will that accomplish, other than more heartbreak?

I don't know. I may just be a fucking monster, but the idea that she might have some notion that there's a Prince Charming out there coming to her rescue feels too uncomfortable to allow.

No one is coming to her rescue. There was no fiancé. This is as good as it gets.

Sorry, princess.

The photo of the trafficker, with his information written on the back, hangs from my back pocket as I walk up to

Hugh's door, and it slides from my mind when I hear the sounds of gunfire. Not real, from a video game, but it's still obnoxiously loud.

I yank open the door and step inside, instantly feeling at home. More so than in the three-bedroom suburban hell I live in for Anya's sake. If I didn't have a teenage sister to care for, it's possible I would've moved in here a long time ago.

It's seven in the evening, but Hugh's youngest brother, Fox, is in flannel pajama bottoms and a wife beater on the couch with his friend, Vlad, who is only slightly better dressed. A cigarette dangerously dangles from Fox's mouth as he stabs at an Xbox controller. Vlad's feet are planted on the surprisingly cleared-off table, his legs spread too wide. It smells like ass in here.

I changed my mind. Anya or no Anya, this place is too much of a bachelor pad. My lip curls, but when Vlad sees me, he doesn't seem to notice my disapproval. He nods.

"'Sup, Mak?"

Jesus Christ.

I raise my chin. "Where's Hugh?"

"Shower," Fox answers. He laughs. "They must've given you trouble today. I could smell brain matter on him from down the block."

Really?

As a reflex, I angle my nose to sniff my shoulder, but I've already showered the gore away. Someone came in to pay a debt but disrespected Nikita in the process. If it were only me, I probably would've let it go, but Roman was around, and I wanted to make a point, prove my loyalty to a fellow lieutenant. If my boss knew how much I despised him, Hugh would be washing my brains off himself right now instead of the man he beat to death with a golf club earlier today.

"Always," I reply, heading for the kitchen to grab a beer.

My eyes find the basement door as I walk past it, a jolt of

excitement making my spine straighten. I continue to the fridge, grab a beer, and when I turn around, I pause.

A petite pair of feet stick out from beneath the kitchen table, and I follow the woman's legs up to her supple ass, hidden by the white skirt of a dress.

I squint and lean toward the table as if that'll give me powers to see through wood.

That isn't...?

Elira didn't seriously leave the basement already, did she?

What the fuck would she be doing under the table?

Fox struts into the kitchen, headed for the fridge, and when he notices where I'm looking, he slaps my shoulder with a laugh.

"She's been doin' that shit all day, man. We told her a dozen times she doesn't have to clean, but she doesn't understand shit."

"Lucky man!" Vlad yells from the living room.

"Yeah, no shit." Fox waggles his eyebrows while looking between Elira's ass and me. "You keep her here as long as you need, my man."

"Ask him if she can cook!"

Fox flicks his eyes toward Vlad's voice. "He doesn't know the bitch!"

Vlad doesn't respond, but Fox lifts a finger when he seems to get an idea. He goes to the cupboard and pulls out a box of macaroni and cheese before tossing it on the counter and going to the table.

Leaning against the counter, I twist off my beer cap and take a swig.

I didn't expect her to leave the basement.

Not today. Eventually, I knew she would cave, surrendering to the tiniest comfort that is the human companionship of a house full of apes, but today, I expected her to be stubborn.

What a nice surprise.

Fox crouches next to Elira and pats her leg. "Hey baby, pause for a second."

I watch her muscles contract. She was already a little tense, but the contact makes her uneasy. Or pissed. Or maybe she just doesn't like being called baby.

His hand is on her the whole time it takes for her to scoot from underneath the table, a scrub brush in her grasp, but he finally pulls his hand away when she recoils from him. Her pinched expression makes me smile, but she doesn't outright glare at Fox.

She *does*, however, glare at me.

What the fuck did I do?

Fox carefully takes Elira's hand and leads her to the counter where the macaroni box is. He lifts the box to rattle it a few times. "*Food.*" He says it loud and enunciated like he's speaking to a hard of hearing toddler who's never seen dried pasta.

I snort. This is fucking *rich*.

He stirs an imaginary spoon in a pot. "Cook. Food." His finger stabs at the box. "Food." More stirring. "Cook."

I cover my mouth as I laugh, expecting Elira to throw another glare my way, but she doesn't. She stares at Fox with eyes convincingly blank.

His head falls in defeat as he lets out a dramatic sigh.

"I'll try," I say, setting my beer on the counter and taking the macaroni box. "Give me a minute."

He grabs a beer from the fridge and makes an expression that shows his doubt. "Good luck."

I watch him walk from the kitchen before turning back to Elira, my lips stretched, but she isn't looking at me, doesn't even seem to register that I'm here. She sets the scrub brush in the sink then goes to the table and pulls a bucket of water from beneath it.

She was seriously scrubbing the floor.

What the fuck?

She pours out the brown water into the sink, then goes about rinsing it.

"You know, you don't have to do that."

No answer.

"Elira."

She tosses me a look like a silent plea for me to shut the fuck up. She really doesn't want people to know that she can understand them.

It's smart, I'll give her that. The less people think she can understand, the more they'll say in front of her. It's how she knew I'd try to kill her. It's how she fooled me so well.

I'd put an end to it if I didn't think it was cute.

The video game starts blaring again, and I shift her way. "They can't hear."

When she goes to put more soap in the bucket, I take her hips and spin her around to face me.

Her eyes widen with fear that eases my grip on her waist, but I don't pull away. I can smell her this close, and the scent has me leaning in even closer, which is ironic with how repugnant she was just yesterday.

I breathe in.

Wildflowers.

"You don't need to clean the floor by hand. Or at all."

Her breath shakes as she looks away uncomfortably. Her chest rises and falls with her heavy breaths, and I bet if I pressed my hand against it, I'd feel her heart racing.

I take a step back, ignoring my hardening cock.

She really cleans up well. Without the dirt or smell, she's... Well, she's beautiful.

"This is where I live now, yes?" she asks, her voice soft but strong.

I open my mouth, ready to tell her no, but I don't know how long she'll stay here, so I nod instead. "For now."

"Then I don't want to live in a home with a floor so dirty a mop won't scrub off all the filth."

I look around. It's definitely a bachelor pad, but there's a housekeeper who comes twice a week, and it isn't 'filthy' by my definition. But okay.

"Besides, what else am I to do all day?" She doesn't look at me when she asks it, and I don't miss the tremble in her voice. "I am only *your* whore, correct? I don't have other responsibilities?"

She runs her nails over her arms as her eyes meet mine. She's asking me something serious, but it takes me staring at her for several seconds before I understand what it is.

She wants to know if they get to fuck her too.

No.

The answer occurs in my mind automatically, but I don't voice it, choosing instead to let her sweat. If she was a true whore, broken in long before she came to me, I don't think I would care. But she strikes me as innocent, naïve, young. She's too pure to dirty.

"Can you cook?" I ask, pretending I didn't fully understand her question.

She swallows and looks away for a moment before nodding.

I hand over the box of macaroni, and she hesitantly takes it. She tucks long, dark hair as smooth and straight as fine silk behind her ear while she reads the back of the box. Her full lips sag as she scans it.

"What about cheese?" she asks.

My eyes pinned to her lips cause her words to delay registering, and it isn't until she looks up at me that I blink and snap back to the present.

"Hmm?"

She flips it over to look at the front. "It says it's to make macaroni and cheese, but cheese isn't one of the ingredients listed."

"It's in the box."

She squints at me. "What?" Her eyes dart to the box as she tears it open and peeks inside. "I don't understand."

I take it from her and pull out the cheese packet, holding it up for her to see. "This. It's powder. You pour it in with the milk and pasta."

Bewildered, she snatches the packet from my hand and tears one corner before pouring a little out into her palm. Her face is the cutest I've seen it when it twists with disgust, making me grin.

"Have you really never had mac and cheese?"

She looks at me like I've just committed a crime and shakes her head. "This isn't *cheese*. This is disgusting."

My chest rumbles with a laugh.

"This is funny to you?" Her eyes are wide, and when her jaw drops, parting those plump, pink lips, I get the urge to kiss her. She looks between me and the orange powder. "You're going to die of cancer at forty."

"That's dramatic and untrue... I have you to take care of me now. I'll make it to *at least* fifty."

After staring at me with wide, disbelieving eyes for a few seconds, she sets the packet on the counter and goes to the fridge.

"Is there another box?" she asks, pulling out butter and a carton of milk.

"Probably."

"Could you get it, please? I want to double your serving of poison."

I feel another laugh coming, but Hugh's sudden presence commands my attention, as well as Elira's.

The milk slips from her hand as she startles, sending it

sloshing onto her dress and spilling on the floor. She gasps before falling to her knees to pick up the carton, but instead of standing, she stays on the floor with her head bowed. Is she afraid of *everyone* more than me? How could that even be possible?

I turn to meet Hugh's inquisitive stare.

"Is she all right?" he asks in Russian.

I shrug. "Just jumpy. Sorry about that."

He waves the apology away before grabbing a beer from the fridge, eyeing Elira as he twists off the cap.

"How long is she going to stay like that?"

"I don't know. As long as it takes for you to leave, I guess."

He takes a pull of his beer. "Those pigs did a number on her last night, huh?"

It takes me a minute to remember my lie. "I got there before they could do anything."

His head tilts. "Makes sense that she'd be more comfortable with only you, then. You saved her."

Right.

"I'm pretty sure it was Nikita who scarred her for life. He had a bit of a temper when Anton brought her to his office last night. He made her clean up the mess."

Hugh nods, still staring at Elira, before chugging the rest of his beer. He grabs another from the fridge then heads from the kitchen without another word.

Once he's gone, Elira quietly starts to clean up. I get the impression our conversation is over, so I pull out the photo from my back pocket and set it on the counter.

"I want you to know, I get no pleasure in being right."

Her eyes move to the counter, but I don't wait to see her reaction, to see her heartbreak. Call me a coward if you must.

I head into the living room with the others and watch Elira disappear into the basement minutes later. My lips feel heavy with a frown, but I fight it. It's best for her to know the truth. Best for me, but also best for her. The truth hurts, but hope gets you killed.

Before I leave, I walk to the basement door to lock it but hover my hand over the knob instead.

Is she crying?

Is she angry?

I'll never know because I walk away, feeling an uncomfortable amount of guilt.

8

ELIRA

$\mathcal{T}$he woman sitting across from me on the bus keeps singing.

It's the same song—or maybe poem—over and over, the same eight *lines* over and over, and although I want to scream at her, I stay quiet.

The woman doesn't deserve my anger, she deserves pity or help if I had it to give. Her hair is matted with dirt and grease like it hasn't been washed or combed in weeks, and her eyes stay open a little too wide, hinting at intoxication.

It's only the two of us plus a couple up front on this 6 AM ride to Bakersfield, California. It's my third bus out of four that I have to take to get to the address on the back of the photo Maksim gave me.

I'm sure Maksim only wrote it as further proof to validate the man's identity, but it felt like a taunt. Like he wanted me to go to this address. Like he wanted me to get myself killed.

I am not a stupid girl, so before seeing this photo, I was prepared to make this my life. To allow Maksim to control me, just as he's doing now with this cruel piece of information. But now…

Now I have something to die for.

"If I were an apple and grew on a tree, I think I'd drop down on a nice girl like me," the intoxicated woman sings.

I turn toward the window and tuck the photo in a metal groove so I can use my hands to cover my ears. I stare at the photographed man dressed in a tux, smiling back at me, filling me with rage I never knew possible.

Daniel Storm.

That's the name written on the back of this photo. The name of the man who stole my life. Not James Anderson. Not my fiancé, my could-be love, my tourist who swept me off my feet. That man doesn't exist and never did.

I'm not convinced Maksim is telling the truth merely because he found a photo of James/Daniel. He could have written a bogus name and address on the back of the picture. But he didn't. This is real. This is truth. I know it because James/Daniel isn't the only person in the photo taken on his wedding day.

His wife is too.

I take in her wedding dress, more elegant than anything I could've hoped to afford, and I channel so much hatred that I wonder if she can feel it.

I hate her.

I hate him.

I hate Maksim.

I hate America.

I hate *myself*.

My eyes nearly close on that thought, but I keep them open as punishment for my stupidity. I'll look at this photo every day until I'm dead, just to remind myself why my younger sisters will no longer have me to provide for them.

Rage spills from my flared nostrils in the form of hot gusts of air, and finally, I'm forced to peel my gaze from the photo when the bus stops. The people at the bus station were very kind, helping me figure out the way "back home," but it's still very confusing even having memorized all the numbered buses.

The bus stops three more times before I get off and wait a half hour for the last one in peaceful silence, no more talk of apples to distract me from my mission.

I just have to see him. I have to see the man who took my virginity before taking my future. I need to have closure. Without it, I'll never sleep again.

My hand absently pats my waist where the kitchen knife is discreetly tucked, then I rest my palms in my lap as someone comes to sit down next to me.

Closure. If that means one of us has to die for me to get it, so be it.

"Where ya headed?" a young man asks me.

I catch his stare out of my periphery and resist the urge to scoot away. "Bakersfield."

He chuckles like I just told a joke, so I look over at his boyish face. Judging by the backpack that sits between his feet, I'd say he actually is a boy. A nice one, I think. There's kindness in his eyes.

But then again, I'm a horrible judge of character.

"You're *in* Bakersfield," he tells me.

Oh. Right.

When I flip the photo over to study the address, the boy peeks at it.

"Damn, nice neighborhood."

My grip on the photo tightens. "Is it?"

"You've never been?"

I shake my head and put the photo away. I think we're going to leave it at that, but when a bus comes, the boy stops me from getting on the wrong one. He offers his assistance and chatters so much during the ride that I long for the apple lady.

But at 7:43 AM, according to the watch the woman at the bus station gave me, I finish the half-mile walk to stand in front of a cobblestone path and look up at a three-story house too big for two people.

Biting my cheek, I drop the photo on the cobblestone and start toward a bright red door. When I make it, I test the knob to find it locked, then I go to the garage. There's a small gap in the bottom that I climb under to find only one car.

What if he isn't even here?

My muscles stiffen at that thought, but I continue on to the door that is, again, locked. It takes me several tries before I finally find a back window unlocked, and I climb through as quietly as I can.

My eyes dart around the home as my heart picks up speed, adrenaline pouring into my blood.

I'm not afraid of being caught. Not even a little. This is too important to allow fear to blind me, so I save the consequences of my actions for a future concern. The only thing I fear now is James/Daniel being away, probably conning a new girl.

He has to die for that. He has to be stopped not only for me, but for the others who would've come after me.

I go to pull out the knife but think twice and take one from the kitchen instead. It couldn't hurt to have two weapons.

I creep through the home, stopping at every doorway to scan the rooms.

My head whips toward noise coming from an open set of double doors just up the hall, and I tiptoe that way with the knife firmly in my grasp.

I peek my head in the doorway to see him.

Him.

Sitting at a desktop computer typing away on the same chat site he used to communicate with me. Typing to someone just as insignificant as I am.

Pain, so much worse than anger, hits me like a gut punch, and I have to cover a hand over my mouth to hold in a cry.

I'm wearing the dress I picked out just for him. *The* dress. The one I decided I'd wear when I met my fiancé in America and the same one I planned to wear on our wedding day.

That dress. I wore it for him then, and I'm wearing it for him now.

When I suck in through my nose, he startles and jerks to face me.

"What the fuck?" His eyes widen as he finds the knife in my hand. "Who the fuck are you?"

My lips part. "Who am I?" I sound too broken to be dangerous, and it shows when he allows his eyes to find my face instead of zeroing in on the knife.

His eyes narrow. "Elira?" With a shake of his head, he holds out his hands and sighs. "Elira, baby, how did you get here? I've been worried sick."

I don't respond. He looks nervous but keeps up with the bullshit.

"The guy we paid at the border said you never showed. I thought you chose not to come, I... I must've called you a hundred times."

"Please stop," I whisper, my lip trembling. It's pathetic. *I'm* pathetic. "I didn't come here to hear your lies. I came here to hear your truth."

"My truth?" He opens and closes his mouth while his eyes keep flicking to the knife. "I don't know what you mean."

My grip on the knife tightens as a wave of anger finally cuts through the sadness, propelling me with bravery. "You *know* what I mean."

His innocent expression finally fades, and he looks down at the knife. "How the hell did you find where I live?"

"My *owner* helped me find you." My accent is as thick as the pain in my voice, so I take a breath and try to speak clearly. "He thought it was funny that I believed you were my fiancé. He laughed at me for not realizing what you'd done."

"And is he," Daniel points to the knife, "dead?"

"Yes," I lie. I want him to be afraid of me. I want him to think it's a possibility that this knife will wind up in his neck.

Daniel nods. "Good for you, kid." He backs into his desk then quickly turns to exit out of the chat that's pinging with messages. "I knew you were different, honey, I really did. I don't want you to think you aren't special to me. You didn't deserve any of this. My…" He blows out a breath like this is hard for him, but it's all an act. He fooled me once, but I can see through the lies with ease now. "My boss made me go through with this. I…" He shakes his head. "I am so sorry."

Bullshit.

I hate you.

I *hate* you.

"I'm so glad you made it here." He sighs and cautiously steps toward me. "Come on, let's go upstairs. I have a drawer full of fake passports you can use to get back home. We'll call your mom too if you haven't already. She must be worried."

"Don't fucking talk about her!" I stab the knife through the air at him, causing him to raise his hands and jump back.

"Daniel?"

I spin toward the feminine voice at my back and lock eyes with a woman who startles when she sees me. She doesn't quite look like the woman in the photo, but my eyes lock onto the ring on her left hand in an instant.

This must be his wife.

She gasps as she backs away.

"It's all right," he quickly says to her. "Darling, it's fine, we're only talking."

"I'm calling the police." She turns to bolt but stops when he screams at her.

"No! *No.* Do not fucking call the police. Just…" Gritting his teeth, he takes a breath. "Just give me ten minutes, babe, all right? Just wait for me in the sitting room. Elira is just about to go."

The woman looks hesitant, but she nods, seemingly obeying the command when she slinks away. I wonder if she has any idea who he is, what he does.

I don't know. Regardless, she feels far from innocent to me. I can feel my hatred follow her, follow that ring I never got to wear, that I was never *going* to wear.

When I turn to him, I straighten my neck and clear away the gunk clogging my throat. "I've heard enough of your lies, Daniel. I want the truth. I've *earned* the truth."

His face sobers as he distances himself from me. Cracking his neck, he seems to be considering it. With a sigh, he meets my eyes. "*Fine.* What do you want to know?"

I lower the knife and try to keep my face neutral, try not to show the undeserving, out of place gratitude I feel. I *need* this. I need this so much more than he knows.

"Why me?" I ask, my heart breaking even as my voice steadies.

"Why you?" He looks annoyed, like at any moment his eyes will roll. "You were available. There is an endless supply of girls just like you."

"No." I shake my head. "You came to my village. You—"

"Okay, let me stop you there. You want honesty, right? You want *the truth*," he mocks, mimicking my accent.

I nod without hesitation.

"I picked a random village on a map, went there, and

67

found the dumbest, most naïve, reasonably attractive girl I could find within the four days I was budgeted to be there. In an *hour* you were eyeing me up outside that cute little restaurant with the qofte like I was a walking visa."

"No." I shake my head. "That's not true."

His eyebrows raise as he smiles. "Now who's lying?"

My grip on the knife tightens while my throat closes. I'm blinded by so much rage that when I lift the knife and barrel toward him, I can barely aim.

When I swing, I slice nothing but air because Daniel easily evades me. He uses my loss of momentum to kick me in the stomach, sending air rushing from my lungs and bile up my throat.

Before my body can collapse, he takes me by my neck and shoves me against the wall, squeezing my throat in a deathly, two-handed grip while his eyes swirl with the most insidious thing… Pleasure.

The woman appears again, but this time the police don't seem to be on her mind, and she doesn't step in to help me. She stands off to the side and meets my eyes, looking uncertain and cowardly, running her nails over her arms out of nervousness. She'll stand there and let him kill me if I give him the chance.

I scratch at Daniel's hands and try to kick him off me, my brain running on pure survival instincts, and I can tell he thinks that he's won.

He laughs at my attempts just before leaning in to lick along my cheek, like he wants to taste all the tears that I've cried for him.

I hate him. But right now, I feel more sorrow than hatred, and more desperation. I feel like my heart was broken before, but now it's shattered, and he's putting the scraps through a food processor. He wants me destroyed, and I can't say he hasn't accomplished that.

He thinks he's won, but there's a vengeful side of me he never got to know. I lost, but I was never going to let him win. If I must lose, he must lose with me.

He thinks he's going to walk out of this the victor, but I know something he doesn't.

I know about the other knife.

9

MAKSIM

*M*y fist pounds on the red door with more anxiousness than I can remember feeling. There are a handful of men combing the streets of Las Vegas, all friends who've agreed to keep the search of the ballsy escapee under the radar for now, but I know in my gut that they'll all come up short.

Elira is here. If not here, then she's lying in a ditch somewhere after the trafficking organization no doubt killed her. With any luck, that's what happened because if I find her alive, she'll *wish* she were dead.

I pound my fist again, my jaw clenching to the point of pain. For all I know, nobody is home. The number I tracked down for Daniel Storm hasn't answered in hours, so it's possible he doesn't even have his phone. He could be overseas.

Then where would she go?

Anger at myself overflows as I reach behind me intent on pulling out my gun to blow the lock off the door, but something from the corner of my eye—along with reason—stops me.

I turn and let my hand fall at my side as a middle-aged brunette walks up in khaki pants and a blue, striped sweater. She wears a wide-brimmed hat even though the sun isn't overhead enough to burn her white, middle-class flesh. A pair of gardening shears hangs from her hand.

"Excuse me," she says, strutting up with confidence that reeks of believed invincibility. "Can I help you?"

I nod to the house. "Do you live here?"

She narrows her eyes like she thinks I'm a burglar who walked right up to the front door. "Well, no, but I'm a good friend of the Storms."

Good for you.

My instinct is to tell her to fuck off, but I resist. I could use her help.

"Storms?" I frown. "He's married?"

She shifts the shears to her other hand. "You're looking for Daniel?"

"I'm looking for my sister. She was out with, uh…" I crook my thumb at the door, "him, but she never came home last night. The location sharing app we have says she's here."

The woman's eyes widen to saucers, but the horror she tries to plaster on her face is too drowned out by excitement. She can't *wait* to tell the girls about this.

"Oh my." The woman presses a hand to her heart. "I knew Henrietta went away to see her mother, but I never would've thought Daniel…" She shakes her head and sighs. "But I guess I *shouldn't* be surprised. A man with a wife as devoted as Henrietta would never fully be able to appreciate her. Life is funny that way, isn't—"

"Yeah, I'm just here to get my sister." I turn to the door and pound but turn back to the woman a moment later, trying to look exasperated. "Have you seen him lately? Is it possible he could've left her alone? I know my sister is in there. The app says so."

71

She peers up at the windows. "Maybe they're still asleep."

"Could you just please—"

"There's a spare key," she says, pointing to a planter in a flowerbed off the porch. "If it's truly an emergency, I don't see why you shouldn't use it."

Her lip twitches like she wants to grin, and I'm too relieved to care about the fucking block party she's probably about to form to watch me drag my whore from this asshole's house. If there's any good that comes out of that, it'll be Daniel's ruined reputation.

I get the key from the bottom of the planter, then nod at the woman who stays rooted in place, excited to see the show. "Thank you."

"Whatever I can do to help. For all I know, your sister could be a child."

She's obviously baiting for more information, but I ignore her altogether as I go inside and shut the door, locking it in case she decides to keep up the good neighbor act and investigate.

The moment I turn around, my muscles tense at the dead woman on the ground. It takes a full second to register her plumpness, her oversized breasts, her highlighted hair that doesn't resemble Elira's.

Her silk robe is sprawled open and is melded with the puddle of blood she's laying in that came from the single stab wound in her stomach.

I blink at the woman, not sure what to make of this, not sure if this is a good sign or bad.

Shaking the woman from my attention, I storm through the house, hearing nothing, seeing no one.

Is there a basement? If there is, that's where he'd take her, if she's still here.

"Elira?" I call, my voice booming off the walls. I stomp

past an open office doorway but halt when a sea of red pulls my attention inside.

My heart pauses. For a full second, I don't think I can breathe.

I did not think I would care if she was dead. Necessary or not, she's a pain in the ass. I warned her not to run, I *trusted* her not to run, and in two days I've turned myself into an absolute fool of a man.

I put that address on the back of the photo. I gave her the information. This is my fault as much as it is hers, so maybe that's why when I see the blood staining the wallpaper, I feel … remorse. Guilt. Fear.

"Elira?" I call, my voice low as I step into the office. Blood has seemed to spray all over the room. It coats the walls, the desk, and the rug. There's so much, the source of it takes me a moment to find.

I look to my right to see the body of a man lying face down, and my very stupid, *very* disobedient 'gift' in a corner of the room. Her face rests against the wall as she stares at nothing. Her once white dress is painted red, the knife that must've slaughtered Daniel and the woman grasped in her palm. It's how I know she's alive. Everything else about her looks lifeless.

"Elira?" I slowly approach her, my eyes running over her to search for injury. She's so covered in blood it's hard to tell. Even her face is a red mask.

I crouch in front of her and gently take the knife from her hand. "Are you hurt?"

"What do you care?" she whispers, startling me. She looks so catatonic, I wasn't sure she could hear me.

I glance over Daniel's body then roll him to get a better look at the cause of death. There's too much blood here for this to have been a quick kill.

When I spot the sliced artery on his neck, the spraying

pattern over the walls makes sense. What *doesn't* make sense is why the man's shirt has more holes in it than I can quickly count.

I lift his blue shirt to reveal over two dozen stab wounds to his torso.

This kill was unhinged. It was brutal. It was *Nikita-level* psychotic.

What in the *fuck*?

I turn my head toward Elira, unsure what I'm feeling at this exact moment.

"He deserved it," she whispers, looking alive for the first time as she peers at her knees in shame. "You don't know how many women he's hurt."

I could ballpark it.

"I know," I say, thinking about what *I* would deserve if she were my judge. She's… This must subtract so many masculine points from my total, but I may be a smidge afraid of her.

Should I kill her after all? If I don't, how long before my torso looks like a cheese grater?

Staring at her sad, hopelessly empty expression makes me want her in my arms. I want to believe he was a villain who deserved this fate while I am a man of higher morals. I want her to see me as a man different from the one she hated enough to stab twenty or so times after slicing his carotid.

I'm both afraid of and impressed by Elira, and although she's proven to be a far worse punishment than Nikita intended, I'm having a terrible time relieving myself of her. She still winds up breathing, in the end.

I wipe the blood of the murder weapon onto Daniel's pants then tuck it into my pocket. "We should go," I say, remembering the woman outside. This just got a hell of a lot more complicated.

"Come on." I hold out my hand for her, but she just stares at it. "Elira…"

"What is the point?" Her voice breaks as a tear rolls down her cheek, turning red as it hits a patch of dried blood. "Leave me here for the authorities. I killed two of you precious Americans, the police will take care of your problem for you."

"Daniel Storm was a trafficker for an organization who won't allow his murder to become known to the public. The police are not your problem, I promise. Now if you want my help, let's go."

"Your *help*," she spews like she's tasted something foul. "Your help involves locking me in another man's basement because I'm too much of a burden to see your own. I'm not your friend. I'm your prisoner. Don't insult my intelligence."

"You'll be my *dead* prisoner if we don't get you out of this house."

"Isn't that the plan?" she asks, giving me a sobered stare that holds no fear. "Or will you be throwing me into a well as promised?"

Frustration builds, and I open my mouth to voice it but pause. Her face is hard, but her eyes are soft. She's brave. And strong. And possibly psychotic.

But she's also just a girl.

"No," I say. "I'm not going to hurt you."

"Right. You've said that before."

I think through my next words carefully, letting my thoughts brew for a minute. Nothing I say will make her trust me. I haven't earned it, and she doesn't appear to be up for giving me the chance.

But she doesn't have much of a choice. She'll never get out of this mess alone. The organization will come for her as quickly as the Bratva.

I stand and turn toward the door. "Good luck, then."

Seconds pass with my footsteps being the only sound. I almost make it to the door before I hear the soft patter of Elira's feet approaching.

Slowing to a stop, I turn to face her.

"Did you mean it when you said you aren't as bad as I think?"

With only slight hesitation, I nod.

"Are you as bad as these men?" she asks, referring to the traffickers.

I do many immoral things, enough that I'm not sure what the honest truth is. I just know the answer she needs to hear.

"No."

Several moments pass while she eyes me, trying to tell if I'm lying, but finally, she gives a curt nod and steps toward the door. "Then I will go with you."

I take her arm before she can walk past me and look down at her dress. When she follows my gaze, her cheeks blush.

"Go find the bedroom and change. Pack a bag of the wife's clothes while you're at it. I don't have anything for you to wear at my place."

She gives me a curious look before leaving to go upstairs.

My place. The thought makes my stomach turn, but I can't ask Hugh to put the girl up anymore. Not after the trouble she's caused.

Roman is out of the question. Everything that has happened since we left the warehouse must be kept quiet, and he would extract everything from her in minutes.

I don't trust her enough to put her up someplace by herself. At any time, Nikita could want to see her, so I really do need her close by.

So that leaves the hypothetical well I spoke of before, or … my place. For now, at least.

I pull out my phone to check my messages. Anya hasn't

texted me since last night when she let me know she wouldn't be home. She's gone more than she's home these days, so … maybe this won't be as bad as I'm imagining. Hell, if Elira is quiet enough, maybe I could keep her a secret.

I message Hugh to tell him I found Elira at a bus stop in Reno, then I shoot Anya a text.

Coming home tonight?

She should be in class, but she texts me back right away. Not a good sign.

Hailey's mom invited me for dinner, sooo...

I roll my eyes. Does Hailey even exist? '**Kay, love you.**

Love you too. Will be home tomorrow. Promise.

She follows that up with three kissing hearts emojis.

I put my phone away and blow out a breath, trying to think of the places in my house I could stash an Albanian whore. When Elira finally returns wearing baggy clothes with a suitcase in hand, I'm prepared to head for a side window that has the least likelihood of a surveillance camera, but she stops me in my tracks when she goes to the woman's body.

She bends over the woman, and with a hand so calm it's chilling, removes the wedding ring from the woman's finger.

She slides it onto her own finger, holding her hand up, twisting it, ensuring she likes the fit.

ELIRA

*H*e doesn't want me here.

I can tell by the tense way Maksim walks in front of me, leading the way into his home. When Nikita brutally murdered a man right in front of him, Maksim casually strolled to dispose of the body, but now his steps seem heavy, and his arms don't sway.

At first, I think his discomfort must be out of sheer embarrassment at the state of the place, but his eyes don't seem to even notice the bowl of milk spoiling on the kitchen bar or the clothes randomly littering the floor. When I look down, I see fresh dirt marks along the carpet from his shoes.

How do these people live like this?

There's a leopard print bra hanging over the back of the couch, and that Maksim *does* seem to catch. His eyes narrow as his lips pull into a frown.

With a sigh, he turns his attention to me.

I raise my chin and brace myself. After everything that just happened, it's hard to believe there will be no wrath to face. The worst part of Maksim is his unpredictability. He could be bringing me here only because his basement has the best equipment for torture.

"Are you hungry?" he asks me.

I don't respond, nor do I allow my guard to fall.

Am I hungry?

Does he know what I just did? It's been hours, and I used the Storms' washroom to clean myself up, but I still smell Daniel's blood. I feel its memory on my clean hands and in my hair. Feel the ring wrapped loosely around my finger that may not have been given but that I feel I've earned.

No, I'm not hungry.

"I'd rather get my punishment over with, if it's all right with you."

Rolling his neck, he ambles past me into the kitchen and over to the fridge. "I told you, I'm not going to hurt you." He pulls out two beers, twisting off each cap as he walks back to me.

"Sit." He gestures to a bar stool and sets one of the beers in front of it.

I want to argue, only because there's a certain level of discomfort involved in obeying Maksim, but I climb onto the barstool and sit anyway. As I pick at the label on the bottle, I chew on my cheek.

I hate to admit it, but when Maksim showed up, I wasn't scared, I was … relieved.

I didn't want to go to prison. Daniel had to die. He had to *pay*. The world will never be rid of all evil, but never again will that particular evil exist, and that was worth whatever price I had to pay. But I'm scared to be on my own here. I'm scared to face an unknown justice system. Or an organization that Daniel belonged to. Or the one Maksim belongs to. I'd rather just face Maksim.

"So," he says to me, making my prying fingers still on the bottle. "That was … interesting."

Interesting?

What does that mean?

I pull my hands away then rest them in my lap while staring at a red smudge of some kind, probably food, on the bar top.

"I won't lie, I'm surprised at what you're capable of. I feel silly for being so sympathetic when you had to see Nikita's unhinged side."

I only mean to scoff in my mind, but it leaves my mouth with such force that it rattles my shoulders.

I'm still staring at the red smudge when Maksim's light blue shirt enters my sight as he leans against the bar toward me. Swallowing, I lift my head to meet serious eyes that wait for me to explain myself.

"You didn't seem very sympathetic," I say, my voice even. I'm not angry. I'm disgusted by this man, but I have no reason to be angry with him. He didn't sell me. He didn't buy me. He doesn't even *want* me.

He tried to take my life, but now he's spared it a second time. He brought me to his home instead of pawning me off to his friends again. Unless his plans for me are more sinister than he's portraying—which would be unsurprising coming from a liar like him—I should consider myself lucky.

Lucky.

Maybe even grateful.

My mind recoils at that thought, unable to go that far, but I do have to admit that, for now, with Maksim is the safest place to be. So I should be kind. Desirable. Listen to my mother.

Be a good girl, Elira. You know what men want.

"I'm sorry." I rest my arms on the bar, trying not to react when something sticky coats my flesh. "I'm sorry I've been troublesome for you..."

When he says nothing, I peek into his eyes to see that

nothing has changed. My words haven't relaxed him. If anything, he looks more guarded.

"Are you angry with me?" I ask, shyly lifting my shoulders.

His eyes narrow, but instead of angry, he looks suspicious, like he's reading right through my attempt at placating him. I must be terrible at this.

I'm just about to stand and go to him, try to use touch to bring down his guard, when he speaks.

"I don't know what to feel about you, Elira." He stares at me a moment before bringing his beer to his lips and taking a long pull. When he's done, he slams the bottle on the counter and roughly takes my arm, dragging me off the stool.

My mouth opens to protest, but I lock the words in my lungs and move my feet when he pulls me down a hall. His grasp on my arm is strong but not exactly rough. Not quite hinting at what he has planned, if it's sadistic or not.

My heart thumps in my ears, and I swallow down words I'd like to spew. Whatever it is, it can't be as bad as the fate I deserve.

Be good. Just be good. At least figure out America, access money, make a connection or two, have *something*.

Then, if and when the time calls for it … I can kill Maksim too.

He throws open a door at the end of a hall and lets go of my arm once we're inside the room. The *bedroom*. A man's, if the clothes *covering* the floor are any indication. There are more articles of clothing on the floor than I own in total, and the four-poster bed that has a wadded-up comforter thrown on top of wrinkled sheets—one corner not even fitted beneath the mattress—is big enough to fit my entire family. The room itself is larger than my home, suddenly seeming cramped with the five of us, and somehow without asking I know this space is only for Maksim.

I want to be disgusted at the wastefulness of it all, especially with the little care he gives his things, but there's a part of me, this part that shames me, that wants a taste.

I wonder if this is what my father's house is like.

When Maksim's hand presses against my lower back, my eyes close. My body tries to recoil from his touch, but I fight the urge and let him silently guide me forward, clenching my hands to keep them steady.

I can guess why a man would bring me to his bedroom. I'm not an idiot. I'm just surprised this hasn't happened sooner.

Be a good girl, Elira. You know what men want.

I move forward toward the bed, leaving Maksim's hand behind to prove my acceptance of this. To prove that I can in fact be what he wants. That I'm a treasure to keep safe and secure instead of a burden to get rid of at the first opportunity.

Unable to help myself, I pull the material that slipped from its corner back to tuck it into place, and I smooth the sheets before straightening the comforter. It's a silly impulse, I know because there's nothing I could do to make this *nice*, but I do it anyway.

When I'm finished with the bed, I turn and sit, staring at my lap to avoid Maksim's eyes.

"All right, then," he says, his tone either curious or annoyed.

My face burns.

"I've got to get going. Thanks to your … *episode* … I'll have to work late, so I won't be back for a while."

I lift my head to look at him, feeling my lips pursed with confusion. Did I read this wrong?

The desire I expect to be in his eyes is nonexistent. He looks serious.

"You can stay at my place for a while if that's what you

want, but you should know, I don't live alone. My roommate is…" He tilts his head like he's weighing how to word this. "Unkind. He and I share everything, including whores, but I know you've had a rough go of things, so I won't mention you if you agree to behave. He doesn't randomly come into my room, so if you're silent, he'll have no idea you're here."

My jaw drops as my veins freeze over.

Roommate?

Share?

I feel like someone just kicked me in the stomach, and I lean forward, pressing my forearms on my knees and breathing through the sensation. I *just* got away from his friends. His supposedly kind friends. This one is *un*kind?

Is it Roman? Is that who lives here?

I feel the blood drain from my face but don't say anything. This is only more reason to get Maksim on my side, get him to start thinking of me as a person or ally or something other than a troublesome, stupid girl.

Maksim walks over to me, but I don't look up until he opens the cabinet door to his bedside table, which is actually a tiny refrigerator. In it are plastic water bottles, beer bottles, and bars of some kind in case the kitchen is too far a walk for a midnight snack, I guess.

I look at the floor.

"The fridge is stocked, so everything you need is in this room. Bathroom is there." I see him point in my periphery to an open doorway. I would be curious about him having a bathroom all to himself if I could breathe. "And if you're feeling scared, there's the closet." Now I look up to follow his finger to a closed door. "There's a trunk inside you could hide in if you wanted to be extra careful. My roommate usually gets home around four, so I'd say listen for the front door, then just play it safe in the closet. Piss in a bottle or something if you have to. Whatever you've got to do." He glances down at his wrist before working the clasp to remove it.

"Couldn't you just tell him I'm off limits?" I ask, my voice high.

"I could." He tosses the watch on the bed. "But I won't. That would involve creating a minor strain on his and my relationship, and you haven't proven yourself worthy of that. Allowing you to hide yourself is as far as my kindness is going to reach for now, and if you act up, I'll take even that privilege away."

"No." I shake my head. "Maksim, I... Please, I won't act up. I..."

I want to be worthy.

The words sound so pathetic. So desperate. They match the tremble in my lip perfectly, so while they kill my pride, I say them aloud.

"I want to be worthy."

Finally, his face begins to soften. He gives a single nod. "That's what I want too, Elira. That's what I've been trying to tell you."

His long legs devour the distance between us in only two steps, and when his hand reaches out toward my face, my eyes close, but I don't flinch away. My ear tickles as Maksim tucks my hair behind it. It's a comfort I don't want but one I think I need. I'd give anything for him to tell me he'll protect me. There are so many men to protect me from.

"One day, all of this will have felt like nothing more than a bad dream. I promise."

I promise.

You lie, Maksim. Your words mean nothing. I can hear the lie in every syllable, feel it in your touch, smell it in the air. It reeks.

He pulls back and turns before I even open my eyes. "I have an alarm system that will go off if you try to leave, so save us both the headache and don't. Just stay in the bedroom, kiddo, all right?"

He looks over his shoulder to see me nod before he leaves, returning a minute later with the suitcase full of Daniel's wife's clothes I stole before he leaves again.

I go to the closet, my eyes popping at the size of the small could-be bedroom, and find the trunk he talked about. I pull blankets along with a shoebox, a couple of tennis rackets, and some other junk out and neatly organize it on a shelf before tucking myself inside the trunk to make sure I'll fit. It's snug, but it'll do for now.

It couldn't be more obvious right now that I don't know what men want, at least not this man.

But I will find out.

11

MAKSIM

"*D*o you think you'll need any to-go boxes?" the waitress with freckles dotting her chest asks. Her tone is purposefully friendly, but she can't hide her impatience no matter how hard she tries.

I've been sitting at this table by myself for forty-five minutes. Thirty minutes ago when Anya claimed she was down the street, I went ahead and placed two orders of her usual bacon cheeseburger and fries our favorite steakhouse makes and have been sitting here letting the food cool for another fifteen.

I don't know whether to be pissed or worried.

"Uh…" I look at the door, willing my little sister to walk through, and when she doesn't, I turn back to the waitress. "Yeah, two please. And the check."

She smiles politely, relief softening her anxious eyes at freeing up a table.

With a sigh, I pull out my wallet and slide my card onto the edge of the table just as the booth rocks with my teenage sister plopping down across from me.

She shoves long, thick blonde locks over her shoulders

and beams at the plate in front of her like I haven't been sitting here for forty … I check my watch … nine minutes.

I could strangle her.

"Oh, thank God, you ordered. I'm starving." She picks up the burger and takes a large bite, moaning as she lets her head fall back, her jaw working as she chews.

The waitress shows up with the to-go boxes and the check, her disappointment now on full display. She gives me a tight-lipped smile before taking my card and walking away.

When Anya sets down her burger, she goes about sucking water through a straw, all the while avoiding my eyes.

"Anya."

Finally, she looks at me, her shoulders straight but her eyes guilty. Sometimes I have no idea if she does this shit on purpose. If she's punishing me. I know that I've failed her, and I wonder if she knows where I went wrong. Because I don't.

She gulps down water then blots her lips dry with her napkin, coating the thing with pink lip gloss. When she sets it down, she swats her hair back dramatically. "Before you *rip into me*, just know that I'm sorry, okay? Hailey and I got caught up preparing for this huge zoology presentation we have in a couple of days, and I'm talking *worth twenty percent of our grade* huge. The reception at the library—that's where we were—*sucks*, so I didn't even take my phone out of my bag and didn't realize what time it was until, like, five minutes after we were supposed to meet. Then," she sighs like the universe has been plotting against her all her life, "*of course*, the Uber got stuck behind a wreck on the way here—right after I texted you—and then my phone died."

She looks at her plate while picking at a fry. "Honestly, I get it if you're mad, but it really isn't my fault that I'm late, so let's just drop it, okay?"

There's a tightness in my arms that I try to loosen by flexing, but it only seems to make my skin feel as if it's crackling. I move my eyes to a television in a corner airing a baseball game and let it distract me for a moment.

She's lying. Obviously. If I texted her right now, her phone would probably ding. I wouldn't be surprised if she pulled it out, forgetting it's supposed to be dead, and started texting right in front of me.

She wasn't at the library. Kids don't go to the fucking library.

If there's a presentation at school, she's probably paid some kid to make the slideshow. This is Anya.

And 'Hailey'... God, I want to kill Hailey.

"Okay," I concede. What am I supposed to do?

She nibbles at fries while I stare at her in silence, trying to think of the right things to say. I wish we were closer. I wish I knew something, anything about her life that I could somehow relate to.

Enough time passes with neither of us speaking that if we weren't used to this, it would be awkward. She dives into her burger, but I've lost my appetite, so I pack mine away in a box for Elira. I wonder if this will be the thing she finally likes.

"Is it okay if I stay at Hailey's again tonight?" Anya asks before taking another gulp of water. "We have so much work to do on that presentation."

"I've never known you to be so studious," I say, unable to help myself.

She smiles, but it's anything but friendly. "Yeah, well, you've always been busy with work. You've never really *known* me to be anything."

Ouch.

"That's not true."

She purses her lips and nods her head in an annoying *sure thing* gesture, and I force myself to let it go. I really can't tell when she's baiting me versus when she's serious, but I've learned not to engage. Or I'm *learning*.

I look away a moment to collect myself before folding my arms on the table and leaning toward her. "So how was school?"

She throws her head back in a cruel laugh, putting her hand to her chest for effect. It's bitchy enough that it makes my teeth grind.

"Anya, I'm *trying*. Please, can we spend a half hour together without fighting?"

"We're not fighting. I'm just not an idiot, big brother. You don't care how school was, so don't waste my time asking."

Don't engage.

Don't engage.

Breathe. Divert. Try again.

Or not.

"If I thought you went to school, I would care how it went, Anya. I would. In fact, if I wasn't fucking *afraid* to hear about the things you do when you *should* be in school, I'd even love to have a conversation about that."

I can feel my anger getting the best of me, can feel the heat in my ears, the tightness in my chest.

Anya slumps in her seat but glares defensively. "What are you talking about?"

I lean toward her over the table, my teeth tightly clenched. "Did you have sex on my couch this morning?"

"*What?*" She rears back, trying to look shocked by the question, but guilt flashes across her face.

"Did. You…" I close my eyes and take a breath, steadying myself. When I open them, I speak calmly. "I found your bra on the couch when I stopped by the house this morning, and it wasn't there when I left for work."

"So? I came and changed clothes before school. What's the big deal?"

It wasn't before school. It was at ten o'clock according to the tracking app. And she's a fucking liar.

"You changed clothes in the living room?"

"What does it matter?" She flings her hands up, her eyes wide.

"It matters because you're full of shit, Anya," I growl, unable to take it anymore. "We have security cameras. Do you really think I don't see you bringing that tattooed piece of shit into my house when you're supposed to be at school?" I lean back and wipe my hand over my face, smearing the images away.

She knows we have door cameras. It would be stupid not to. What she doesn't realize, and what I don't plan on telling her, is that there's a camera in our living room and throughout most of the house. Except, of course, her bedroom and bathroom.

"Don't call him that," she growls, her black, chipped nail polish catching my eye as she grips the table. "You're not half the man that Tanner is."

I laugh. "I thought his name was Hailey."

"Fuck you." She shoves her plate my way, knocking silverware onto the wooden table. It makes enough commotion that I look around to see we've caught the attention of a few diners nearby.

I lean in and lower my voice, determined to have the last word. "If I could stop you from whoring yourself out to low-life trash, I would. But since it doesn't seem I can, I just ask that you stay off my *fucking couch*."

She stands abruptly, her perfect, ivory cheeks now a rosy-red color. The table rattles when she slaps her hand against it and leans toward me. "You don't have to worry about that because I won't be coming to *your* house ever again. I *hate* you."

Her eyes, so blue and fierce, show every bit of the hatred

she claims to have for me, but they also shine with pain I know in a moment I'll regret bringing on.

As soon as Anya storms away, the waitress returns with my card, as if she knew better than to interrupt our argument. We could've used the interruption.

I follow after Anya and see her climb into the passenger seat of a raised pickup with an obnoxiously loud idle. I don't have to guess who that is.

"Anya," I yell, walking to the truck, but she slams the door shut, and the truck roars away.

"It's your house too," I say to the air, letting my shoulders sag.

But that isn't what I said, is it? *My* house. *My* couch.

I let out a sigh and shake my head before heading home, heavy with regret.

* * *

WHEN I OPEN my bedroom door and don't immediately see Elira, my muscles wind tight. A flicker of panic tightens my chest.

"Elira?" I call, walking to the bathroom and peeking inside the empty space. I go to the closet next, remembering suggesting to her that she hide inside. She may have heard me get in and thought I was my 'roommate.' Having her hide in a closet is probably overkill. With the way things with Anya went tonight, she won't be back for a while. But what would I tell her if she *did* find Elira?

I don't want to think about it. I'd rather Elira just hide.

My breathing becomes shallow as I scan the empty closet. *Shit.*

But the alarm didn't go off. How could she...?

My eyes find blankets stacked on a shelf that shouldn't be there, and I remember the chest. It commands my attention now, my head tilting as I stare at the four by three box. Jesus, she actually stuffed herself in there?

I go to it and open the lid to reveal a cramped Elira with her eyes clenched shut as if she still thinks she's hiding from me.

"Hello," I say, barely hiding my amusement.

She opens her eyes and turns her head toward me. When she speaks, her voice is a cautious whisper. "Is he here?"

"No, he's gone for the night."

She lets out a relieved sigh before slowly untangling her limbs and lifting herself out of the chest. I consider helping her, especially when her face twists with pain, but I stand still. When she's finally upright, she presses her hand to her lower back and cringes, arching backward as if her body is a glow stick and she's trying to light up the sky.

I assumed she heard me come in, but she doesn't look like she just jumped in that chest.

"How long have you been hiding?" I ask, stepping from the closet and welcoming her out with me. Even knowing my fake roommate is gone, she still seems hesitant. She isn't nearly as afraid of me as she is of my imaginary friends.

"Since three."

My face has been soft, merely curious, maybe even a little amused, but now I feel my skin tighten.

"What?"

She glances up at me while following me from the closet into my freshly cleaned bedroom. I don't know how I didn't notice it when I walked in. The floor is bare as well as my nightstand, and after a quick sweep I still don't have a clue where any of my shit went. I'm a little too stunned to care.

Three? It's nine. She's been in there for six hours?

"You said he usually comes home at four."

"I said…"

I said he doesn't come into my room.

I don't finish the sentence. I'd be an idiot to. Am I even *sure* Anya doesn't come into my room? How would I know when there's no camera in here? Wouldn't it be safest *not* to assume these things?

It isn't as if I'm forcing Elira into a box and locking it for hours at a time. If she feels it's safest to do that all on her own, who am I to stop her?

"Well, he isn't coming home tonight," I say instead of finishing my thought.

Her arms cross over a white blouse a couple sizes too big, and it draws my attention to the oversized slacks she's wearing as well, but they don't hide the subtle curve of her hips. The wife's clothes remind me again what this girl is capable of.

Even in ill-fitting clothes, her beauty still strikes me. I don't know if it's actually her looks or if I'm imagining things after what I now know about her, but her eyes hold a fierceness to them that I know without a doubt could never be tamed. Her lips, full and supple, are either great for sucking cock or merely a cover for vicious teeth.

This girl isn't a whore. She's a vixen.

I gesture toward my bedroom door and walk that way. "Come on, I brought food."

Her feet patter after me, soft and light like a mouse (or an assassin) to the kitchen where the to-go box awaits on the bar. Elira silently slides onto a stool without needing the command and stares at the Styrofoam container with suspicious, disapproving eyes.

When I slide it to her, she carefully opens it, her eyes softening when she sees food that must look edible by her standards. I watch with a curious amount of anticipation as she picks up the burger.

I lived in Russia until I was nine years old. This is not my home country. But still, as she bites into that burger, I wait with a strange feeling as if it isn't only the food she's judging, it's me. So far, I am what she knows of America, and I do not impress. It wouldn't matter if it didn't remind me so painfully of my own experiences.

With that thought, a memory flashes that I immediately shove down, choosing instead to focus on Elira. That life was decades ago. It's over. It's done.

As she chews and swallows, she gives me no indication of what she thinks. No expression, good or bad, crosses her features, and for some reason, it irritates me.

"Well?" I ask, realizing I'm leaning toward her on the bar.

She looks up as if she's just noticed I'm still here. "Hmm?"

I splay one of my palms. "What do you think?"

"Oh." Her eyes dip to her lap while she tucks hair behind her ear. "It's, um. It's good. Thank you."

Thank you?

A little red flag waves in my mind, and I find my eyes constricting slightly. She's being especially polite this evening.

"Of course," I say through my growing suspicion.

I watch intently as she eats the burger like the good girl I know she isn't, just waiting for some kind of snarky remark to come from her. But it doesn't, and not knowing what has caused the sudden change in demeanor makes me uncomfortable.

My eyes lower to her tits. "I liked the dress better."

Wiping her mouth with the back of her hand, she looks down at the blouse, baggy in the chest.

"This is umm…" I wave my hand at her while I pretend to be thinking of a word. "Less than flattering."

"Oh…" She crosses her arms over her chest, apparently finished with her food. "I'll wear it tomorrow for you, then."

I'll wear it tomorrow for you, then.

What the fuck is she doing?

"I'd rather you wore it now. Or nothing at all." My voice is cold and reprimanding, as if she did something wrong by looking anything less than the sexy piece of ass she's supposed to be. I only mean to poke, to test, to tug that fiery girl out of her just to make sure I still have her figured out.

But my cold words, the thought of commanding her to take her clothes off, the thought that she may one day listen, heats my blood. Desire starts to crackle inside of me as I watch her, waiting for the fireworks to go off.

She looks at me with an expression as cold as my voice. She looks pissed. Her eyes hold a contempt that brings a comforting ease to my confusion, revealing that she was merely forcing herself to be polite. Maybe she's gotten smart. Maybe she isn't trying to be the manipulative little minx I know she can be.

I can't help but smile.

But then, as one corner of her lip crooks upward, my smile falls. She stands like she's about to call my bluff.

Her eyes never leave mine as she unbuttons her slacks and lets them fall off her hips into a puddle on the floor. I try to hold her stare, but my gaze betrays me and wanders to her long, slender legs. Her white, cotton panties are simple, as I guessed they would be. On another woman, I might like a thong, but it wouldn't look right on her. She's... I don't know. Different.

She lifts the blouse over her head next and tosses it to the floor before standing straight and peering into what I'm sure to her must look like weak, hungry eyes.

I am not this man. I *abhor* men who could let something as abundant as pussy bring them to their knees, but I'm ashamed to say my knees are shaking.

Fucking. Bitch.

"Is this what you want?" she asks, her voice silk. She's proud of herself. She'll lock herself in a box for six hours to avoid being fucked by a man she's never seen, but for me, she'll strip to only her panties as a way to tell me to go to hell. Strange, isn't it?

I don't answer. My voice would be even weaker than my eyes, so instead, I just take her in, looking over her perky tits outlined with a bikini top tan. She must've swam hours and hours in the Adriatic Sea to get that hourglass figure.

She's looked confident up to this point, but as she walks to me she's cautious, and the triumphant gleam in her eyes fades. She pauses in front of me, inches away, and says nothing, just stares at me, waiting. Waiting for me to make my move.

I do.

My hand, having a mind of its own, reaches out to caress a lock of her soft, dark hair. When I drop it, I move the back of my fingertips to her ear, down her neck, over her collarbone, her shoulder, then dip it part way down her arm.

I breathe in her scent, leaning in without thinking about it, and let my hand brush across her chest.

My cock strains against my pants, begging, *demanding* to take what's mine. What appears Elira is offering.

When I look at her face, my eyelids drooping, I see her eyes closed and her lips shut tightly. I can't tell if she's afraid, but I'd guess she's more expectant than anything. Then again, I'm not sure what she expects. I'm not sure what *I* expect.

I've never had a whore, never wanted one. The type of man who desires to own another human being is the type of man too weak to stand on his own. How pathetic it is to need to have full control over someone in order to have influence.

How pathetic it is to have to own a woman in order to get her to fuck you.

Surely, I can do better.

I look away, a breath stuttering past my lips as I let my hand skate down her side before I pull it away.

"That's better," I say, taking a small step back and clearing my throat. "You could stand to eat more. You're a little far on the thin side, but getting rid of the frumpy clothes is a good first step."

She opens her eyes, and I grin in anticipation of seeing her anger, but it isn't there. Her brown eyes go wide before they drop to the floor, and she covers herself in what looks like shame.

Fuck, too far.

She turns and scurries toward the hall.

"Elira, wait."

I stride after her, and when I take her shoulder, she spins to face me but doesn't meet my eyes. "I'm *teasing*. I'm sorry, I… I don't know why I said that."

She shakes her head, still not looking at me. Her cheeks are bright red. "I'm your whore, Maksim. You're allowed your preferences."

"No, you…" I look up, searching for words, not quite sure why I'm explaining myself. Maybe it's because of my night with Anya. Maybe I just can't take being this big of an asshole in interactions too close together. "I was trying to get a rise out of you, Elira. I like it sometimes when you're fiery, that's it. You're not too skinny."

"You said you…" She closes her eyes a moment as her fists ball in frustration. "You said you wanted me to be good."

"I know." I nod. "And I do."

"But I…" She looks down and gestures at her naked chest. When she looks back up, she has a desperate gloss to her eyes, and her lips are parted. "I don't understand what you want from me."

When she blinks away moisture that her lashes collect, my words catch in my chest.

What do I want from her? Honestly?

Nothing.

"Maksim, please," she cries, stepping toward me and clinging onto my shirt. My eyes widen with confusion. This is a side I've yet to see from Elira, and I've seen her in much more desperate situations. "Please, just tell me what you want me to be."

Putting my hands up, I try to coo. "Okay, calm down."

She takes several deep breaths, but they seem all but calm. I glance down at her chest before removing my shirt and handing it to her. She pulls it over her head in jerky movements.

"I am *sorry* about the skinny comment, okay?" I say with regret.

"I don't care about that!" Her eyes pop like her head is exploding, sending me back a step. "I was *standing in front of you naked*, and you still didn't want me. What am I supposed to do differently? Please, I… I'm so confused."

I stand with my head tilted for a moment, trying to process that.

Did she *want* me to fuck her?

No. No, I'm certain of that. The tightly closed lips, the clenched eyes… No, she didn't want it.

So what exactly is the problem?

"What do *you* want, Elira?" I ask, just as confused as she is.

She shakes her head. "I'm the whore. It doesn't matter what I want."

"It does if I say it does."

She narrows her eyes. Once again, I'm the enemy. "Fine, then I want to go home." Her eyes soften. "Please."

"No," I automatically say. "Not that. Obviously not that."

Her shoulders slump as if she really believed she had a chance, but it doesn't work that way. If it did, I wouldn't be here either.

She closes her eyes, and after only a few moments, opens

them with a new strength straightening her shoulders. "I want your protection."

From? I almost ask, but it's unnecessary. My imaginary roommate is the least of her worries.

When it comes to the Bratva, yes, she needs me. Her life would be worse off without me being in it, but my boss has locked that into place for her, so she need not worry.

But that organization... They will come. I would bet my life Daniel had security cameras just as I do, and his associates will be tracking us soon enough. When that time comes, she'll need me to not give her up, which would be my get-out-of-whore-free card that has not slipped my mind.

Now I understand the politeness, the eagerness to please, the desperation.

I must take too long to answer because her eyes leave me, and she purses her lips.

"You have no idea what this is like," she whispers, pushing hair out of her face with a shaking hand. "To you, this is one big joke. You can *tease* me as you call it and mock me, but you have no idea what it's like to be at the mercy of another person. You have no idea how terrified I am, all the time, and still, you joke..." She shakes her head, then angrily swipes a finger beneath both eyes.

I take her hand and gently put it back at her side before stepping within inches of her. She cranes her neck to look up at me.

There are so many things I could say. So many lies I could tell. I don't know this girl. Before a few days ago, she was nothing to me. She didn't exist. And if I'm honest with myself, if she had never tried to kill me, if she hadn't piqued my curiosity and earned my respect when she revealed herself to be a fighter, she would still not exist to me.

But she does exist to me. I see her. I see her pain. And as much as she'd never believe it, I do care.

"I know what it's like."

She blinks, then furrows her brow with confusion, but I don't explain further. It's been a long day, and I'm tired, too tired to dig up old wounds just to prove to her I know what pain feels like.

I allow my gaze to linger on her for a few more seconds before I pry myself away from her questioning gaze to go to my room, shower in mind, surprised when Elira doesn't follow.

12

ELIRA

I still don't know what Maksim wants.

It's been four days since he brought me to his home, three days since I offered myself to him. We're settling into a routine like roommates would, barely speaking to each other, barely *looking* at each other.

I listen for the front door vigilantly every day in the morning and early afternoon while I'm outside of the bedroom. I clean, organize, listen to music on an iPod I found in a hallway drawer, sometimes turn on the TV, sometimes cry, sometimes scheme, other times go through Maksim's things, searching for clues to piece together who he is.

I've found some interesting things. For instance, there's a box of tampons underneath the bathroom sink—not the one in Maksim's room—along with a host of female bath products in the tub. I've found lip gloss tubes forgotten about in drawers, a nail polish stain on the rug that took forever to get out, then there was that bra on the couch the first day.

It's safe to say a woman stays here frequently, maybe even lives here, so I think Maksim must have a girlfriend, unless the things belong to the girlfriend of the roommate I've yet to encounter (thankfully).

It would explain a lot. Why he didn't want me to stay here, why he doesn't want me *period...* I keep finding myself hoping she'll find out about me and dump him. If he doesn't take an interest in me soon, I'm going to give up on him. I grow more anxious by the second counting on his protection.

Around three in the afternoon, I go to the bedroom closet and wait until a quarter to four to climb into the trunk. Maksim is usually home by six thirty, so it's only about a two and a half to three hour wait, which is better than what the alternative could be.

Once he's home, we eat food he picked up from a restaurant while I question if my tastebuds will ever adjust to the enormous amounts of sugar. If he had anything in the fridge, my digestive system would be less of a wreck, but I haven't complained. There are so few ways into Maksim's good graces and many ways out of them.

But if I didn't care about his good graces, my throat would be shredded from screaming.

Even now, my face tics at the dirty footprints leading to the couch. The TV blares a news program loud enough for my grandfather in his grave, but Maksim doesn't seem to pay attention to it as he types away at his laptop, filthy shoes balanced on top of the coffee table.

He looks well put together today in his blue slacks and white shirt that hugs his biceps, but what was he doing, foraging through a jungle? Better question, how is it possible that he doesn't notice the trail that could be avoided by simply *taking his shoes off at the door*?

Tipping my head toward the ceiling, I take a deep breath. When I lower my head, the first thing I see is that damn trail of dirt, and although I know I should let it go, I clench my jaw and walk to the closet to get the vacuum.

His head turns my way when the vacuum starts up, and I spot a tiny glare like I've sparked irritation for breaking his concentration. Yes, because the TV is somehow soothing while the vacuum is a disturbance.

I turn my head so he won't see me roll my eyes. He doesn't tell me to stop, so I carry on, hoping he sees exactly the mess I'm cleaning up. Maybe he'll have the sense to avoid this in the future.

When I bring the vacuum in front of the couch, his jaw is tense, but he doesn't look up from the computer. His feet are planted on the floor now, blocking my path.

I hold the vacuum still and wait, staring at him. Eventually, he looks up, glares for a moment, then lifts his feet back to the table while I finish vacuuming.

Once I'm finished and the vacuum is turned off, I peek at Maksim's irritated face, aimed at the monitor, and suppress a smile.

I should not be glad to annoy him. I shouldn't. This is the opposite of my objective.

But… It can be fun, and this is the most we've interacted in days. Even at dinnertime, we eat in separate rooms. We sleep in separate rooms, him on the couch, me in his bed.

Some interaction is better than no interaction, right?

No, probably not.

After putting away the vacuum, I go back to Maksim to take care of the problem at the source. Carefully, I pull one shoe at a time off Maksim's feet while he stares me down.

"What are you *doing?*" he scowls.

His shoes dangle from my fingers, held out from me like they're toxic, and without answering, I turn and walk them to the front door. Maksim springs off the couch to follow me.

"Elira."

After neatly lining the shoes up at the door, I stand and gesture to them. *"Look."*

His blond eyebrows bunch together as his nostrils flare, his gaze not moving from my face.

"Your shoes go here. Or you can take them off and walk them to your closet, but when you wear them inside, you track dirt in. All you have to do is take your shoes off at the door, and your carpet will stay fresh. I won't have to interrupt what you're doing to clean up the mess."

His eyes are wide, and his lips part as he gives his head a small, incredulous shake. "God, you are such a bitch."

My throat constricts, and instinctively my shoulders lower, but I hold my expression neutral. The way he says it, so matter of fact, hurts worse than if he'd screamed it.

"Honestly," he says with a huff. "When you were doing this shit at Hugh's, it was kind of cute, but Jesus Christ, is *anything* good enough for you?"

I force myself to scoff, hoping my words don't stick in my throat. "I wouldn't say I ask for much."

Maksim rears his head back. I wait for his next retort, brace myself for it, but instead of speaking he shakes his head and pulls out his phone. His fingers tap away while I die a little inside.

I don't need much.

I *don't.*

These people, all that I've seen so far, have more things in junk drawers than I've ever owned, and I need none of it. Is cleanliness really so much to ask for? Good, clean food, a clean home, an honest man?

No, it isn't. Fuck him.

"What about you?" I ask, venom on my tongue.

He slips his phone in his pocket and looks at me with blank eyes. "What about me?"

"I've been quiet for *days*." I wipe my sweaty palms over the white dress he asked me to wear then never mentioned again. The one that took hours and a bottle of bleach to get the blood stains out of. "I've cleaned your home spotlessly, I haven't complained, I've been good. What more do *you* want?"

He rolls his neck, feigning exhaustion. "Jesus, not this again."

"I'm serious."

"I know." He looks me up and down with contempt that makes me want to cower. "Save yourself some dignity and keep your clothes on this time."

Anger, so hot it burns my eyes, ignites, and I clench my fists. I could hit him, and I half-consider it while thinking through words meant to bite, but my train of thought is halted, my anger snuffed when I hear something behind me.

The door.

I spin in time to see the knob twist and the door begin to open. My legs propel me backward into Maksim before I scramble around him and sprint for the bedroom.

My heart pounds so hard against my chest it hurts, and a fearful chill covers my flesh. Maksim's words are a distant memory as I climb into the trunk and shut the lid, praying he'll spare me.

Why did I do that?

Why did I fight with him?

I cover a hand over my mouth to muffle a cry as I shake and wait for my fate. I know the person at the door must've been the roommate. Who else would just walk inside?

And now he knows I'm here.

I cry harder, so hard I bite my hand instead of using it to muffle my sounds.

* * *

Maksim

MY LIPS ARE SPREAD WIDE in a grin, and a chuckle lodges in my throat, held there tightly until Elira is out of sight. It erupts as I turn to Alik, a Bratva enforcer, but my amusement doesn't rub off on him.

He stands like a statue with mismatched eyes—one brown, one oddly red—so cold, I'd think something was wrong if it wasn't his usual composure.

"What was that?" he asks, nodding toward Elira's ghost.

I turn to the side as a silent offering for him to come in, and he obliges, strolling into my living room with his hands tucked away in his jean pockets.

"*That* was my greatest pain in the ass."

"It looked like I scared her."

"You did. Want a drink?"

He gives a single nod before roaming his gaze around my home, studying it as Alik does most things. This isn't the first time he's been here, but you wouldn't know it by his never changing, curious gaze.

I walk to my liquor cabinet and pull out a bottle of Belvedere before retrieving two glasses.

"Should I apologize?" he asks, his tone neutral. I'm unsure if he's capable of empathy or remorse, but with the work he does for me, I highly doubt it. There's a reason I prefer him out of all the enforcers the Bratva has. He isn't sadistic, and therefore wastes no time, but he isn't the slightest bit hesitant to commit acts of violence that would make any other man cringe. His complete detachment from humanity makes him utterly efficient.

"No, that was the point of asking you to walk in without knocking. I wanted her to think you were someone else."

"Ah," he says, sitting slowly on the couch, sliding his eyes over the empty walls. I wonder how long they would linger if

I had photo frames or something hanging up. "You wanted to scare her."

I don't answer. For some reason, saying it out loud makes me feel like an asshole. I pour the drinks then walk his to him.

Long fingers wrap around the glass when I hand it to him, and he gives me a tiny quirk of his lips and a tip of the glass before drinking. I sit in a recliner adjacent to him.

He stares into his glass when he brings it down. "What a cruel game."

I feel my face tighten as my eyes slightly narrow. Maybe I was wrong. Maybe he does have a sadistic side.

"Right… So what did you find out?"

Looking up at me, he folds his legs and rests the glass on his knee. "They know little."

"Little?" I raise a brow. "Little is not nothing."

Without breaking eye contact, Alik slips his hand into his pocket and pulls out a flash drive that he tosses to me. I catch it with one hand before studying it as if the information is written on the outside instead of hidden within.

"The organization caught most everything on security footage, which you guessed, but nothing I found points to them knowing your identity. They do know the girl's, but their assumption is that she's on her own. They don't suspect she's with you."

I shift to face him fully, my brow furrowing.

He goes on to explain without me needing to ask the question.

"The footage that they have is on that flash drive." He points to the device in my hand. "Watch it and you'll see why. There's a video of her murdering Daniel Storm, *to put it lightly*, but part way through, blood covers the webcam, so it ends there. The only other camera on the property is a door-bell camera that catches you entering with a key several hours after the incident. They know you were there for her, but reason would suggest she was already gone and is likely still on the loose, given what she's capable of."

I lean back on the couch and blow out an amused gust of air, bringing my glass to my lips but pausing.

They still don't know who I am, don't even know that I have her.

Smiling, I take a sip of the vodka.

"The wife is calling for vengeance."

Wiping my lips on my shoulder, I shrug. "So let her."

"She wants them to harm the girl's family. An eye for an eye."

I huff. "They're in Albania. That's too much of a hassle."

"For the organization, possibly. For the wife, possibly not."

Tension suddenly appears in my neck, and I roll it out. "What are you saying, Alik?"

When I look at him, his shoulders rise and fall. "I don't know, boss. I'm just here to give you information."

For several moments, I just stare, and he stares back with empty eyes that would give away nothing of what he's thinking if I didn't already know.

He's thinking it might be a good idea to kill the wife.

It's an idea. But I don't like it.

Right now these people don't believe Elira has help. I kill the wife, that changes. I kill the wife, and immediately, my identity becomes loads more important. They don't just find me, they find Nikita. I was prepared to face this with him, but fuck, if all I have to do is claim not to have her and they'll leave it be, I could avoid that exchange altogether.

That organization is not going to go to some village in Albania just to slaughter some girl's family to avenge some cockroach on their payroll. He was a trafficker. He made them money, yes, but believe me, if he was that important, they would've found Elira by now. They were probably relieved to see his death was one of revenge instead of a message for them from rivals.

They aren't going to Albania. The wife flying over to kill Elira's family also seems unlikely, unless she's as crazy as Elira. She's emotional. She lost her husband. It'll pass.

Alik finishes his drink in silence, then I walk him out. As soon as he's gone, I put the flash drive in my laptop, too curious not to take a peek.

I skip over the doorbell stuff and go straight to everything caught on webcam.

The hairs on my arm raise as I watch her with Daniel's hand wrapped around her throat. When Elira pulls the knife from beneath her dress and rams it into his side, a shooting pain occurs in my stab wounds. I find myself absently touching my bandages.

I can see now that she went easy on me that first night. That, catching me off guard, she could've killed me if she'd had it in her. In the video, she looks crazed as she shoves the knife into Daniel's abdomen, over and over and over, so fast he doesn't have a chance to fall.

When he stumbles backward, his hand on his stomach, his head downcast, she takes a strong step forward and slashes the knife across his carotid, sending blood spraying. He spins on his way to the floor, splattering the camera and effectively blocking what happens next.

But I saw the body, so I know. She stabbed him at least a dozen more times.

Shaking my head, I close my laptop. I throw a look over my shoulder at the hallway that leads to my room where she's hiding, terrified of a monster that doesn't exist. Once again, I consider killing her before she gets the sense to kill me first.

And once again, I can't bring myself to do it.

13

ELIRA

"*L*ook, it's Diellza," I say to myself, pointing out the glass sliding door that leads to the back patio up to a cloud in the clear blue sky with two jutting, white puffs that look vaguely like rabbit ears. My lips spread into a soft smile as I pretend to be home, to be speaking to Bora, my youngest sister, her stuffed rabbit named Diellza clutched tightly to her chest.

My heart aches, but I don't let my smile fall, not yet. I've spent too much time ruminating on loss, on regret. I don't feel like being sad today.

"I bet you're doing fine, *zemer*." I have to fight to stretch my lips. I picture Bora and Asher back home with our mother, sitting at the dinner table envious of the life I'm living. Asher's hands will still be sticky from collecting honey in the hives we harvest on our property, and Mami will be scolding her for not already washing up.

I smile at the defiance I know will be in her eyes as she stomps to the washroom, returning with her frizzy hair and dirty face from a day of exploring and working with animals she was born to love. She'll tease Bora for still clinging to a stuffy at the age of eight, and now that I'm no longer there, Mami will have to be the one to remind Asher of the photo we keep on the mantle of her sucking her thumb at age ten.

I thought I wanted more than that life, but now when I close my eyes and I breathe in, I long for the smell of the apple tree in our meadow and the gnawing of the goat's teeth when it mistakes my shorts as food. I miss the stickiness of honey and the feel of the warm sun on my back. I dreamt of being served important dinners among colleagues, but I'd kill to be slaving away in a crowded kitchen among friends again, preparing a feast for locals and tourists alike.

But I won't think about that too hard. Not today. Today I will smile, remembering the softness of Bora's chestnut hair, the shade of our father's—a man she never got the chance to meet—as I carefully wove it into two braids.

A sigh rushes past my lips as I open my eyes.

God, I miss them.

A sound snaps my attention to the front entryway, and I push off the wall to sit up straight, my spine erect, the hairs on the back of my neck standing at attention.

I've had this same physical response a dozen times already today, so I'm not actually expecting anyone to be there. My guard has been raised since last night, not allowing me to relax for more than a few minutes at a time. I dozed off in the closet only to snap awake a hundred times over until morning came.

I'm exhausted, but as far as I'm aware, safe.

Only this time, the reaction isn't in vain, the stimulus not imagined.

The front doorknob rattles like someone is unlocking it, and although it's probably Maksim, my eyes pop. I jump up from my spot by the back door and rush toward the hallway, but the front door opens before I get there.

I press my back against the hallway wall and put my hand

over my mouth, my heart beating wildly while I wait to hear signs that whoever is here saw me.

A beeping sounds, the alarm Maksim talked about, but it stops a few moments later after a succession of beeps.

"Now," a young woman says. "Where were we?"

She giggles a moment before the giggles turn to moans that move this way. As quietly as I can, I creep to Maksim's room and open the door only enough to slide through, hoping the couple doesn't hear the noise.

I didn't hear the man's voice, but he must be the room-mate. Surely Maksim wouldn't bring a woman here, not unless she's cool with him having, um, me.

When they stop at one of the other rooms in the same hall, it confirms my suspicion that it's the roommate. It's the only room in the house that I haven't explored, which I assumed is his bedroom. I wouldn't have dared to go in there even if it wasn't locked.

I go to hide in the closet, but sound draws me back to the door to listen. They're yanking on the roommate's bedroom door.

"What the fuck?" the young woman growls.

The roommate chuckles. "It's locked?"

"He locked my fucking door?!"

Her door?

My face pinches with confusion. Huh?

The woman kicks at the bedroom door multiple times. "Stupid fucking piece of shit asshole!" She groans loud and dramatically, so much so that I start to question whether she's a woman at all. She sounds younger.

A child?

When angry feet stomp this way, I scramble away from the door and rush to the closet, barely tucking myself inside before the bedroom door bursts open. My fear draining, I watch through the crack in the closet door as the girl viciously tears open Maksim's nightstand drawer in search of something.

Meanwhile, the guy I'm no longer sure is the roommate and old enough looking that I wouldn't call him a boy, flops down on the bed and stretches out, lacing his hands behind his head and crossing one dirty sneaker over the other.

"I don't know, babe. This is better anyway."

She pauses what she's doing only long enough to glance at him and let out a feeble laugh. "Right."

I shift to get a better view as she walks around the bed to the other nightstand. Instead of rifling through this drawer, she rips it out entirely and chucks it on the floor in a rage. When the contents scatter, she drops to her knees and searches.

"Mmm, jackpot," the guy says, hopping off the bed to retrieve a package of condoms off the ground. He pulls one out and waves it at her, his eyebrows wagging.

"Gross." She lets out another feeble laugh. "Just give me a minute. I know the key's around here—"

"How is it gross?" He arches backward and gives her a chastising look that makes my head tilt and my curiosity pique. The fear I had has vanished.

Her shoulders hunch slightly, and she laughs. "Those are Maksim's."

"Yeah, I figured."

"Right, so I mean…" She waves her hand like it's obvious.

"Oh my God, you're such a kid." The guy, the *asshole*, laughs at her, shaking his head as he tosses the condom on the bed.

"Oh really?" she asks, her face reddening. "Well, then what does that make you?"

Smiling, he takes her face in his hands and laughs when she pulls away. "Babe, come on, don't be mad."

"I just don't know what you mean by that." Now she sounds whiny. Young. Way too young to be with him.

He looks sleazy. Tattoos are not inherently bad, in fact, they can be kind of hot, but not on him. On him, they look like a means for hiding needle holes. They poke out of the top of a ratty T-shirt with an unfamiliar band on it and go all the way down both arms. His hat is the cleanest article he's wearing, and it can't be for shading him from the sun because he's wearing it backward. It looks like its purpose is to tame greasy, reddish hair.

"I just mean you can be a little immature." He runs his hands down her sides, resting them on her hips, and when she lets him, I frown. "Don't get me wrong, you're way more mature than most girls your age, but... Babe, come on. A condom is just a condom. It all comes from the same store, and that shit costs money. Not all of us have a big brother to foot the bill."

A big ... *brother*?

Maksim?

My heart speeds up, but this time it has nothing to do with panic. Heat spreads to my ears, but I don't move. I barely breathe.

It all, in an instant, becomes clear.

There is no *fucking* roommate. *She* is the roommate. Not a man, not a girlfriend, but a sister. She's the reason he didn't want to bring me home. She's the one I've been hiding in a motherfucking trunk from.

I turn my head on impulse to glare at the trunk.

I'm gonna kill him.

I'm *going* to kill him.

That *son of a bitch*.

To quote his sister, that *stupid fucking piece of shit asshole*.

I would growl if I didn't still want to stay hidden.

Why do I want to stay hidden? What the hell are *they* going to do?

I turn my head back to peek through the crack at the two. The guy's mouth is on her neck now, and he fondles her as he coaxes her back onto the mattress. When he moves to her mouth, she kisses him back, but I can tell even through a crack in a door that she's uncomfortable.

"Tanner." She grabs his hands when he pulls her shirt up. "Tanner, wait."

He leaves the shirt alone but moves to kiss her mouth, I'm assuming to shut her up. It suddenly feels wrong to watch this, but I can't look away. Even in my limited experience with men, I know what's happening. Even with this being Maksim's sister, someone I could hate for the crime of loving him, I care.

He lifts up her skirt and grinds on top of her, ignoring her meager protests.

Yell, I want to shout. I want to tell her to be stern. *Loud*. Insistent. But I stay put instead and watch, my heart pounding.

"Tanner." She pulls her head away so he can't claim her mouth again and speaks louder this time, but she follows his name up with a laugh to soften her tone. "We're not seriously going to fuck in my brother's bed, are we?"

"Shhh, baby." He puts a finger to her mouth before replacing it with his lips. After a minute, he turns their bodies so her head is on the pillows, blocking their faces from my view, but I no longer want to see.

I can feel the heat in my cheeks when I step back from the door and listen to sounds that turn my stomach until I can't take it anymore.

Without caring about the consequences or even knowing what they'll be, I sneak from the room and hurry to the front door. The idea of simply leaving crosses my mind but only for a second. It was never a real option anyway.

Taking a deep breath, I open the front door and slam it as loud as I can.

14

ELIRA

I wonder, had I not known exactly what was going on, if I would have been able to feel the tension in the house with the same intensity as I do after the door slams shut.

It wasn't particularly loud before, but a dreadful silence casts over the space as I picture the panic Maksim's sister must feel believing that her brother just arrived home.

I walk to the kitchen at a leisurely pace and open the fridge door, pulling out items only to put them back in as if I'd just arrived from a store.

Panicked footsteps shuffle down the hall just before the back door slides open, and I think for sure the sister is gone when I hear the faint *click*. But when I turn toward the living room, I see her scared, timid form appear.

Her face sags when she sees me, but then it goes taut with worry. She spins to face the front door, her hands pointed out like she's bracing for something. She looks like she's about to run.

"Maksim isn't here," I say to calm her nerves. At the same time, a vehicle roars, and I mean *roars*, to life outside, pulling my gaze that way. Tires screech, signaling the successful escape of her boyfriend.

When the sister turns to me, she looks more confused than afraid. There's a bite in her voice when she speaks. The timid little girl is long gone, and I have become the enemy. "Who the hell are you?"

Woah. Potty mouth.

I smile and try not to let her brazenness remind me of Asher. "My name is Elira. Who the hell are you?" I ask the question in a calm voice, as if I'm simply not familiar with the foul language.

Her jaw drops like she wasn't expecting me to say that. After what she just went through, and after what I know she'll go through again and again by having sleazy boyfriends like that, I wish I could hug her.

But that, unfortunately, is not how you reach a teenage girl like this one, nor Asher. Not yet. You must earn her respect before she'll gift you her vulnerability.

She crosses her arms over her chest and glares so intensely, I question if she's trying to melt my mind or something. "I *live* here."

"Ah." I nod. "Maksim's sister. I did guess that."

"Anya," she corrects, shifting her weight.

She's uncomfortable with me being here. Does he not usually have girls over?

"So I guess you're the fuck of the week?" she asks.

Oh. Maybe he does have girls over.

I stare at her, keeping my face neutral. She speaks with such a snarky tone, but there's a pain beneath her words that peeks over that hard exterior she's trying so hard to put off. I bet she fools most people so well.

If he does have women over, I don't think she likes it.

"No," I say, unsure what I *should* say. "We're friends."

She quirks a brow and juts out her hip as she adjusts her

crossed arms. "A friend who shows up unannounced when he isn't here to rifle through our fridge?"

I glance at the open refrigerator and put the rest of the groceries away before closing it.

"I brought groceries, actually. I just came back from the store."

"Where the fuck are your shoes?"

'Fuck' now too?

I turn to her and glimpse my bare feet. "It's rude to wear shoes into others' homes. It tracks in dirt."

She laughs and leans against the bar. "Where did you get that idea? Your accent is thicker than *Maksim's*, so obviously you aren't from here."

"I'm from Albania," I say, proud.

She stares blankly. I bet she couldn't point to it on a map.

"Why are you here?"

I shrug. "My father is American, so I suppose you could say half of me is too."

A beautiful curtain of blonde waves shimmers as her head tilts, and she peers at me hatefully through blue eyes. "Cool, but why are you *here*, in my home, bringing shit to my fridge, dragging your dirty feet through my house? Women don't hang out here during the day, so I know my brother's dick can't be that good. What, are you fishing for a green card or something?"

Now my neutral expression snaps. My eyes go wide, and I feel the blood rush to my ears. A powerful surge flows through my hand, tempting me to slap her.

Why are these people so. Fucking. *Arrogant*?

My teeth grit, and I inhale, ready to growl, but I've had enough fights with Asher to know it's a mistake. She's pushing me. She's trying to get a reaction. She *wants* this.

I don't have to fight hard to tame my anger because the fire in her eyes dwindles without me speaking a word. Her eyes aren't on my face anymore. They've lowered, to the left of me.

I look down, tensing when I realize what it is she's looking at, but it's too late to rip my hand out of sight. The shiny diamond I stupidly have worn on my left hand since confronting Daniel, the one I was sure I'd earned, seems to gleam brighter than ever in the light of the kitchen.

"That's it, isn't it?" she asks, her voice low and weak. She clears her throat, but she isn't hiding her pain well anymore. When she looks me in the eyes again, she forces herself to stand straighter. "So what, my brother bagged a mail-order bride? Is he that fucking pathetic?" She laughs a sickly, cruel laugh.

No.

I open my mouth, ready to correct her, ready to set the record straight, but something stops me. This is Maksim's sister. If I tell her the truth, he will no doubt kill me. My only option is to lie.

I could tell her I'm someone else's wife, but I can see in her eyes she's already made up her mind. It wouldn't make sense. Whose wife would I be? Why would I be here? How would I answer these questions?

Anya shakes her head in disgust, but she waits for my confirmation. She cares. I see so much pain in her eyes that my heart grants her sympathy I wouldn't know was possible for Maksim's kin.

And even though I *hate* him. Even though I think he's slimy, he's scum, he's as pathetic as this girl pretends to believe he is … I don't *want* her to know the truth about him.

"Your brother loves you," I say, my voice soft and soothing.

She scoffs, looking away so I won't see her eyes water.

"He does, Anya. You are the most important person in his

life, and he would never do anything to intentionally hurt you."

"Do you even know my brother?" she spits, whipping her hair off her shoulders and slapping the bar top. "I mean, besides the fact that he's an American who can grant you citizenship? Do you *know* him? What kind of man do you think needs to ship a woman overseas because *all* the other women in this country wouldn't want them? Do you think he's a *catch*?"

She laughs and drags her hands down her makeup-caked face. "Has he told you what he does for a living? Because as soon as he does, you'll run. I promise you, you'll be on the first flight back to Armenia."

"Albania," I correct, walking toward her. "And I wish that were possible."

Her lips purse while she waits for me to clarify.

I lean toward her on the opposite side of the bar. I can feel my face perfectly relaxed even as my mind rejects what I'm about to say. *I fucking hate you, Maksim.*

"Yes, I know what your brother does for a living. His boss introduced us."

Anya pulls back slightly, like the mention of Nikita scares her as much as it does me. I don't imagine she knows much about the man, but enough to know she should be wary of him.

I sigh. "Can I be honest with you? You seem, uh…" I pause as if I'm searching for the word I know hits hardest for her. "Mature. I think you can handle the truth."

She seems to stand taller, putting on a brave face as she nods.

"Back home, I wasn't um…" I look down for a moment in false shame. Again, fuck you, Maksim. "I wasn't free, Anya. There were very bad men there who wanted me to do things for them, to make them money. Do you understand?"

Her shoulders slump, and her face twists with pity as she nods.

"I met an American man there, also not a good man, but he agreed to marry me so I could at least be free of the monsters in Albania. When I got here, our engagement fell through, and I was going to have to go back."

I look off, willing tears to gather in my eyes as I paint my enemy a hero to this naïve girl. The man who wanted to kill me after telling me salvation was on the other side of a hill.

Fuck you, fuck you, fuck you, Maksim.

"Then I met Maksim," I say, a longing quality to my voice that makes me want to vomit. When I look back at Anya, I take her hands. "Please, you must understand, I *begged* him to agree to marry me. He was terrified of what you would think, but I told him about the horrible life I lived before, and he felt sorry for me. He *saved* me, Anya. Your brother is a good man... The best I've ever known."

Puke. Vomit. Hurl.

"Wow." She looks down, then up at me, her cheeks pinkening. "I... I'm so sorry. I had no idea. All that shit I said..." Her eyes well with tears. I let go of her hand to cup her porcelain cheek.

"You couldn't have known," I say with a sad smile.

"Still, that was..." She shakes her head and pulls her hands from me to pat her chest, free from a bra. "Hold on a sec, let me get my phone. I want to put your number in, and I'll give you mine. I can't really stand to be around my brother lately, to be honest, but if there's *anything* you need... I mean, this is a new country, right? Maksim is always working, so if you need anyone to show you the good malls or something, I'm your girl. Unless, you know, you have other friends already or—"

"I have no other friends." I smile and pray she doesn't

start another awkward ramble. I *really* guilted her, didn't I? She'd feel even worse if she knew the truth.

This is good, though. She's a child, but someone to show me this city is exactly what I've been needing. And *she* knows the passcode to the alarm system.

Maksim will kill me for this, but he has no idea how much he owes me.

"And that would be *great*. I've been almost nowhere, so I'd love to get out."

She nods with a smile, happy to have something to relieve her guilt. Her eyes pop when I don't say anything further. "Oh, you mean *now*?"

I shrug. "Unless you have school to get to?"

With a wicked grin, she shakes her head and steps toward the hallway. "Just let me grab my phone and clean up. I took a nap on Maksim's bed and am a drooler, so I have to throw the comforter in the wash. You don't happen to know where the key to my room is, do you?"

"Sorry, hon, don't have a clue. Do you want some help?"

"No!" She nervously laughs. "No, thank you. I'll just be a minute."

Without another word, I walk to the hallway dresser I've been using to sort junk and pull out a pair of flip flops I found shoved beneath the couch days ago. They're a size too small and obviously Anya's, so I hope she doesn't notice, but even if she does, I suppose it doesn't make much of a difference. Even in my lies, I'm a pitiful whore.

I wait for her by the door, my fingers tingling with excitement. I'm sure there will be hell to pay for this, but for now, I'm going to enjoy my first real day in this American city.

15

MAKSIM

*C*hinese takeout hangs from my arm, the plastic bag rustling, as I step up to my front door only to find it unlocked.

My chest seizes, my eyes glued to the gap where the deadbolt should be in place, and for a moment, I'm frozen.

Anya…

I swing the door open and step through while telling myself not to panic. Elira has been stuffing herself inside a trunk in my closet, so that's where she'll be.

Except, the moment I smell food, *real* food cooking, I know that isn't the case. I halt in the hallway and listen to the sound of Elira's voice. She sounds like she's explaining something, and I stay perfectly still with my ear craned that way until my little sister's voice replies.

Fuck.

Fuck, fuck, fucking, fuck.

I walk that way as calmly as I can, unsure what I'll do when I arrive in the kitchen. A protectiveness takes over me that makes me question why I was foolish enough to let Elira live, to bring her here of all places, to ever think this could work.

Now I have to kill her. Now, having the audacity to threaten my relationship with my sister, with the only thing in my life that matters, it becomes obvious.

What did she tell her? What kind of lies will I have to tell Anya now?

When I step foot into the kitchen, resting the bag of takeout on the bar top, both women turn to look at me.

I expect anger. Repulsion. I expect at least one slap in the face from Anya, maybe one from Elira if she's feeling ballsy.

I'm not prepared for this.

My face is hard, my chest open and broad even with how tight it feels. I expect the very worst, so when Anya smiles, *smiles* at seeing me, my brain tumbles with confusion.

"Hey," she says as if my whore is not standing next to her in our kitchen. As if I'm not an even more despicable human being than she pegged me for just days ago. As if she hasn't ignored every call, every text, every apology I've tried to give since we last spoke.

"Elira's teaching me to make baklava." She gestures to the stacked dough on a pan in front of her while beaming. I don't have any idea what to make of that, so I simply stand in shock.

Huh?

"Oh," I say at last, and if it's possible to fumble on a single word, I succeed.

The timer on the stove goes off, making Anya jump with excitement. Elira pulls out a pan of something with an incredible smell I can't yet appreciate properly. She sets it on the stove and tosses the oven mitt on the counter. I don't miss how she avoids my eyes and has neglected to greet me the same as I've neglected to greet her.

"Oh my God." Anya hops in front of the pan and waves

the steam toward her face, leaning her head back and breathing in deeply. "This looks *amazing*. Mak, come look."

She tosses me a smile over her shoulder, something she hasn't done in ... I can't remember. When she was a little girl, she used to look at me like I was her world. She used to squeeze my hand extra tight when she was excited, pulling me along with her, throwing me that same smile, bursting with joy she couldn't contain.

I had no idea how much I missed it until just now.

I walk to the stove, avoiding looking at Elira as much as she avoids me then look down at the dish. It has a yellowish, solid yet creamy top that looks unfamiliar. Whatever it is, it smells good.

"It's tavë cosi," Anya tells me. "Lamb and rice with a yogurt/egg mixture on top."

"Wow."

Where the fuck did the ingredients come from? I turn my head to Elira, but she doesn't meet my eyes, of course.

Did she fucking leave the house?

"Tomorrow we're going to make blini. Like Mom used to make."

My eyes widen for half a second before I neutralize my expression. Anya doesn't talk about her mother. Ever. Not to me. I didn't realize she even remembered her mother, let alone her blini. She was only three when her parents died.

Discomfort washes over me while I try to debate what to say.

"Cool."

When her face falls, I open my mouth to say more, but nothing comes out. Now I can feel Elira's eyes on me, intruding on something so private that, to her, must feel basic. That's what she's been since she's entered my life, one big intrusion.

Bitterness tries to curl my lip, but I keep my attention on

Anya and give up on saying anything further about the blini. I don't want Elira anywhere near her, certainly not near a hot stove or kitchen knives.

What the fuck is Elira's game plan?

I don't know, but this can't continue. *She* can't continue. With a glance her way, I debate what to do. I could kill her myself as soon as Anya inevitably runs to her boyfriend, or… I could just give her back to the people who really want her. All it would take is one phone call. Hell, one text.

Nikita will understand. He will think I'm weak for allowing her to get away, but when he sees the video, he'll understand that she isn't a typical woman. He'll respect my decision and find another way to punish my other choices.

"I'm gonna step outside," I say, eyeing the exit. When I slip out the back door, I pull out my phone and search for the contacts I originally got when I looked for Daniel Storm's identity.

The door slides open, and I watch Anya come through and shut it before walking to me with her hands behind her back, her head shamefully bowed.

Okay, seriously, what the fuck is going on?

"Hey." I lower my phone. "Are you okay?"

She nods while chewing on her lip, but when her face ripples with an impending sob, I widen my eyes and open my arms for her as she crashes against me. She hugs me tight, tighter than I can remember, and cries against my chest.

"I'm so sorry," she mumbles before sucking in a deep breath.

I smooth my hand over her back, at first awkwardly, but then my eyes close and I squeeze. My chest aches at the tension that's been so tightly wound between us, and although the hug is still fresh, I get the sudden dread that this will be the last time I ever feel her arms around me. It doesn't feel possible for us to ever be close again, so this small taste is almost too painful to bear.

"I'm sorry too." I run my hand down her hair and squeeze. "I know I'm not enough for you, Anya. I know you need more. I'm so sorry for the things I've said to you and the things I have and haven't done. I swear to you, I'm trying."

She pulls away and shakes her head, wiping fresh tears from her eyes. "No, that's bullshit. You're more than enough. I just treat you like shit because…"

She looks off like she's ashamed, and again, I search for words to make her pain go away, finding none. I'm terrible at comforting her.

She looks up and takes a sharp breath. "Because I thought you were a bad guy. Because of your job. I thought…" She shakes her head. "It doesn't matter what I thought. I said awful shit to you, and it turns out, I'm just a shitty judge of character. You were right about Tanner. He's a lowlife asshole."

I stare at her, more confused than I was when I walked into my house.

She hates me because of my job? Okay. That's fair. But why does she suddenly think she was incorrect in her assessment?

"Elira told me everything," she says, answering my unspoken question. Sort of. It actually makes me more confused.

"What is *everything*?"

Her long eyelashes flutter as she hugs her stomach. "She told me about the men in Albania who took her freedom and how you agreed to marry her so she wouldn't have to go back there. She told me you saved her."

She said I…

I slowly blink while I try to wrap my head around that, but the look my sister gives me makes it difficult to question the warped reality for long. She's looking at me like I'm *her* savior. Like I'm suddenly worthy. Like I'm…

Like I'm her brother.

"Just so you know, I'm not angry," Anya says, holding her hands up. "I get why you didn't tell me about eloping and the green card stuff. But I hope now that I know, maybe we don't have to hide so much from each other anymore?"

She gives me a tiny, hopeful smile as she says it, tears glistening in her eyes.

Finally, I have no hesitation to speak. I nod, my throat feeling smaller. "I'd like that very much."

Again, she throws her arms around me, and I hug her back, my eyes drifting to the glass door. I spot Elira watching us by the hallway. She walks away as our eyes meet.

She is a clever, *clever* bitch. Telling my sister we're married, making herself a more permanent marker in my life, buttering Anya up, ensuring herself extra security. Well done, Elira. Well done.

I try to make myself angry, but it's hard when I feel like for the first time in a very long time, the war between my sister and I is at rest.

I slip my phone into my back pocket, no longer intent on making a call.

After all, what kind of husband gives his own wife up?

16

ELIRA

*W*hen I lay my head down for the night, I'm content, with the most peace I've felt since leaving Albania.

It isn't *real* peace. I couldn't begin to know what true peace feels like. But it's better than fear of someone sneaking into Maksim's bed in the middle of the night. It's an inkling of safety.

Anya loves me.

I smile at the thought, my mind taking me to the mall today. She used her brother's credit card to buy me enough things that Daniel's wife's clothing is now obsolete. I've never spent so frivolously in my life, and I could lie here with my lip curled, pretending the overconsumption disgusts me, but not today. Today, I feel like royalty. Today, I feel *great*. Even within this shitty existence.

Breathing in, I no longer smell Maksim on the freshly-washed pillowcase. In the morning it'll be my own scent rubbed off on the satin, as if this is my bed. For a moment, I pretend that it is. For a moment, Anya is my sister and today was one of many outings to look forward to. I'll be sending Mami a check tomorrow and a photo for Asher just to tease.

It's a nice fantasy. But, of course, Maksim has to ruin it.

The bedroom door opens, announcing his arrival, and I sit up in bed, tugging the comforter to my neck. He showered a while ago, so he's in athletic shorts and a white T-shirt now like he's about to go play futbol.

"What do you want?" I ask, my tone sharp and accusatory.

He shuts the door and glares at me before strutting to the bed. "What do you mean, what do I want? This is my room."

He pulls his shirt over his head, revealing the tattoo across his pec and enough muscle to make me uncomfortably look away.

"Aren't you sleeping on the couch?"

He huffs, but it isn't obnoxious like normal. It's muted, like he's afraid Anya might hear. "Six hours of marriage, and I'm already in the doghouse?"

Now I look at him, my head tilted with curiosity.

So... Anya told him. I'm surprised. Not that she told him, but that he didn't bring it up sooner or that he doesn't seem angry. After what looked like a heartfelt conversation, the two siblings came inside and we ate together at the table, listening to Anya ramble about our day. Maksim was noticeably quiet. I kept searching for signs of anger but saw none.

Maksim throws back the sheet, revealing my camisole and baby blue velvet shorts in the process. I quickly cover up. He seems to notice my discomfort by the look he gives me but says nothing as he climbs into bed next to me and rests his arm behind his head on a pillow.

"You're a clever girl, Elira," he says, his voice smooth enough to send a tingle running across my shoulders. "Telling my sister we're married so that you're harder to get rid of... Now if my wife suddenly disappears, I'll have explaining to do."

Leaning back against the headboard, I run my hand over my knee. "Believe it or not, Maksim, my own safety had little to do with it."

His head lazily turns my way like he isn't convinced but is going to hear me out anyway. He thinks the worst of me. I can see that. I suppose I think the worst of him too.

I hold up my left hand to draw his attention to Daniel's wife's ring. "She saw this and assumed you gave it to me... Should I have told her the truth?"

He says nothing, just stares at me, waiting for my explanation. I can see it on his face. See him waiting for my ulterior motive. For some reason, it stings.

"I went with the explanation that made you look the best."

"Why?" he asks, his eyes narrowing with skepticism. It's a fair question.

I shift the comforter for no other reason than to busy myself while breaking eye contact. My heart swells thinking of Asher, my fantasy of bringing her a better life vaporized. In reality, I'll probably never see her again, never speak to her. And I damn sure wouldn't want her to see a picture of this.

"She reminds me of someone I know... It seemed like she was hurt by the idea of you not telling her about me, and I didn't want to make her pain worse."

I don't look at Maksim, instead choosing to keep my eyes forward. I can picture his skeptical face and nearly hear the condescending tone of his voice before he speaks his next words.

"Thank you."

My eyes widen in surprise at the softness in his voice, so soft it was barely audible. When I turn his way, it's him who isn't looking at me. Instead, he stares at the ceiling. I've seen him serious, but I've never seen him this soft.

"I didn't do it for you," I say because I have to. I don't

want to fight, but I don't know how ready I am for a truce. "You let me squeeze myself inside a trunk for hours at a time out of fear for a roommate who didn't exist."

His eyes close as he sighs. "You took the wedding ring of your trafficker's dead mistress after you brutally murdered her… In hindsight, bringing you here at all was beyond reckless, but forgive me for at least taking precautions for my sister's sake."

His fist, lazily tucked beneath the blanket, connects with my gut without ever moving. I bite my lip and suck in a breath through my nose to quell the sudden blow. His opinion, of all people's, shouldn't matter, but…

That woman, Daniel's mistress, apparently, was not innocent. She stood there, watching Daniel strangle me, and if I hadn't pulled a knife, she would've let me die.

I play with the ring on my finger, suddenly feeling ridiculous for taking it. If that wasn't his wife, then this isn't even his ring. And now, because of my lie, I'm stuck with it. Stuck with a false ring in a false marriage with a man who believes I'd harm an innocent teenage girl.

Does he *really* believe I'd hurt her?

The shame twisting my gut suddenly releases as anger takes hold. If he was afraid for her safety, he would have killed me. No person would put their sibling in harm's way. I'd slit Maksim's throat in a heartbeat if he went near mine.

"You're so full of shit," I growl, his eyes snapping open when my voice climbs high. "Terrifying me over a fake roommate was never about *safety*. You didn't want Anya to find out your dirty little secret, you asshole."

"Okay." He sits up, holding his hands up as if to pacify me. His eyes dart to the door every other second. "Calm down."

"*Do not*. Do fucking *not* tell me to calm down."

"Elira."

"Admit it." I whip toward him fully, my chin high and arms

crossing over my chest. "You lie *constantly*. For once in your life, I want you to admit the truth. *Then* I will calm down." A surge of power races through me that feels like a high I'll never stop chasing. It didn't cross my mind until now just how powerful a position it puts me in, having Anya in the next room, but the frantic way Maksim looks toward the door makes it obvious.

He *cares* what she thinks. She is his weak spot. His Achilles heel. His...

My eyes widen as I realize it.

Be a good girl, Elira. You know what men want.

Maksim doesn't want a whore. He doesn't even want a woman to claim. He doesn't crave power. All the preconceived notions I've had about men have gotten me nowhere with him.

But now, *finally*, I know what he wants.

Her.

And with the way she was talking today, he has no clue how to bond with a teenage girl. From what I saw at dinner... He's hopeless.

"Okay." He nods, his hands still raised, his voice low. "That was a lie, I'm sorry. I just..."

I shift to sit on my heels. "You just what?"

His eyes close. Finally, I think he's about to tell the truth. "My relationship with Anya is holding on by a thread, and I don't know how much more it can survive."

There's pain etched into his face that sobers my anger, along with the surge of power. I relax my posture, sinking into the mattress and slumping my shoulders as I watch his inner turmoil move to the surface. I get the strange urge to touch the lines of his face, as if it'd let me feel the vulnerability within, and it hits me out of nowhere just how human he is. Feelings and all.

"Today was the first day she's hugged me in..." he stares

off like he's trying to recall the last time, "a long time." He looks at me, his eyes holding a humanity that makes me shrink. I thought I wanted honesty, but this is... Life is easy when we dehumanize each other. When we reduce each other to future victims, to objects to conquer. What he's doing right now is messy.

"I don't know what your reasoning was," he goes on. "Whether it was selfish or if you really did give a shit about my sister's feelings or something else, but ... she likes you. A lot. And she likes the version you painted of me... If you keep this going, at least for a while, I'll give you whatever you want."

"*Whatever* I want?" I ask, my throat closing and heart quickening.

He nods. "I'll personally drive you to the airport."

My lips part, but I force my excitement to stay locked inside a box in my heart. This is Maksim, the crusher of dreams. He could be lying. He's *probably* lying.

I swallow. "You're saying I can go home."

He looks up and scratches the back of his neck while I stare intently, my hands gripping the comforter while forcing my breathing to stay even. He's lying. Right now, he's coming up with another lie.

"Eventually, yeah." He brings his eyes back to me. "Obviously, this isn't something I can force you to do. But..." He looks away again, lost for words.

I think I get it.

"You want me to help you repair your relationship with your sister."

"No." He snaps back to me, but then his shoulders fall. "I mean, I don't know how you could possibly do that."

My lips lift at the nervous way he rubs at his arm, the slight blush in his cheeks. Maksim, the man I watched casually clean up a dead body, is nervous, maybe even embarrassed.

"By talking you up and making you seem like a world class husband."

He lets out a stilted laugh, not looking at me. "I wouldn't get too carried away."

"Maksim."

He rests his hands at his sides as he looks at me. The nervous edge to his features settles at the seriousness in my voice.

I take my time speaking, my eyes pinned to him. "What you're asking me to do is not nearly as difficult as you think it is... But I won't help you for another second without some assurances that you aren't going to fuck me over."

He raises his hand. "I give you my word."

"Your *word* is not going to cut it for me." I lift my chin. "I need more than that."

His eyes narrow as if he's confused. "Like what?"

When my mouth dries, I run my tongue along the roof of my mouth, searching for moisture. I did not anticipate having this much power, but I know exactly what I want to do with it. It's the same thing I wanted when I came to America. Never could I have predicted that I'd actually get it.

"I want a bank account in my name and my name only that has monthly, automatic transfers set up to my mother's account. I want you to allow me employment and also match what I earn." I suck in a breath and continue before I can judge his reaction. "I want to be allowed a cell phone, regular access to communication with my family, and a plane ticket to visit them in three months... If you grant those things, I will trust that when the time comes for us to cut ties, you will do so without putting a bullet in my back."

He raises a brow and stares like he's waiting for me to go on. "Is that it?"

Should I ask for more?

I blink, searching my mind for what else I could ask for, but he interrupts before I can find something.

"I have a few requests of my own."

I shake my head. "You don't get to make requests."

He laughs. "You finally have some bargaining power, kid, I'll give you that. But let's not pretend I have more on the line than you do. We're talking your freedom versus my relationship with a moody teenager here."

"That," I point at him, "is a bluff. That's another thing I want. *Honesty*."

He rolls his eyes. "Are you telling me I'm wrong?"

My lips pinch as I consider it. No. No, he isn't wrong.

"Fine. What do you want?"

He takes a moment to smirk before replying. "Your employment must be at one of the Bratva's businesses. It'll be easier that way. I'll be able to adjust your schedule and pay you under the table so we can avoid the annoyances that come with you being an illegal immigrant. Plus, I like to be able to keep an eye on you." He winks, the playful, obnoxious Maksim returning. To my surprise, I'm not immediately annoyed.

"Fair enough," I say.

"I want us to sleep in the bed together."

I shake my head. "I'll sleep on the floor."

"Ah, so no deal?"

When my eyes constrict, he smiles like he's amused. Again, I'm not annoyed. It's weird.

"*Fine.*"

He nods victoriously, but then his composure falls some. He looks like he's about to ask me for something serious. "I want us to start over…"

His eyes implore me with such intensity that I look away. I saw him first as my enemy, then as a tool with such ferocity that the idea of seeing him as anything else seems wrong.

"Look, you don't like me. I get that," he says. "I'm not a big fan of yours either."

"Wow, thank you."

"*But* all the fighting we do in private is going to bleed into times we're supposed to look … you know, happy. I think we should try to become friends."

I almost laugh. "You're gonna make me puke."

He goes to smile but then changes his mind, rubbing his jaw instead. "I don't know, maybe that's too much to ask."

Yes.

Probably.

But… We could try.

It's a much better situation than I was in yesterday. Or even hours ago.

I tuck my hair behind my ears and twist my lips as I consider it, consider *him*. I don't think it would be easy. Too much has happened. Too many unkind things have been said, too many threats have been made.

But… There are a million things I want to experience in this country, starting with this city.

I could use a friend.

With a sigh, I hold out my hand, and Maksim stares down at it with his brow furrowed.

"Hi," I say, my voice as awkward as you could imagine. "I'm Elira."

17

ELIRA

THREE DAYS LATER

*M*aksim, Anya, and I sit on the couch, our feet propped on the table—even mine—as we let our minds deteriorate while staring at moving pictures on the screen.

Our bellies are full of borscht, a Russian soup I learned only today how to make from the woman I now work with at a bakery owned by the Bratva. Anya's initial excitement to learn to cook seems to have worn off, and after kneading dough all day then preparing dinner with only Maksim's poor attempts at helping, I'm exhausted. Which feels *amazing*.

I peek over at Maksim, his eyes glued to the screen, although I doubt he enjoys this movie as much as Anya does. It was her choice and is a bit too sappy for a ruthless killer, but you never know. We never had a TV back home, so I really can't say what I prefer, but this is nice.

No fighting. No danger. Just three people on a couch, *faking it 'til we make it,* as Anya likes to say.

When her phone buzzes, Maksim's concentration breaks,

and we both look at her as she picks it up, but I quickly turn back to the TV.

"Who is it?" Maksim stupidly asks.

I nudge him, but he only shoots me a dagger before looking expectantly at Anya.

Give her space, you idiot.

"No one."

Her fingers tap the screen while her brother continues to intrude. He even goes so far as to lean over me to peek at the message.

When I pinch his arm, giving him a threatening, 'are you insane' look, he backs down, but his muscles are still tense. Even having no idea what went on between Anya and her boyfriend in his bed, he is still this overprotective. It would be ridiculous if his instincts weren't right.

"I really like this movie, Anya," I say in an attempt to diffuse the tension brewing in the air.

"Uh-huh, Ryan Gosling's a babe." She nods along with her words, never looking up from her phone. As soon as her fingers stop moving, my spine tingles with a rumble coming from outside.

Beside me, Maksim fumes, but Anya hops up before he can mention the tell-tale sound of the boyfriend's truck.

She stuffs her phone in the back pocket of white shorts that show off her ivory skin before training her eyes on me sheepishly. "I'm actually gonna take off for a bit, so you two enjoy it."

She doesn't even make it a step before Maksim is up and blocking her way. "You're not going anywhere."

Instead of her eyes widening like I expect them to, they narrow. She isn't surprised a bit. "Excuse me?"

"If you don't have the self-regulatory skills to stay away from things that are bad for you, then I have to make your decisions for you. You're grounded."

"Grounded?" Her jaw drops with a laugh. "How are you going to ground me if you're hardly ever here? How exactly do you plan on enforcing that?"

Maksim gestures to me, and I glare at him, wishing to be left out of this.

Anya rolls her eyes and turns to walk away, probably headed for the back door.

I expect Maksim to chase after her, but he stands his ground. "I hope you're prepared to support yourself, Anya, because if you walk out that door, I'm not going to sit around waiting for you to come back this time. Your phone and credit card will both be turned off before you get to wherever that dirtbag is taking you."

This has Anya's attention. She grinds to a halt, her shoulders lifting as her back constricts, and when she spins, her eyes look like glass.

"Sitting around waiting for me to come back?" she asks, stomping his way. "You don't even *care* when I leave!" I cringe at the high pitch of her yell, but Maksim doesn't even flinch. "You went off and got married, you stupid fucking *asshole*!" When she reaches him, she slaps her hand at his chest, tears pooling in her eyes. He just stands there like a statue, looking exactly as she's accusing him—uncaring.

Oh, Maksim.

"Of course he cares," I chime in, unsure if I'll regret it. The kid likes me, but I'm still new. This isn't my business.

Anya predictably looks at me like she's about to spew venom, but I go on.

"He's an *idiot*, obviously, but, honey, if your brother didn't care, he wouldn't be trying to stop you right now." I frown and go on before she can throw a retort my way. "I thought you realized that boy wasn't good for you."

"That *boy* has a name. His name is Tanner, and neither of you even know him. You're both judgmental pricks, and I fucking *hate* you. Just…" Her hands fly up as she growls and prepares to storm away again.

Even as my stomach twists, I nod. "You're right."

That surprises her. And Maksim.

"What?" he snaps while Anya gives me a skeptical glare, her arms crossing as she turns to face me.

I show her my palms. "Neither of us know Tanner. Why don't you invite him inside so we can get to know him a little better?" I smile and gesture to the TV. "Maybe we could all finish the movie?"

She blinks at me then shakes her head in disbelief before striding to the back door.

"Anya!" Maksim yells, storming her way.

I rush to get in front of him and put a hand on his arm.

"Get out of my way," he snarls.

"*Stop*. Just let her go."

"Anya, I swear to God—" The sound of the sliding door slamming cuts him off, and when he turns to head for the front door, I grab his arm and pull.

"Maksim, stop it. That's enough."

He jerks out of my hold. "You don't even know her."

"*You* don't even know her," I counter. When he makes it to the front door, I let out a frustrated groan. "You're her blood. She'll forgive many things, but if you hurt that boy, you'll never stand a chance of earning her trust."

With his hand on the knob, he fumes. The truck rumbles away without him moving, and as soon as the sound ceases, he roars and barrels his fist into a wall, caving in the sheetrock and making me flinch.

Closing my eyes, I count to five, then I slowly make my way to him and put my hand on his shoulder. He stands unmoving.

"Maybe that's the problem," he says, his voice low, defeated. "I'm not her blood."

I stare at him questioningly, but he gives no sign of explaining further, so I don't press for details. "You're her brother. Blood or not."

When he turns to me, I see pain I didn't know he was capable of. I find myself nudging closer, moving my touch to his arm. The warmth of his skin on my hand feels oddly pleasant.

He sighs. "What do I do now?"

I frown, thinking about him being on his own raising Anya all these years, clueless and helpless. When did their— or her—mother die exactly?

"Now you wait. You check in. You show her you're here for her whenever she needs you, without judgment."

He rubs the back of his neck, pulling away from me in the process, and it gives me a feeling of loss that I try to immediately shut down.

"What if she doesn't come back?" he asks.

"She will."

He slowly lowers his hand, asking the question without words. *How do you know?*

"Text her. Tell her you love her and to be safe. Don't shut off her phone or do anything that would push her away, and she'll come back. I promise."

He nods, accepting the suggestion. "Okay."

His eyes lower to the little space between us, and we look away like we just realized how close we're standing. I feel my face get hot as I take a step back.

"So what now?" he asks.

I meet his eyes and tilt my head. Didn't he just ask me this? "Now you should send the text. Then just wait for Anya to make her move."

"No, I mean, what do you want to do now?"

Oh… Of course. My face grows even hotter with embarrassment.

He glances toward the door. "I don't mean to ditch you, but I'm not in a movie watching mood."

I nod like I understand even as my throat tries to close up. "You're leaving?"

His lips part, but then he just nods.

The blue eyes that apparently hold no genetic ties to his sister kick me in the stomach now. Never would I have thought that I'd want Maksim's company, but... I don't know. I thought we had a moment of civility just then.

I smile like he just made my night and turn to walk down the hallway. "Have a good time."

A second passes. Then another, the only sound my bare feet padding on the carpet.

"Come with me."

I halt in my tracks, not turning around when I speak. "What?"

I feel him near me. "Come with me to Hugh's. You can pretend not to speak English still, if you want to, but... We're supposed to be friends, right? How are we going to do that if we don't get to know each other?"

"So stay here, then."

"I can't."

My brows pinch. "Why?"

"Because this place makes me feel like a fucking American."

I twist my lips while I ponder that.

"If you decide you don't want to be there, we can leave... Who knows, maybe it'll be fun."

I've been around those men. It's hard to imagine having *fun* in their vicinity.

But days ago I thought the same of Maksim.

Am I really considering going back there?

My heart races just thinking of it, but still, I take a deep breath and turn around.

"Sure," I say, not sure at all. "Just let me change."

18

MAKSIM

*E*lira leans slightly out her open window, staring out at the lights and chaos on the strip. Her hair waves in the light breeze, and I crane my neck to peek at her curious, wanderlust face, a smile curving my lips.

This isn't the way to Hugh's place. In fact, this adds at least an extra twenty minutes onto the drive, but something pulled me here anyway. I remembered the first night we met, wondering what she thought of the Vegas lights even as I was slowly bleeding out, and all at once I had to know.

"What are you thinking?" I ask as we pass the mini Eiffel tower, going at a snail's pace behind traffic.

She sits back in her seat to peer at me. "You Americans are flashy as hell."

I laugh, but it grates my ears when she calls me an American. As if she's stripping me of my Russian identity, yanking me from my home all over again.

But I know what she means.

She turns back to the window. "Is Chicago like this?"

"Chicago?"

She nods. "One of your cities. Am I saying it right?"

Chicago. So many memories in Chicago. I spent nine years of my childhood only two hours away from the Windy City but didn't set foot in it until Anya and I ultimately called it home at age eighteen, her a tiny three-year-old. My first home as a free man, but freedom came with the brutal price of poverty and the unknown territory of surrogate fatherhood.

But the memories that assail me aren't all bad. Some are good.

"Yeah, I know Chicago. I'm just wondering why you care."

She glances at me a moment, something indiscernible in her eyes before turning back to the window.

I stop at a light and watch a group of women wearing hats with dicks flopping from the bills run across the street, ushering the center of attention wearing a pink sash I can guess says something like 'bride to be' on it.

"No, Chicago is much more serious than Vegas. And the winters are too cold," I say.

A shiver spreads over my shoulders, but I shove down the memories pushing to the surface, reminding me why I prefer the suffocating desert to the mere sight of snow.

Elira doesn't seem to hear me as she intently watches the bachelorette party, her eyes wide with curiosity. I suppress a laugh and drive on.

When we make it off the strip and are on our way to Hugh's, she relaxes into her seat.

"So you've been?" she asks, making my brows raise.

"To Chicago?"

She nods.

"A few times, on business."

"*Business?*"

I give her a crooked grin and speed the car up instead of

answering. The engine roars, drawing her attention, and when the car accelerates to sixty-five, she starts to look nervous.

"Should you slow down?"

I gun it to seventy-five. "Why do you want to know about Chicago?"

Her eyes flick between me and the road. "What are you doing?"

"Asking you a question."

I slam on the pedal again, pushing it to eighty and veering around several cars.

Elira presses her back into the seat, her chest rising and falling quickly, her head turning to look behind us.

"Maksim, slow down," she says, her words clipped with panic.

"Why do you want to know about Chicago?"

"I'm serious!"

I laugh and slow only to take a corner at a speed that has Elira falling into me, her scent sobering me a moment. It's like a string that attaches to a piece of something in my chest and tugs me in her direction.

"Okay!" she yells. "Okay, I'll tell you!"

I slam on the brakes, my car skidding to a stop at a red light. I turn to her and smile as she places a hand to her chest, panting.

"Are you *insane?*"

I point at the stoplight. "You have until the light turns green, sweetheart."

She looks between it and me, her mouth open. When her face lights up with a green hue, I shove my foot on the gas pedal and laugh when she gasps.

"My father!" she blurts out.

My smile slips as I ease off the gas.

She stares at the glovebox. "My father lives in Chicago."

I ease the car up the road, my mind fogging. "He's an immigrant?"

She doesn't answer for a long time. Not until I pull onto the curb in front of Hugh's place and shut off the car, regretting teasing her. She's just … a locked safe. It feels hardly fair that she knows my life while I know nothing of hers.

"He's from this country… He and my mom were never married under the law, but they loved each other, and he visited many times a year. My entire life, my mother has only been with my father."

I nod, unsure how else to respond. She sounds defensive, but I'm not sure why.

"My mother is not a whore," she snaps like my nod was somehow offensive.

My eyes widen, and I blink. "I never said she was."

"You didn't have to."

"Elira," I say, dumbfounded. "I…"

I what?

What are the right words to say?

"How could I judge your family when mine is so grotesquely on display for you?" I settle on.

Her angry face begins to relax.

"I'm sorry I pried…"

"You should be." She glowers. "You could've gotten us killed."

My lips curve without my command. "Then tell me on your own next time. It's uncomfortable having you know all my dirt without having any idea who you are."

"Your discomfort is my satisfaction." She unbuckles her seatbelt, her lips tugging into a mischievous grin, then throws open her door.

Amusement warms my smile and flushes my face as I

open my door and hear the music from the backyard disturbing the would-be quiet street.

* * *

Elira

LAUGHTER.

Loud. Masculine. *Deep* laughter.

That—mixed in with Russian rock music—is what I hear past the wooden fence, and it chills my bones thinking about what could elicit those laughs.

I see the faces of the men who came to pluck us one by one from the truck in my mind and wonder how different these people could be. They exist in the same world. They play by the same rules.

They're the same. *Of course,* they're the same. Maksim is different because he has to be, because that life wouldn't work with the one he's trying to fake for Anya, but these men are freed from their restraints. They can do whatever they want.

What was I thinking coming here?

I slow to a stop. "Maybe coming here was a mistake."

Maksim's hand presses to my lower back, and while a day ago I might have wanted to jerk away from his touch, it feels comforting now.

"Ten minutes." He urges me forward with him. "If you want to leave then, we'll go."

My feet shuffle while my heart pounds. "How do I know you're telling the truth?"

"I swear it on my father's grave."

I huff. "For all I know, you could've killed your father yourself."

He laughs, but I'm serious. I don't trust him. Even if he told me he swore on Anya's life, I wouldn't trust him.

As if he can read my mind… "Just trust me, *lislchka*."

That is a command I cannot obey, but my feet move as he guides me to the gate. He opens it to reveal probably fifty people, *too many people*, men and women. Some wade in the pool, some are on chairs surrounding it, a few people are on the roof like I saw that first night. Few seem civilized, most are loud, all have some sort of alcohol gripped in their hands.

I cross my arms over my chest and bite my lip.

"*Brat!*"

My eyes snap to the man I know to be Hugh with his huge palms spread wide as he bounds this way, a smile stretched across his face. When he reaches us, I step to the side.

"*Dobro pozhalovat' drug.*" He and Maksim exchange a back slapping greeting, and Maksim grins before speaking Russian so quickly, I can't even discern what syllables he uses.

It didn't occur to me until now that I rarely hear Maksim speak Russian. Now, though, it slips off his tongue effortlessly as he exchanges what I assume are pleasantries with the giant. Finally, when he remembers I'm here, he side steps to me and puts his arm around my shoulders. I would shrug him off if my body wasn't frozen in fear.

Why did I come here?

"You remember Elira," Maksim says as if I was a guest of honor here at one point.

I can't find it in me to smile politely. I watch Hugh's reluctant expression for only a moment before ducking my eyes and wishing I had a watch so I could time ten minutes exactly.

"I didn't realize that was her name," Hugh says, sounding uncertain. Maksim hasn't told him a thing about me. Nothing.

I don't know why that hurts.

Maksim squeezes my shoulder. "Yes, I guess I never properly introduced the two of you. Her English was um…"

He leans in to my ear, kissing me with his breath. It feels intimate in front of all these people. Wrong when I know what they must think happens in his bedroom.

Neither my 'elevated status' at Maksim's house nor our agreement matter. To these people, I'm his whore.

"Do you speak English yet?" he asks, his voice gentle, caring, soft.

Does he not know the vile things his friends think, or does he simply not care? Does he realize how uncomfortable I am?

"*Lislchka?*" he whispers, concerned.

No, he has no idea. This is the clueless Maksim we're talking about.

Taking a sharp inhale, I lock eyes with Hugh who studies not me but Maksim with curious eyes. I don't see what benefit it gives me to hide my comprehension anymore, so instead of answering Maksim, I try to be brave and hold out my hand.

Hugh looks down, *way down*, at it.

"Pleasure to meet you," I lie, my words crystal clear.

He blinks, looking at Maksim for answers, but when he doesn't get them, he shakes my hand.

"You as well."

Hugh pulls away and speaks to Maksim in clipped Russian, which feels a little rude but unsurprising. When he's finished, he addresses me with a half-hearted smile. "Enjoy the party."

When he's gone, Maksim turns to me. "Thirsty?"

"What did he say?"

His eyes blank. "What?"

I nod at Hugh's back. "What did he say about me?"

Maksim chuckles nervously. "Nothing. He was telling me something about work. Don't worry about it."

"Is it time to leave yet?" I turn longingly toward the gate, my lips dipping into a frown.

I hate these people. *Hate* them.

"Elira?" a new voice, feminine and unfamiliar calls.

I turn toward a woman in a tight black skirt short enough to reveal all if she so much as bent over a sink and a shirt with so many holes she may as well have just stuck with the hot pink bra she displays beneath. Her eyes are like raccoons with dark makeup, and her hair is gathered on top of her head in a bundle of brunette curls, except for a few pieces streaked pink that she lets frame her face.

She fits in with the other women here—and this city for that matter—just fine, but she strikes me as unique, flashy, bold in a way that makes me wonder how bland Maksim must think me. Not that I should care.

I cross my arms protectively over the simple yellow summer dress I bought while shopping with Anya and raise my chin in acknowledgement.

The woman beams.

"Cherish, *zdravstvuyte*," Maksim says before turning to me and gesturing to the woman. "Elira, this is—" She throws her arms around me before he can finish, making me stiffen.

"I'm Cherish." She pulls back with her hands on my shoulders. "Sorry to interrupt," she bashfully says to Maksim, but he waves it off, bringing her attention back to me. "I'm Zinovy's girl. He told me you were new to the country and a…" She glances over her shoulder, and I follow her gaze. Hugh stands with Zinovy, the skinny man who treated

Maksim's stab wounds. Hugh must have asked her to come talk to me.

When she turns back to me, there's a quizzical look on her face. "Do you speak English?"

Chewing on my inner lip, I nod, and for some reason this elates her. She claps her hands enthusiastically before taking my arm that's still crossed. "Great! Let's go get a drink. You have to show me how you make your detergent. I'm *obsessed* with the smell."

I look at Maksim with wide, imploring eyes, but he only gives me an encouraging smile as he lets Cherish whisk me away.

Inside is hardly quieter with its own music blaring through a speaker, but it's at least less crowded. Cherish guides me into the kitchen, cluttered with liquor bottles and garbage, then she plucks a couple of red cups off a stack.

She crooks a brow at me. "What's your poison?"

I give my head a tiny shake, my lips parting.

Poison?

"What do you like to drink?" She smiles, keeping her tone light. "Sorry, I forgot, you aren't from here."

From the sound of her accent, she isn't from here either. She's Russian. So not exactly out of place.

"I know American lingo," I say, somehow offended. There was a time I wanted so badly to fit into this country, so badly to belong. Felt as if it was my birthright even. I copied my father's speech, studied fiction novels, practiced, believing one day I would come here... And all to end up hating it. "I just don't drink poison."

She giggles. "I meant alcohol."

"Exactly."

Her eyes widen at that, but she isn't discouraged. She walks to the fridge to retrieve a bottle of orange juice. "I got you, girl, don't worry."

I give her a grateful nod before opening the pantry in search of the baking soda. When I find it exactly where I left it, I pull it out.

"What are you doing?" she asks, pouring white alcohol into both cups along with the orange juice.

"No, I don't…" I reach for the cup, but I'm obviously too late to stop her.

She smiles. "Trust me, you *need* this."

That feels like an insult.

She nods at the baking soda. "What's that for?"

"It's one of the ingredients for the laundry detergent I make."

Her head tilts as she looks at me like I'm the last puppy in a box for sale. "You are so cute."

I frown. "What do you mean?"

She takes the baking soda from my hand and replaces it with the cup of what even she admits is poison.

"I only said that so Maksim wouldn't ask what we talked about." She takes a drink of her cocktail and rests it on the counter. "So give me the good stuff."

"The good stuff?"

She nods and twirls her hand. "Yeah, you know, what's it like?"

"What's what like?"

Her jaw drops, and she looks away like she's thinking. "*Girl*, come on, we're all on the edge of our seats here."

I shake my head. "I'm sorry, I just don't know what you're talking about."

"Sleeping with Maksim," she drones like it's beyond obvious. "That man is a *conquest*, my friend. Many have tried and many have failed. There's a rumor that he doesn't like Russian women and another that he doesn't like women at all. Don't tell him I told you that, of course," she says, more seriously. "I don't believe it. Actually, I thought maybe he just had a thing for Italians until recently. He's *impenetrable* to our group. But…"

She opens her palms to gesture to me. "Here you are, showing up with his arm around you, staying in his home while even his closest friends aren't invited there. You must have a magic coochie. Please, tell me your secret. I'm *dying* to know."

I shake my head. "It isn't like that at all."

"No?"

Again, I shake my head, looking down at the dull orange drink that suddenly tempts me.

"Am I making you uncomfortable?" Cherish asks, excitement missing for the first time from her voice.

I shrug. "I just…" I don't know how to finish other than to say yes. Of course. I don't know her. I don't know them. As much as I don't trust Maksim, I trust him more than these people, and I'm not going to expose what could be his secrets.

What *are* his secrets?

They know he has a sister, right? Is it such a big deal if perhaps he isn't a man whore?

But then there was the box of condoms in his drawer.

Could he be gay?

No. No, I've seen too many erections to be doubting his sexuality.

"I get it." She raises a hand. "Sorry, babe. Zinovy always says I can be a bit much." She chuckles, but it's nervous. "Do me a favor and don't tell Maksim I asked all this, okay? I like to think I'm one of them, but he's a lieutenant, which makes him automatically terrifying. Girls like us have to look out for each other."

Girls like us?

Is she a…?

It doesn't matter. She's a woman in this world. I know what she means.

"I won't say anything," I assure her before my own question strikes me. "What's a lieutenant?"

She shakes her head, her lips pursed. "It's just a ranking in the Bratva, and it means he did a lot of nasty shit to get here. If you don't already know, trust me, you don't want to. He's…" She sighs. "I don't know. Just be careful and don't piss him off. I think you've figured that out by now."

No. Not in the slightest.

"Right."

What kind of nasty shit?

Do I really need to ask? Murder. It's murder. I already knew he was capable of that.

Still, the chill in her voice has me peeking at my cup and taking a sip.

She squeals with delight and pats my shoulders. "Attagirl. Now come on, let's get back before the boys wonder what's taking so long."

* * *

Maksim

I HALF LISTEN to Zinovy rattle on about the state of his motorcycle he wrecked last night, pulling at his shirt to reveal road rash on his side.

My attention keeps drifting to the back door where Elira disappeared, and when she finally re-emerges onto the patio, I search for signs of distress. One arm is wrapped around her stomach while the other holds onto a Solo cup. She follows Cherish with her head down, looking uncomfortable but not terrified, so maybe that's progress.

I prepare for her to ask me to take her home, but when she reaches the circle of lounge chairs where we've gathered, she perches on the end of mine and doesn't say a word, instead glancing at Zinovy as if she's politely listening to his story.

When I nudge her, she looks at me.

Are you okay, I mouth.

She doesn't answer right away, but after a few moments she nods, and it's like a valve is opened, releasing a breath caught in my lungs since we arrived.

I scoot over in the chair and pat the tiny space beside me, knowing she won't fit. After chewing on her lip in contemplation, she crawls up the chair to flatten against me, half her body lying on mine.

I wrap my arm around her shoulders but don't smile, don't even look at her. Her body is tense, and so is mine, like we're in agreement that this was a stupid idea. Any minute I think she'll move back down to the edge of the chair, but she stays rigid in place, probably too afraid of embarrassing me to move.

Minutes go by like this. Minutes that feel like hours.

I could get up to go to the bathroom. I could put an end to this misery for both of us.

"Do you have the highest ranking here?"

I tense, startled at Elira's voice, and finally look at her. She peers at me with soft eyes I hardly recognize on her, eyes that massage my muscles, relaxing me in the chair. The discomfort is still there, but her question brings enough relief that I'd answer anything she asked right now.

"Yes," I say, although I'm unsure where her question came from.

She looks around. "Then why is your home so much smaller?"

An unexpected laugh rumbles up my chest, and I just barely quiet it to keep the attention off us.

"Sorry, I don't mean to be rude," she says, her shoulders caving.

I shake my head. "It's fine… I chose a smaller home because I didn't want to spoil Anya. Her mother dreamed of her living a normal, boring, American childhood, and I tried to make that a reality. I failed, but I tried."

Her nose wrinkles in the cutest way. "I don't think you failed. How could you have failed what you haven't finished?"

I shrug, relaxing more into the chair. Her body doesn't feel so stiff anymore. It molds to mine, and without thinking, I tug her closer without her seeming to notice.

"This was your stepmother?" Elira asks, bringing me back to our conversation. I don't want to talk about this or anything now. The silence was grueling with the discomfort, but now, this isn't so bad.

"Hmm?"

"Anya's mother. She was your stepmother?"

Elizabeth's image comes to mind, her blonde hair that reminded me of my own mother's, her kind smile. The puffy dresses she always wore, even when she worked in her garden.

I remember being in one of the fields, sweat seeping from every pore of my body, mouth bone-dry, skin hot as an iron. The house was so far away that people were mere sticks as they came toward the fields, and you never knew whether to fear or to feel the relief of company.

Those puffy dresses made her stand out, and I always knew to expect water soon. Cold. *Iced*. Not the drippings from the rain buckets but fresh from the well.

I hadn't known English when I came to the farm, but I knew that her words, slow and enunciated, were kind.

My fellow unfortunate bunkmates taught me to speak the language, but she taught me how to read and write. She snuck books and food to me. She invited me into her home when her husband was away.

She was not my mother, but she was kind. And when she had a child of her own, she did not forget about the young boy in the barn. She introduced me to the new baby, Anya, as her son while I stood as a statue holding the child for the first time. Later, alone in the barn, I wept. I had siblings somewhere on Earth and parents who'd long forgotten me, but that was the first day in years I felt the warmth of a familial bond. I was someone's son again. Soon, I felt like a brother. I had family. And this time, it seemed, they wanted me.

"No," I say at last, letting the image of Elizabeth fade. "A foster mother, I guess."

"Oh." Elira considers this. "So you were adopted?"

I nod, but an imaginary boa constrictor wraps around my chest and begins to squeeze. I don't like talking about this. "Sort of."

She opens her mouth, and she might say something, but my attention is completely diverted to the out-of-place figure entering the yard.

I can feel Alik's presence the moment his boot crosses the threshold.

Eyes like lasers do a single sweep of the area before landing on me. He doesn't bother motioning for me or head this way. There's no one else at Hugh's that he'd be here to see.

Something's wrong.

I dart my eyes to Elira, silencing whatever she was saying. "I have to go."

"What? Where?"

I get up without replying and walk to Alik with Elira on my heels. "Hugh," I call, gesturing to Elira. He goes to lead

Elira away, ignoring Alik when he shakes his head and waits for me to reach him.

"We're going to need the girl," he says.

My spine stiffens, and protectiveness starts to flare. "Why?"

His eyebrows raise as if to tell me not to shoot the messenger. He isn't here on behalf of himself. He's delivering Nikita's orders.

If Nikita is sending Alik, it's bad.

"The trafficking organization has arrived." His eyes drift to Elira who's still being led off by Hugh. "They want their whore back."

19

ELIRA

aksim doesn't tell me why we're leaving, but I sense the tension between him and the man who walks just ahead of us, stopping at a running SUV parked in the driveway.

I go to walk past the SUV, but Maksim takes my arm and squeezes it gently to stop me. He flashes me a brief, serious look that hints at danger we must be in before he opens the door for me.

Swallowing, I drop my head and climb in, scooting to the middle so Maksim can get in beside me while my pulse quickens. Neither of the two scary looking men in the front seats acknowledge us.

The man who led us to the SUV opens the back door on my other side then climbs in next to me, shrinking the would-be large space with his suffocating presence. I purposefully don't look at him and sit as far away from him as possible, pressing myself into Maksim who doesn't wrap his arm around me like he did before. Back when things felt safe, nice even, just for a few fleeting minutes.

What is going on?

The SUV pulls out of the drive and crawls down the street more terrifyingly than when Maksim was speeding us here. The man—or demon, I'm not sure which—beside me doesn't move. I know because I watch him closely out of the corner of my eye. As far as I can tell, he isn't even breathing. Maybe he isn't human. That would explain the one weird, red eye and sharp cheekbones that belong more on a fictional figure than on a man. Dark hair hangs ominously, like he's trying to hide the evil bursting from his red iris, but it only adds to his villainous look. My eyes scan his all-black clothing for a minute before moving away.

He looks like a killer. *Feels* like a killer.

Why are we with a killer?

I peer at Maksim, hoping he can read my thoughts so I don't have to voice the questions.

His jaw is set, and his posture is perfect. He looks as all business as the other men, if not more so. As I study him staring straight ahead, I search for fear or uncertainty, but I see nothing but confidence.

More than that. It's hard to put a word to it, but he looks … in control? Is he in control?

I don't think so. But the dominant vibe he puts off says otherwise. My heart starts to slow as Maksim's aura envelops me, pushing away the fear of the other men.

He'll protect me.

It isn't my head that thinks this, it's my gut. Or the fact that I'm useful now. Or it's wishful thinking.

In any case, my breathing evens as I stare straight ahead just like everyone else.

The sun has set, and the city lights are out of view by the time we reach our destination, which is not a random spot in the desert to dump our bodies.

It's a mansion.

Not a house. No one would ever call this place a house. It

isn't until the driver pulls up to the gate and says Maksim is here for Mr. Petrov that I realize this isn't some sort of hotel.

The gate opens, and we roll toward the monstrosity, lit up like someone forgot to turn the lights off in every room. A long row of cars are parked along the driveway, but we pass them all and pull up to the front, just in front of the door.

What is this place?

The demonic man is the first to step out, and the two up front follow shortly after. Maksim opens his door but leans toward me to whisper his first words since we left Hugh's.

"Keep your head down and be silent."

That's it. That's all the wisdom he imparts on me before he slips from the SUV and holds out his hand for me, his face stern as the day I met him.

What's going on?

I want to ask so badly, but I can tell he doesn't want me to. He wouldn't have waited until we had the briefest moment alone to speak to me if it didn't matter.

I take his hand and let him help me out then shuffle behind him up a set of stone steps to the door. The two men who were up front are on our heels.

The demon leads the way inside while I walk so closely behind Maksim that my crossed arms graze his back.

Seductive instrumental music plays throughout the place, and people mill around, but I don't look at them, instead keeping my head down like Maksim said to. It strikes me how easy it is to listen to him now when days ago it felt impossible.

Even walking through halls, I still can't tell what this place is supposed to be. It seems like a party venue, but we can't be here for that. The farther we walk, the more the music and voices fade, until it's gone completely and we've come to a sliding, wooden door.

The demon leads the way inside, but I'm hesitant to

follow Maksim this time. The hairs on my neck stand up straight, and my feet naturally shift backward. Something tells me not to go in that room.

Maksim pauses to look back at me, but instead of saying anything, he just looks at me seriously, his eyes slightly wide, his jaw clenched.

Sucking in a sharp breath, I follow him inside, halting when I spot the familiar cane leaned against a purple velvet chair, one of four in the room.

"There she is," Maksim's boss, Nikita, says. His voice slithers down my spine like a snake, making me want to frantically bat it away, but I stay perfectly still until the man behind me pushes me forward.

Nikita wraps his arm around my shoulders and leans on me like he's replacing me as his cane. "This is the ruthless murderer you've been searching for?"

His tone is light, but his words make me jump. I look up at the two angry men he's speaking to and recognize neither, but I know who they must be.

The organization.

Oh no.

I snap my head toward Maksim, but he doesn't seem surprised. He stands fairly relaxed with his hands clasped in front of him.

"This bitch brutally murdered one of our men," a man with a triangle of moles on his cheek grinds out. "We'd appreciate it if you kept your tone respectful."

"*Ah.*" Anger, just a touch, brews beneath that one syllable, and I feel it in Nikita's firming hold. "Of course." He removes his arm from my shoulders and uses it to shove me to the floor so abruptly I yelp.

"Fucking whore," he spits, but he sounds more mocking toward the men than serious. Still, I prepare for a kick or shove or something more.

Behind me, the younger man around my age from the SUV snickers.

Tension builds in the room so quickly, I wonder if I'm imagining it and can't help peeking at Nikita who stares at the young, snickering man with a death stare that freezes my blood.

"You're new," he says like he's observing it for the first time.

"My nephew, sir," the SUV driver nervously answers for the young man. "It's his second week. He doesn't know any better. Please forgive him, Pakhan."

Nikita nods slowly. "You're man enough to work for the Bratva but not to speak for yourself?"

The man, now looking more like a boy, fumbles with his lips. "I…"

"What's your name, son?"

The young man clears his throat. "Stephen."

"*Stephen*. Do you have a gun, Stephen?"

Stephen's face reddens. "Of course, sir."

"Could I please see it?"

Hesitation. So much hesitation. The fear in Stephen's expression makes me nauseous with how contagious it is, how much it fills the room. Everyone here knows what he's thinking.

He takes his gun from his waistband and walks it to Nikita, clearing his throat again and trying to walk tall in a surge of bravery.

Nikita takes the gun. "Thank you, son." He smiles before clapping Stephen on the shoulder, then he turns to the driver. "Sean, were you the one who vouched for Stephen to get into the brotherhood?"

Sean, afraid but holding his chin up, nods.

"I thought so."

Nikita aims the gun at him and fires before Stephen can suck in a breath to yell out. But before he can try to stop Nikita, the demon is there, holding him back. Nikita hobbles to the uncle and fires bullets into his body until the gun clicks.

I stare down at my shaking hands, my head so low I could fall forward at any moment, and try to be invisible. The growing sense of *déjà* vu overwhelms me as I silently work on the plea to give Maksim so he'll never make me see this man again. Never take me here.

What if this is it? What if Maksim doesn't protect me?

What if he can't?

My stomach winds tightly, and I bite my lip while staring at the snow-white rug that will need a jug of bleach before the night is through. It makes no sense why Nikita doesn't have all red or black carpeting with as often as this must happen.

The gun thumps on the floor, and Nikita must give an order to the demon because a crack sounds, silencing Stephen. I regret the moment I look behind me to see Stephen's head awkwardly twisted in the demon's grasp before he drops.

The soup I had earlier rises up my throat, and I slap a hand over my mouth, facing forward and seesawing air through my nose. I swallow and close my eyes, focusing on the ringing in my ears to distract me from everything else.

But it doesn't work. Nikita's voice pierces through the noise I try to create in my mind, demanding my attention.

"So where were we?" he asks. "Oh yes. The great loss of one of your men. Very serious. I can understand how you feel. Just today, I lost two."

My eyes grow wide at the deadpanned statement, and I look to the outsiders for their reaction. They seem uncomfortable. *Very* uncomfortable. They exchange a look with each other then shift as they face forward, one's Adam's apple bobbing.

"Please, gentlemen, *sit*." Nikita warmly waves to a set of purple velvet chairs like he's inviting in close friends. He hobbles to the one with the cane but continues standing until the other men, including Maksim, have sat. There's the slightest bit of relief that crosses Nikita's expression, like standing caused pain that he'd never admit to.

I'm off to the side of the room but not far from the men's minds, so I eyeball Maksim and wish he was closer. Wish he'd give me some indication as to what he's thinking. What he's planning.

You're going to help me, right?

Please help me!

Finally, he seems to hear my internal pleas because he meets my eyes and pats the side of his leg, a silent 'come here' command.

I'm too afraid to stand, somehow feeling like that would draw too much attention to myself, so I crawl to Maksim, quickening my pace to pass Nikita along the way.

Maksim parts his legs so I can situate myself between them. I hide my face against his knee before inhaling the scent of safety. Days ago, I disliked having his scent on his pillow, so close to me in bed, but now when—if—we go home, I want it there. I'll breathe it in, bottle it up as a perfume, be grateful to keep it for the rest of my life if I can.

"Aww, isn't that precious," Nikita teases.

"Look, we don't want to take up any more of your time. We just want the girl back," the guy with the moles bravely says.

Maksim's large hand runs over my head in a pet I didn't know could be so comforting. "You say that as if we've stolen her."

"No, of course not." The other one laughs nervously. "We aren't saying that."

"*They* can't really say anything," Nikita cuts in. "Apparently, we aren't important enough for the boss to come down here to speak with us. These are his *representatives*."

"Daniel Storm, the deceased, is not important enough, sir," Moles says. "I assure you, it has nothing to do—"

"Yes, that's great. Alik…" I lift my head to watch Nikita motion to the demon. "Could you please escort these men outside to wait while I speak with my lieutenant?"

I expect an 'of course, sir,' but Alik just glances at the other men who reluctantly stand from their seats and follow him out the door.

Once they're gone, Nikita rubs his temples and growls something in Russian. I think he's talking to Maksim, so I startle at a sound behind the chairs and peek around to see a half-naked woman filling two glasses with clear liquor. She was here the whole time? Was she hiding?

"Explain something to me…" Nikita takes a glass from the woman. She hands the other to Maksim before kneeling at Nikita's feet. "This trafficker apparently lived in Bakersfield, California. How the fuck did this foreign, non-English speaking cunt find her way to the exact address of the man who lured her to America?"

"I had no part in the kill." Maksim doesn't hesitate, and it makes me stiffen. He knows what he's doing. He *must* know. He doesn't sound fearful at all.

But what if he doesn't sound fearful because he isn't going to lie for me? What if he's going to let them punish me, like I *should* be punished, like Daniel needed to be punished?

No. No, he wouldn't.

He'll protect me. I'm safe.

On impulse, I push my head into his hand. He rubs his thumb over my scalp.

"But I did give her the opportunity to do it herself... I gave her the address to the man's home, not thinking she'd go through with it. I was mocking her more than anything because, before I enlightened her, she believed he was her fiancé. I apologize for my recklessness. Clearly, I underestimated her, but when I went to pick her up, she had been there waiting for me for hours. She's as obedient as a whore can be, despite the unfortunate miscommunication."

"Unfortunate miscommunication." Nikita laughs and relaxes his head back. He mutters something in Russian, a command of some sort that has the woman at his feet crawling between his legs and unbuttoning his pants. My eyes widen, and I sharply turn my head away.

"She isn't a problem for us, Pakhan," Maksim says, unfazed by what Nikita is making the woman do. I take another peek at her bobbing head before looking up at Maksim to see some sort of reaction, but there is none.

"Maybe not, but she does present an opportunity." Nikita continues when Maksim remains silent. "Vengeance is a powerful need. They'll buy her back from us for far more than we paid."

I search Maksim's hardened features in the silence, wishing we were back home, wishing I had caressed that face when it was flooded with sadness and vulnerability. I'm so scared, my teeth hurt from clenching so hard, and a whimper crawls up my throat.

All the arguing we've done. All the remarks I've made. All the things I've taken for granted. I want to take it all back. I want him to take me home. Hug me. Tease me. Make me angry. Anything but make me fear for my life.

My fingers dig into Maksim's calves, a desperate plea that he doesn't react to.

"I wish to keep her."

Nikita's brows raise. "We have other whores, Maksim.

You can take your pick. Here…" He pushes the woman's forehead away from him, sending her tumbling onto her back and leaving himself exposed. "Take this one."

"No, thank you."

When Nakita's eyes narrow, my lungs shrink with fear not just for myself, but for Maksim. Nikita just murdered two different people for reasons I'm not even sure of. Maksim…

What if he hurts Maksim?

I close my eyes.

"Why?" Nikita asks.

When Maksim shifts, I jump, but he just grabs his phone from his pocket and messes with it for a minute.

Once he finds what he's looking for, he hands the phone to Nikita—now dressed—who takes it and squints at the screen.

"She's incredibly unique. Fierce but obedient. There are few women who hold my attention, but I've come to quite enjoy this one."

Nikita's head rears back as he watches the screen. "Hmmm."

"I recognize that I made a mistake and am prepared to pay whatever cost to make this go away."

Nikita doesn't reply. His eyes are glued to the screen as a minute ticks by, then another. Finally, he hands Maksim his phone back and locks eyes with me. If I could, I would look away, but he roots me in place, searing me with so much lust, I wonder if I prefer his murderous looks.

"Fine," he says. "Pay the bastards whatever will keep them from contacting me again and you can keep her."

He grabs his cane and uses it to stand. "I'll show Miss, um…"

"Elira," Maksim offers.

"I'll show Elira around while you work out the details. I

171

hope you'll be joining us this evening?" Nikita drags his eyes to Maksim.

"Of course," Maksim says, but he sounds anything but certain.

Joining them? Joining them where?

`I should be relieved. I *am* relieved.

I'm going to live. Maksim is going to keep his promise to me. He's going to protect me.

But that knowledge can't give me the sweet relief my rigid body craves when Nikita extends his hand for me, ready to lead me away from the only person I feel safe with.

I silently plead with Maksim for help, but he nudges me away and stands, walking around me to leave me alone with the worst man I've ever met.

My stomach sunken to the floor, I bite my lip hard and take Nikita's hand.

20

ELIRA

*N*ikita smells like evil.

Every time his hand smooths across the back of my neck as he leads me down the hall, I inhale the scent of his cologne sharply, and every time I think it must be custom made. They couldn't be selling Nikita's scent commercially; no way.

Then again, maybe it isn't the scent that's evil. Maybe it's just when it's on him.

"This way," he coos, guiding me toward voices with his hand curving around my hip. His cane clicks on the tile insidiously with each step, but he walks at a surprisingly brisk pace. Whatever happened to him hasn't slowed him down.

People appear as we enter a large, impressive room dotted with leather couches and chairs. At first, I think nothing of the people, noticing the gigantic white rug Nikita must have a thing for and the glass wall revealing a rectangular pool on the other side of it so large it extends out of sight.

But then I hear more than a voice, it's a moan, and my

eyes glue to a fully nude woman swaying her hips to the instrumental music. My eyes dart around, finding couples, *groups*, naked, their bodies melding together.

Not everyone is like this. Some people are fully dressed, conversing like nothing is happening, and some are half-naked in pieces of lingerie like the woman who was with Nikita before. I can't believe anyone could just stand there talking like nothing is happening.

My face gets impossibly hot, and my eyes naturally find my feet. I try to block out the noise, all of it.

I want to go home.

Now.

I want to watch that dramatic movie Anya chose and plan what to have for dinner tomorrow and pretend Maksim isn't the kind of man who comes to places like this.

That thought is ripped from my mind, it feels like a *luxury*, when Nikita's hand slips under my dress and runs to my rear, sliding beneath my panties to feel skin felt by only one man before him.

He squeezes and moves us to a wall so he can rest his cane against it. "You fooled me that first night, didn't you?" he asks me, staring down at my chest when he uses the back of his deft fingers to slide my straps off my shoulders, making my summer dress sag and catch on my chest that heaves with each quick breath. "You can understand everything I say."

I stare straight ahead, my hands bunching into fists so they don't shake. My throat is a pinched hose, so I nod.

Nikita rubs his thumb across the top of my dress, leaning in to smile against my face. "Sneaky little bitch."

I feel it when his smile falls and close my eyes, bracing for pain.

"I must admit, I wrongly assessed you. You are … quite a woman."

What?

"I think you and I could have an awful lot of fun together."

His words, along with his breath, sting my face like he bit me, and I clench my eyelids. I try not to consider what he's saying, try not to picture it, but it's hard. He could be talking about sex. He could be talking about torture. He could be talking about anything.

"Open your eyes."

His voice isn't harsh, but I obey the command immediately anyway, opening my eyes wide as if that makes any difference.

"If you could pick anyone in this room, who would it be, and what would it be with?"

Huh?

My wide eyes soften as I turn to search his face for meaning.

He smiles, reading my mind, then he reaches into his inside jacket pocket to reveal a knife. My lungs harden to concrete, and I get the overwhelming urge to flee, having to fight myself to stay still.

I stare at the knife like it'll stay out of my body as long as I don't take my eyes off it.

"Blades are my first choice," he says, turning it over in his hand. "Small ones. Your kill would've lasted much longer if you'd used a less lethal blade, and trust me, you want it to last longer."

I don't grimace. Don't puke. Don't react at all to what he's saying. My heart beats wildly, and blood whooshes in my ears, but I listen and hope like hell I don't look anything like I feel because... Because I don't think he's trying to scare me. I think he's bonding with me. And I'm a smart enough woman to know not to reject him.

He thinks I'm a killer.

Which makes sense because of what happened, but ... I'm

175

not. I'm *not*. I'm… I never would have done that if it wasn't deserved.

I'm not *Nikita*.

But he wants me to be. For the moment, he wants me to pretend.

Where is Maksim?

"So?" Nikita asks, nodding toward the people. "Who would it be, and what would it be with?"

Wheezing in a breath as quietly as I can, I turn my stiffened neck toward the room.

He wouldn't make me kill someone for real. This is hypothetical. An exercise. A game.

It's fine.

Just say something.

I scan, searching for someone who looks unkind, deserving of this hypothetical fate, until I find the perfect person.

The demon.

Alik.

He's slunk back in a chair by himself in a far corner with a drink resting on his knee. Fully clothed. Merely taking things in like a creepy voyeur.

I don't know him, but I bet he deserves to die.

"Him." I point at the demon.

Nikita follows my finger and chuckles. "Alik?"

I nod. "With a gun. Quick, efficient, middle of the desert."

"*No*." I flinch at his disapproving tone. "Don't be a coward. This isn't a kill for work. It's for play."

For play.

This man is as sick as I imagined.

I nod like I now understand the rules, but I'm regretting my choice. I'm still sure this is just an exercise, but on the off chance he chooses to tell Alik about this or push me to act this out, Alik could break my neck as easily as he did the young man's.

"With a fire poker. First to take out the knees, then the genitals. I would wait for his cries to stop before finishing the job on his face."

Nikita inhales a deep, intoxicated breath then lets it out on a sigh. "That's a sight I'd like to see."

Oh no.

Hypothetical.

Hypothetical. Hypothetical. Hypothetical.

"Take off your clothes," Nikita commands, his breath hot, his tone fierce. If he'd said this ten minutes ago, I would have struggled not to break into tears, but now I'm relieved. I'd rather do *anything* except enact this sick fantasy game we're playing.

I pull my yellow sundress over my head and step out of my white cotton panties, unsure where to put both but dropping them when he slaps my hand.

"Good girl," he growls, caging me in, his eyes hungrily taking in my breasts. I close my eyes as he squeezes both nipples then lowers one hand to what he's famously dubbed my *cunt*.

I turn my head and swallow a whimper when two fingers invade me, pumping into me like I belong to Nikita. My body burns as his rough touch scratches and rubs an area unaccustomed to this sort of intrusion, and I fight the desire to push him away, to move, to scream.

It was better with James/Daniel. He was not perfect. I didn't orgasm the way I'd read about in books or been told about by friends. But he was slow and fairly kind.

Nikita is not slow nor is he kind.

"Do you want my cock?"

He says it like a question, but there's only one correct answer.

177

One I can't give.

If I open my mouth, I'm afraid it'll come out as a cry. My lip trembles, and I suck in a sharp breath, tilting my head back so he doesn't see.

A hand weaves into my hair before balling into a tight fist. It jerks my head to the side, sending a shooting pain through my scalp and a gasp soaring past my lips.

It isn't Nikita. The large body of a man crowds the two of us before I can register who it is or what's happening.

"Starting without me, slut?"

Maksim's hot, angry voice seethes in my ear. I don't even try to make sense of it. Relief floods me as I meet his eyes, leaning into him.

He stares back with a hardened expression that would make me cower if Nikita didn't have his hands on me. When his hand wraps around my throat, all I manage is a whimper as he yanks my body roughly away from the predator and pins me against the wall.

Nikita merely laughs coldly and watches as Maksim unbuttons his pants and yanks down his zipper.

My jaw drops.

What are you doing?

He shrugs his pants over his hips, revealing himself as carelessly and confidently as Nikita had.

Just like Nikita.

He's just like Nikita.

No.

No, he isn't.

I clench my jaw and listen to the voice deep down inside of me that trusts Maksim, spreading my legs wide on its command when Maksim presses himself against me and lifts me up against the wall.

When his mouth claims mine, I don't resist. His kiss is

rough, *brutal*, and I can feel myself cringing, but I put my hands on his face and lean into it.

His erection strokes the sensitive flesh Nikita just assaulted, and I clench my eyes shut, waiting for pain.

When he thrusts, I gasp, but he doesn't enter me. He slides between my legs with a grunt while his hands dig into the flesh of my rear.

It's an act.

A *show*.

He's protecting me.

I rip my mouth from his to tuck my face in the crook of his neck so Nikita doesn't see my face twisting with gut-wrenching relief. I hug Maksim's neck, squeezing hard each time he rocks my body with his thrusts and hope he can sense my gratitude. Hope he knows I know what he's doing.

I kiss his neck, to add to the display at first, but then because I want to. I want his smell, his skin, his arms, the faint taste of his sweat, his roughness, his jokes, his vulnerability, his lewd remarks, his…

His everything. Right now, I want his everything. I just want him to take me home, and I want most of all for him to be nothing like the man watching us.

My heart quickens as I peek at Nikita to see if he's still there, and sure enough, he is. My head whirls the other way in a panic, my mind drifting to the possibilities of what comes next.

Will Nikita wait for this to be finished?

Will he want me next?

Maksim can't continue this forever.

"Look at me, *lislchka*."

My eyelashes flutter as I focus on Maksim.

"You are mine."

Those words, those possessive, dehumanizing words,

smooth down my back in a sweet, assuring caress. I know what he's saying to me.

I will protect you.

From the organization.

From Nikita.

From everything and everyone.

I hated him. I hated him more than I thought possible to hate a man. I planned to kill him. If I hadn't recognized I needed him to do exactly what he's promising me right now, I probably would've already done it.

A week ago, I would have glared at these words he's speaking.

Tonight, at this moment, the back of my throat feels full.

I close my eyes and press my lips to his, tasting a man I feel I'm meeting for the first time.

His movements falter like he's surprised, but he quickly recovers, kissing me back as he jerks his strong hips against mine.

My lips part as an invitation that he greedily accepts, dipping his tongue into my mouth to stroke me.

I move my hands to his face to feel the roughness of his stubble, the hardness of his jaw, smoothing my thumbs over his cheeks and pulling him in closer.

Desire relaxes my body while simultaneously winding my core. My nipples pebble as they graze Maksim's chest, but I still feel Nikita's hands on me. I feel his prying. His greed.

His phantom touch haunts my insides, and the more warmth Maksim ignites, the more attention is drawn to those areas.

I don't want to feel Nikita. I don't want him to be the last man to be inside of me, to be the hand I feel.

I want Maksim.

The more he kisses me, the more my body undulates to grind with his, craving more than a charade.

Maksim's thrusts gradually transition from rough to rhythmic, angry to passionate, and he must sense the shift as an issue because he breaks our kiss and looks to the side for Nikita.

He's gone.

I search over Maksim's shoulder to find Nikita by Alik, his hungry gaze taking in the room. He seems to have moved on.

Maksim finds Nikita as well and goes to set me down, but I stiffen and dig my hands into his shoulders, halting him.

When he narrows his eyes at me, confused, my cheeks heat.

"He could still be paying attention."

My voice squeaks, my face growing even hotter as I hear how uncertain I sound. These people are disgusting, coming here, having sex in a room full of others, probably not all consensual. But... Would it be so terrible if I didn't want this to stop?

Maksim's eyes light up. He nods, lowering his gaze to my lips, my breasts that ache at his attention, down to our hips.

When he puts me on the floor, I deflate, but then he crooks his arm beneath my knee and lifts, making me gasp and almost topple over if not for him grabbing my shoulder to steady me.

Letting go of my shoulder hesitantly, he pushes his tip against my opening that feels slick, welcoming. I close my eyes and relax while he rubs himself over my entrance then glides his shaft over my clit.

My head tips back against the wall, and I sigh at the sensation as he starts to thrust slowly, grinding himself against a magical bundle of nerves I've yet to explore with another person.

Maksim's lips, now tender, find my neck, and he kisses me like he's tasting me, his tongue swiping each time. It's silly, but it makes me want to cry. I didn't think I cared what the pigs thought of me when I was being sold, but being made to sit in filth and constantly being appraised as disgusting must have stuck in my mind somewhere because it feels good that he wants to taste me. That he *wants* me.

That I'm his.

When his kisses reach my collarbone, I puff out my chest for him. He uses both hands now to lift me up, his arms hooked beneath my thighs while I wrap my legs around his waist.

I watch, mesmerized as he takes my nipple into his mouth to cause a sharp, pleasant sensation that travels inward and down to my swollen clit. When he sucks, I gasp, fisting my hands into his hair and tugging, unsure if I'm pulling him away or closer. Either way, he doesn't stop.

He licks and sucks my nipple until the other screams with deprivation, and then he grants it mercy, causing the same sharp sensations to travel down to my clit that begins to feel so full, it aches.

I catch the sight of people over Maksim's shoulder but don't care. They don't matter. Nikita doesn't matter. The past doesn't matter. My body cares about none of it. It only cares about here, now, replacing the phantom touch in my core and relieving the ache in my clit.

"Touch me," I say, breathless.

A wave of self-consciousness passes through me as his eyes find mine, but I can't regret my words. I need this too badly.

His head tilts. "Am I your whore, *lislchka*? Do you command me?"

"Please," I groan, arching my hips toward him.

Take the ache away.

Take his touch away.

Please.

He stares at me a few more seconds, a man unaccustomed to being told what to do by a mere woman like me.

But there's hunger in his eyes. I'm guessing he's hungry enough to listen.

He shifts me so he's holding me with only one arm while my back is pressed against the wall, then with a delicious slide of his hand up my thigh, his fingers find my sex.

Not making me wait another second, he slips one finger inside me and starts to massage my walls, making my eyes heavy and my body sag. Desire builds, but more than that, my body breathes a long sigh, the recent violation no longer as pronounced.

Maksim seems to search for something, and when sparks fly in my core, zapping my arms and legs and making me jerk, I know he found it.

"Mmm," I moan, my back pressing against the wall as he strokes me faster.

When his thumb moves to my clit, I cry out.

"Is this what you wanted?" he asks, slowing his pace so he can rub teasing circles around my clit.

Yes.

"Hmmm?" He shoves another finger inside me, and I knock my head against the wall.

"Yes!"

I must look ridiculous, and I know he'll be smirking, so I keep my eyes closed as he brings me more pleasure than I've ever felt in my life.

I think of all the times people whispered about my mother behind her back, calling her a whore. She chose an unconventional route of picking a life partner, unheard of in our culture. Sex outside of marriage is shameful. Having children outside of marriage is an abomination.

I vowed to never have either. If for no other reason than to never be looked at the way my mother was. I would not be a whore. I would wait until marriage. And I got close. I waited until my engagement, too afraid that without sex, the marriage would fall through.

But now it seems it was all in vain. I'm in what must be a whorehouse, acting exactly that, with my legs spread wide for a man who claims he owns me.

And the worst part is, I'm not hating it.

My body lifts, my chest rising as Maksim brings me to a precipice, the tension in my core wound so tightly, there's no room for more.

I dig my nails into his shoulders and open my mouth in a strangled cry. I do my best to keep quiet but fail miserably as my body pulses and squeezes around Maksim's finger.

When my hands slip off Maksim's shoulders, I feel the sweat on my neck and notice it beading on my forehead, sticking to my back, moistening the backs of my knees. I'm covered in it.

I'm panting as I come down from my high and terrified that I won't be able to stand, but Maksim must sense this because he doesn't put me down.

My eyelids flutter, finally looking at Maksim again as he picks up my dress and panties then shifts me in his arms. He carries me out of this hell without a word to the demons in it.

He doesn't speak, so neither do I. I wouldn't know what to say.

Thank you?

Does this change things?

Where do we go from here?

I doubt he has the answers, so I let him carry me to safety, snuggling in his arms.

Arms that for the very first time, I feel I can trust.

21

MAKSIM

*M*y eyes close as I listen to Elira's soft, relaxed breathing, a stark contrast to how it was on the way up. She had clung to me then out of desperation, but now, cradled in my arms in the back of Hugh's SUV, she's relaxed to the point I think she may be sleeping.

Hugh drives us to my home in silence, never uttering a question about what took place at Nikita's. He won't ask. We won't speak a word of it unless I bring it up.

But he'll be curious. Tonight, when we arrived at his house, he asked a question I wasn't sure how to answer.

Have you fallen for the whore, brother?

He asked it playfully, as a reference to my arm around Elira, as an acknowledgment of her presence there at all. Now I wonder what he must think.

Elira shifts in my arms, hinting at her wakefulness, but I don't look at her. I keep my eyes closed while I try to answer Hugh's question for myself.

Have you fallen for your whore, brother?

No.

Elira is … useful. She's useful. Necessary even. Anya likes

her, she likes the version Elira paints of me. Elira keeps my house a level of clean I had no idea I enjoyed. She cooks food I didn't realize I'd missed. She makes my home feel more alive, less like a suburban box I force myself to crawl into every night and more an actual home.

So she matters. Apparently, enough that I'm willing to go home a hundred thousand dollars poorer, the agreed upon cost of Elira's vengeance. But have I *fallen* for her? Am I even capable of that?

No. Of course not. That would be ridiculous.

I open my eyes and roll my neck, suddenly feeling better at the revelation, but when I find her staring at me, my arms wrapped around her stiffen.

Her irises are caramel swirls that are lighter than I've ever seen on her. She blinks slowly, never looking away, like she's allowing me to gaze at those swirls she's been hiding from me. I'm so used to seeing her guarded or angry or defensive, occasionally afraid, but never, ever like this. Never so open, so vulnerable, so … *trusting*.

My skin crawls, but I don't look away. I *can't*. The urge to shove her away from me twitches my muscles, like my body is rejecting the closeness I enjoyed only a moment ago.

She doesn't speak.

Neither do I.

But I wonder what she's thinking. I wonder what that was back there, what it meant to her, if anything at all. I wonder if another man has ever made her come.

My eyes drop to her lips while I consider that, welcoming the oncoming sensations massaging my balls. Lust feels so much more natural than the things those caramel swirls have me questioning. It feels *right*. Like I should've been fucking her all along. Like we have so much to make up for.

Pretty, long lashes flutter as she must feel my cock harden beneath her, but she doesn't move. Interest sparks on her face, making me regret texting Hugh to pick us up. Suddenly, he feels in the way.

My eyes drift up to Hugh, but when Elira shifts, grinding her ass against my cock, my eyes snap back to her.

I must look intimidating because her cheeks redden, and she shrinks back like she's embarrassed. She reacted this way earlier too, when she wanted me to keep kissing her. *Touching* her.

What I wouldn't give right now to taste her…

But no. She's been selfish plenty tonight.

Taking her knee, I rock her body gently to rub her against my dick like before, just enough that she gets the message. Her uncertain eyes relax with interest, and she perks up as she wraps one arm around my neck and subtly grinds her ass against me.

It's nice, but it only has my eyes locking onto her lips, even fuller than I remember.

"Stop," I say, my tone low and sharp, before I lose myself and start fucking her mouth in the back of this SUV.

She freezes, her sweet body tensing in my arms, and her shoulders hunch like she's a dog I've just reprimanded. Yesterday, she would've glared, probably shoved herself off of me, and stared out the window with her arms crossed. *Now* she cares what I think. She wants my approval, *needs* it, and fuck if that doesn't turn me on.

Hugh pulls into my drive less than a minute later, and I throw open the door before urging Elira out more eagerly than I intend, causing her to stumble.

I nod at Hugh through the open window. "*Spasibo.*" *Thank you*.

He nods in return, his eyes finding Elira before he drives away.

"*Go,*" I command, giving her back a small shove. My cock

strains when she obeys, hurrying toward the house like the good girl I know she isn't.

It isn't her fault, I know, but out of nowhere, I feel deprived. Hungry. *Starving.* I want her, just like this, obeying my commands, eager to give my cock attention.

Jesus fucking Christ, I want her.

Pushing her aside, I rip my keys from my pocket and jab the lock before flinging open the door. Elira flinches when it slams into the wall, but still, she doesn't say anything. She arches her shoulders and hurries past me when I angle my body to the side.

"Get in the shower, *lislchka.* I want all the filth of tonight off of you."

Without looking back, she turns the corner to my bedroom, the smooth curve of her hips tempting me each second. Without her in my sight, I can remind myself a hundred times over why I haven't already fucked her, why I should breathe, relax, have a drink, let my desire settle.

She's young.

Inexperienced.

Timid.

She may be mine, but she's no whore.

Still…

She wants me. I could see it all over her face, feel her excitement in the air. She wants more than the pleasure my hands can give her. She wants my cock.

Who am I to deny her?

* * *

Elira

WATER SPLASHES ONTO MY FACE, tiny droplets clinging to my lashes to make me blink every few seconds while I listen carefully for any noise outside of the shower.

It's been minutes, and I haven't touched the soap. Haven't even moved to fully wet my hair. I just listen, waiting, wondering what comes next, unsure of what I want.

My nipples are erect and throb under the spray of the shower, and my sex, satisfied less than an hour ago, feels painfully neglected yet again. My body knows what it wants.

But my mind… My mind is struggling.

We're home. We're safe.

He protected me.

I can trust him.

But…

But what, Elira? What is the problem?

The door to the bathroom opens, making every muscle in my body tense like I'm afraid of the man I seem to be craving so intensely. And all at once, I get what I'm afraid of.

What if I'm *wrong*?

What if he *is* like those other men? *Just* like those other men?

What if I'm a fool?

I swallow as the shower curtain is pulled open and a blur of skin and muscle steps inside behind me. My eyes close as I shift forward and tilt my head up to let the water sprinkle my face.

Maksim's hands, large and rough like they've known hard labor, circle my hips and run up to my breasts.

The ache in my nipples intensifies as he cups both breasts and squeezes, his palms pressing against the sensitive buds, while nuzzling his chin into my shoulder.

"Do you want me?" he asks, more like growls, in my ear, causing my spine to shudder.

I don't answer. Don't know how to.

He removes one of his hands to thread it through my hair

and yanks my head back from the spray, pulling a gasp from my lungs.

"Do you want me?"

His words, so demanding, so forceful, remind me of Nikita's.

Do you want my cock?

There was only one correct answer then. Is there only one correct answer now?

Maksim keeps a tight grip on my hair while shoving his other hand between my legs, relaxing when he finds the heat and liquid he left me with.

"You are so sexy, *lislchka*." He runs his fingers up my slit to a spot only he has claimed. My tensed body begins to relax as he uses a finger to rub a circle over the tender nerves, lighting up my pleasure sensors while dampening the pain in my scalp. "I know you want me. Just say it. Say it and maybe I'll be nice."

Nice.

Maksim is many things. I don't think he's a bad man, but it's hard for me to see him as *nice.*

My eyes roll as he works me, my body feeling heavier than before. I could lie to him, but what would be the point? "I want you."

"Good girl," he whispers, massaging the sting from my scalp. Those two words send warmth through me that leaks out onto his hand when he slips a finger inside.

My lips part with a moan as I lean into him, letting his body and his strength hold me up.

"Tell me you're my whore." His words are almost snarled, his breath hot, even as his finger fucks me lovingly.

I'm no one's whore.

I almost sneer it. Almost.

But he feels too good. Too right. It isn't even my choice at this point. My body has made up my mind for me.

Tomorrow, I will be his equal.

Tonight, I am whatever he wants me to be.

Arching my hips when he fucks me deeper, I close my eyes and moan. "I'm your whore."

He groans, swiping the hair off my shoulder before his lips hungrily make a trail to my neck.

The sensations he brings me curl my toes, shake my knees, sink my eyelids, but abruptly, his hand leaves me.

"On your knees, *shlyukha*," he growls, whipping me around and pressing on my shoulders so I'll lower to the tub.

I don't know what *lislchka* means, but on Maksim's lips, it sounds endearing. I feel safe, special, in a way. I don't mind it, certainly don't hate it.

Shlyukha, however, is not a term of endearment. From my time with the Russians, I can confidently say it means something along the lines of 'whore.'

Water trails down my face, gathering in my eyes so I close them, but it's gone when Maksim takes my chin and yanks me out of the stream.

I open my eyes to take in his length, large and intimidating in his grasp. I can feel his arousal making the tub feel smaller, my nipples tighter. My core grips at what isn't there.

Maksim squeezes my jaw so I'll open my mouth, and I look up at him, searching for... I don't know what I'm looking for, but all I see is lust. Pure, powerful lust as he presses himself to my mouth, urging me to open wider.

His eyes close as he fills my mouth, and mine would do the same, but panic sweeps me. It's silly, but I get the sudden fear that I'm not going to do this right. That I won't bring him the same pleasure he brought me. That I'm a letdown, the lust in his eyes nothing but buildup that will lead to disappointment.

I shouldn't care. There are so many things I shouldn't care about that I keep finding myself worrying over.

"*Fuck,*" he groans, opening his eyes as he pulls out and pushes into my mouth again. He looks down at me and says something in Russian that doesn't sound like a command, nor is his voice filled with anger. Just lust.

He shoves in hard, hitting the back of my throat and making me gag around his length. I try to pull away, but he fists my hair and holds me in place without a word.

I look up at him, feeling tiny compared to his six foot plus frame, and even smaller in this position. He appears so much more controlling than normal, more … I don't know, scary. It makes me want to hide while at the same time makes my nerves feel tight, ready, *wanting*.

He's … sexy.

Powerful.

Mine?

Or am I only his?

"Hold still, Elira," he says, his commanding tone making me tense. My name sounds strange on his tongue now. Like a naughty word that gives me chills.

Holding my chin, he thrusts into my mouth while I fight my gag reflex, but the more I fight, the farther he pushes until I realize he *wants* to make me gag.

His length bounces in my mouth each time I choke, and his hips pick up their pace, his hands taking my head while he pumps into me.

I stop worrying about him grading my performance when I finally realize that he doesn't give a shit. He has no intention of giving me any amount of control. He wants to use me. Fuck me. Treat me like a *shlyukha,* like a whore.

Is that *all* I am?

Will he discard me after?

Maksim rocks into me hard, stilling with one hand holding my chin up while the other grips my hair. An explosion of warm, salty goo fills my mouth, and I close my eyes as I swallow it down.

"Mmm," Maksim groans before muttering a string of Russian he must not intend for me to understand.

Fear, the real kind, not for my life but for my pride, worse my *heart*, comes barreling in. It turns my cum-filled stomach when Maksim pulls out of my mouth and shuts the shower off.

I'm a soaked mess on the tub floor, my hands wrapped around myself, unsure if I should be ashamed or content.

What happens now?

Will he just leave me here? Will he keep calling me *shlyukha*? Is that my new name?

My eyes clench shut when I remember the men from tonight, the ones he must have had to pay off in order to keep me alive. I don't know how much it was, but it must've been years' worth of work that I'm doing in the bakery. It'll take my life to pay Maksim back.

I won't be able to send money back home.

Everything will be different.

My bargaining power, my freedom, it's... It's gone, isn't it?

I am *shlyukha.*

Shame washes over me at not only what I just did, what I enjoyed, but at how long it took for me to realize my incredibly obvious reality.

I am *shlyukha.*

I am *shlyukha.*

I am *shlyukha.*

"Elira?" Maksim towers over me like a king, a *master* I may as well call him.

Sobs erupt from my mouth, shaking my shoulders. I hug myself to control it.

"*Elira*." Maksim crouches beside me and goes to put his hand on my shoulder but hovers it inches away. After a moment, he sighs and mutters under his breath. "*Topoy grebanny idiot.*"

I squeeze myself as he stands, expecting him to leave, but he grabs a towel and wraps it around me before lifting me gently and carrying me to his bed.

I bite my lip, silencing my cries as he lays me down and pulls the covers over me. His hand feels warm covering my shoulder, but when it leaves, my body cools.

"I'm sorry, *lislchka*," he says with regret straining his voice before his presence fades.

I roll over to face his retreating form, confusion and fear making me sick to my stomach. I'm terrified to ask what I think I already know, but watching him walk away feels worse.

"Maksim."

He stops and turns to me, his face twisted with concern.

I stare at his handsome features, my protector, my house-mate, my owner.

I don't want to know.

But I have to know.

"How much money did you have to pay those men?"

He frowns as he comes toward me and sits on the bed. "It doesn't matter."

"Of course it matters," I say, my voice weak.

He's quiet for a moment, but then, "A hundred grand."

My breathing stops.

One hundred thousand dollars.

My life. That's what it cost, my life. Maksim puts a hand on my leg at the sight of tears filling my eyes.

"The money doesn't matter, Elira. I have a much smaller home than I can afford, remember? You can't imagine how much money I've put back."

"But it's *your* money," I counter. I look pointedly at the

bathroom. "How many times am I going to have to be your *shlyukha* before you're paid back?"

When a moment goes by, I wonder if he's doing the math. How many blowjobs equal a hundred grand?

"Look at me."

No.

I keep my watery eyes on the bathroom entrance, afraid of what I'll see if I meet Maksim's gaze.

"Elira."

"*No*," I grate out. "Say what you must, but I've done my duties for the night."

Out of the corner of my eye, I watch Maksim rub the back of his neck and feel his frustration brewing.

Letting out a gust of air, he scoots onto the bed to lay down beside me while I twist to face away from him.

Still, when his arm wraps around my chest and hugs me closer to him, I don't fight it. I close my eyes and let him hold me, kiss the top of my head, bring me comfort I desperately need.

"I'm sorry. I thought…" He sighs. "You want me. I know you want me. I was a little," he pauses briefly, "*rough*, and I'm sorry for that. I'm not good with women. I don't even know how to *begin* to be good with women. My experience is less than ideal, but that isn't the real problem here. You're in your head right now, and you need to get out of it."

"What the hell does that mean?" I snap, even as I press myself against him like I'm afraid my harshness will push him away.

"It *means* you're so concerned with believing I'm the enemy that you can't just accept me as your friend. Get over the idea of being owned. It's happened. It's done. Stop crying over it like it's the worst thing that could ever happen to a person."

A dry laugh bursts from my mouth. "That's easy for you

to say, isn't it? You have *all* the control. You could kill me right now just because you felt like it, but you want me to what? To—"

"Do you think that I couldn't kill you even if you were free? Fuck, Elira, you *are* free. You're not locked up here like a prisoner. You have a job, access to family overseas, and in six months, you can do whatever the fuck you want. Is that not good enough?"

I flip over to face him, my eyes shooting daggers. "I have a job you gave me with hours you set. Access to my family in the parameters you—"

"Okay, stop." He rubs his temples.

"It's not freedom, Maksim. I don't expect you to understand, but please, don't tell me that's freedom because it isn't."

When he drops his hand, his jaw is clenched. "Fine. Then go."

The tightness in my face relaxes, but it transfers to my chest, making it hard to breathe. "What?"

He waves to the door. "You want your freedom, have it. Goodbye."

I look between him and the door, my gut churning.

"What are you waiting for?" he asks, goading me. "*Go.*"

"I can't," I say, my voice small.

The organization.

The Bratva.

I can't *leave*. I need him. He knows I need him.

That's his point.

"Get the fuck out of my house," he snaps, sitting up and flinging his hand toward the door. I flinch at the anger in his tone and slowly stand from the bed.

Where? Where would I go?

What would I do?

How long before they found me?

"Maksim," I whine, the fear in my voice pathetically apparent.

He's quiet for several seconds, the only sound my heart beating in my ears.

"Come here," he orders, his voice calm but commanding.

My shoulders sag with relief as I climb onto the bed and crawl to him, not stopping until I'm safely wrapped in his arms, feeling like an idiot.

His hand smooths over my back, leaving a trail of warmth that melds me to him.

"You think I don't understand," he says, his voice soft and low. "But I wasn't *free* when I came to America. I was angry and scared, just like you. I fought it for a long time, just like you."

His words spread confusion through my mind, making my eyes squint, my head feel cloudy.

What?

"I promise you, lislchka, I am not your devil... Your fear has eyes like bowls but does not see a crumb."

I pull back to look in his eyes, not to see if he's telling the truth. I know he's telling the truth. There was a time I didn't believe the words passing Maksim's lips, but now, I know he wouldn't lie, not about this.

I stare wondrously at the vulnerability I knew would be on his face and reach out, cupping his handsome cheek and smoothing my thumb over bone. I spot curious lines for the first time. "What happened to you?"

His eyes don't hesitate on me longer than it takes for him to register my question. He turns away, his firm cheek pulling from my hand.

I don't ask again. His face, his reaction, is enough to show me he'll never tell.

22

MAKSIM

ONE WEEK LATER

*E*lira stares out the plane window with her spine straight like clouds are somehow interesting, but I wonder if she's actually studying them or if she's lost in her head.

The girl is an enigma to me. She claims I hide things from her because a week ago I didn't want to tell stories of my past, all the while sharing little of hers.

The week hasn't been bad, aside from the fact that Anya still hasn't come home. Things with Elira have even been, dare I say, pleasant.

We talk a bit, almost always about me or America or something that doesn't matter. She steers clear of Albania, like it isn't safe to mention. The woman has walls, but I can tell her trust for me is building.

It's … nice. Nice to come home to someone. Nice to have someone to worry about Anya alongside me, or better yet, to talk me down.

We eat together every night, mostly Elira's cooking, but we went out once. I felt her discomfort like I was transported back in time, and it was my own nerves set on fire. All the people, all the noise, the chaos of it all. I figured she wouldn't want to leave the house again for weeks.

Then yesterday, out of the blue, she asked me to take her to Chicago. To find her father.

I was going to say no. Opened my mouth with the word balanced on my tongue.

I know this is going to come as a surprise, but my job does not offer vacation days. Or sick days. Or a 401k. I have responsibilities that don't allow me to catch a flight to another city to take my foreign whore to see Daddy Deadbeat.

But her eyes… Her soft, caramel eyes pleaded with me, opening up a door she's never let me through before. This matters to her in a way I could never understand. When I left Russia, I had no plans to see my father again. No desire to make the effort. He did not love me, and that was something I accepted before the plane touched the ground.

Elira is a little behind.

But we've been here before. I've already crushed her by pointing out her unrequited love. If this is what she wants, what she *really* wants…

Well, we're sitting on a plane bound for Chicago, aren't we?

She's quiet the entire plane ride, but when we descend, I can feel her nerves. Her palms flatten on her knees, subtly patting away sweat.

I check my phone, unsurprised to see Anya hasn't returned any of my calls. The tracking app shows she's actually at school.

I type out a message.

Just landed. Should be back tomorrow morning. I love you.

Within seconds, it's marked as read, but I don't expect a reply. I'm about to put my phone away when it dings.

Can you bring back Piggly Pie?

In the middle of a busy airport, I'm so caught off guard that I freeze to reread the reply.

Finally, after a week, she speaks to me.

Piggly Pie. I'd all but forgotten about the little bakery around the corner from the one-bedroom, roach infested slump we lived in when we first left the farm. It was a time I only remember as miserable and terrifying, dragging around a three-year-old, trying to find work, sorting through the dark web and black market, anyone who could get me paperwork I'd never had to have.

Every night, I would stare out the window of our apartment we had sublet with a handgun behind my back and Anya in my arms, tensing every time I heard footsteps pass our door. I was eighteen, just a kid back then. It would take a year of petty crime as a way to survive before I'd be introduced to the Bratva. First as an associate, then as a soldier in Chicago before meeting Hugh and transferring to Vegas. Then finally, under Nikita's father, I became a lieutenant. If I'd known a man like Nikita would become Pakhan, I would've gladly stayed in Chicago, tainted memories or not.

That's all I thought the place was for me. Tainted. Struggle. Suffering. Those pastries Anya's talking about were pulled from the trash cans, I'm ashamed to admit. The owner used to throw away stale scones at the end of the day, and every morning, Anya would have one for breakfast.

Eventually, I was caught, with Anya in tow to make things worse. Instead of shooing us away, the woman smiled kindly and left the boxes on the curb the next day. And the next.

When I made enough money for us to move from the apartment, Anya still wanted her scones, so every Sunday, we stopped in for one, my head hung in shame, the woman smiling kindly.

Now when I think of it, I smile and send a reply.

Okay.

"Maksim?" Elira calls, sounding nervous, probably because people are getting irritated.

Thanks... Love you too.

I stare at my phone another second before putting it away and continuing through the airport.

* * *

Elira

I WONDER what happens if you puke in a rental car.

Do you have to pay extra? Can they tell? Does it leave a smell?

I've never owned a car, but last year Bora got sick all over her bedspread, and it took multiple washes to get the smell out.

Glancing at the controls on the door, I press and pull on one until the window lowers, but the clean air doesn't quell my nausea. If anything, it worsens it.

It smells like flowers and money. We left the busy city my father used to describe to me a while ago. Now we're surrounded by towering houses with pristine lawns and long driveways to park SUVs I once heard dubbed, "mommy cars."

Maksim says he found my father's address, but there's no way he got it right because the car is slowing, and the line on the GPS is shrinking.

"This is it?" I ask. "This is the neighborhood?"

Maksim nods. "Just up ahead."

"That can't be right." I look around for an apartment complex, a side road, a guesthouse where they keep the peasants, something that would make more sense, but my mind can't think right now. I'm too wound up, too nervous.

It's been over a decade.

A *decade*.

What if he doesn't recognize me? I've grown so much, matured from the little girl I was back then. Do I look like the photos he keeps on his mantle? Would he know my voice or my eyes?

And what about Maksim? What if he's as abrasive as Maksim is with his sister's boyfriend? What if my father doesn't want me to leave?

It could be a problem, but I can't help but feel the tiniest bit giddy at the idea of it. At the idea of living here, being away from Las Vegas and instead living in Chicago with my father. Maksim offered me my freedom a week ago. There should be no reason he would rescind that offer today.

There are so many things I want to say. So much I want to know.

What happened?

So many things could've happened. People get put on no-fly lists for ludicrous reasons. People suffer financial hardships. He could've lost his phone then subsequently lost my mother's number and been unable to afford to fly. His family lives in another country as him, not a different state. It isn't as easy to come see us, there are more things that could go wrong.

I forgive him. That's the biggest thing I want to say, that I forgive him. I will get a job here that will pay enough to fly him to Albania to be with my sisters and mother who have missed him as dearly as I have.

At last, we will be together, and I will thank Maksim for that for the rest of my life.

When the car stops, I look over at Maksim, planning on telling him this, but when I spot pity, I look at the house instead.

It's similar to the houses on either side of it except it has a basketball hoop bolted to the top of the garage and a convertible in the driveway along with the mommy car.

A memory snaps to my mind, my hair whipping around crazily in the back of a red convertible with toddler Asher beside me and my parents kissing in the front seat. My father was spoiling us with a trip to Tirana for Mami's birthday. We were going to eat at a fancy steakhouse and stay in a hotel with a pool. It felt weird, like we were playing pretend or had won some lottery, but it's one of my favorite memories because my dad is in it.

I keep staring at the black convertible.

"We can go," Maksim says like he's reading the situation. Like he thinks my heart is about to break. "I know the city better than I let on before. I could show it to you."

Does my father really live here?

Why is there a basketball hoop?

"Elira?"

I climb out of the car, ignoring Maksim's offer, and walk toward the convertible. My lips numb when I read the 'my kid is an honor's student' logo on the bumper.

This can't be his house, but I still run my finger over the decal, my heart pumping hard.

The front porch looks like something out of a spring catalogue ... flowering plants, a welcome sign, a mat that says Home Sweet Home. It's perfect except for a set of muddy roller skates laying on their side.

I blink at them and ring the doorbell.

A girl, younger than me but older than Asher, probably seventeen or eighteen, opens the door wearing black shorts and a blue top, a uniform of sorts. Her chestnut hair the same shade as Bora's is up high in a ponytail, and when she speaks, braces shine.

"Hello, can I help you?"

"H-hi," I stumble, taking hold of my wrist. "I'm looking for Joshua Martin."

She turns her head to yell inside. "Dad!"

Dad.

My heart swells until it's in my throat. I don't say anything else, but she doesn't seem concerned anyway because she steps out of the way when the man I've looked up to my whole life steps to the door with a friendly smile.

"Hello." He holds the door open. "Can I help you?"

I blink at him, and in the silence, recognition registers on his face, twisting his familiar features from friendly to horrified.

The girl, his daughter, my half-sister, is back carrying a futbol as she slips past him out the door with a younger boy behind her. A woman scoots out the door next, pulling a purse onto her shoulder. She looks like she's in a hurry, but when she spots me, she strains a smile. "Hi there."

My father turns to her, his face instantly cooling. "Honey, do you have a twenty? One of the schools has a boy whose mother has ALS, and they're doing a fundraiser."

I die inside. I can feel it happening, feel the cells in my heart giving out one by one. He isn't breaking me, he's just slowly suffocating me, starving each cell of the love I've needed all these years. Love that he's had but given to these people instead.

He isn't on a no-fly list.

He hasn't suffered financial strain.

He just ... doesn't want us anymore. He wants to stay in this big house, drive nice cars, and let his unwanted children in Albania struggle.

I whored myself to come to this country. To work for money to send back home.

And he just ... bought fucking plants. And a convertible. And a big fucking house for a stupid fucking wife.

She digs in her purse. "Uhh."

"Oh, never mind, I've got it," he says, pulling out his wallet. "I'll be right there, honey."

"Okay, hurry. Bentley's soccer game is at six."

She smiles at me like it's obligatory but then hurries off toward the family car. The kids are already inside as she starts it up and waits on her husband to get rid of his bastard child she doesn't know exists.

"Here," he says, yanking all the cash from his wallet. He shoves it at me. I don't even look at it. "Take it," he urges.

My eyes stinging, I take the bills.

He nods, looks frantically at the car, then sighs. "Look, kid, I'm sorry you came all the way here, but that's all you're getting out of me. Your mom is in Albania. She isn't legally entitled to child support, and for all I know, I'm not even your biological father. So … don't come around here again, all right? If you do, I'll have to call the police and report you for trespassing."

More of my heart dies.

And more.

And more.

Who knew I had so much left?

He looks between me and the car, opens his mouth like he'll say something else, then gives it up and walks away.

I don't move. Just stay rooted in place while he gets in his family car and goes to his daughter's soccer game.

The daughter who, all her life, has mattered.

Not me. Not the Albanian girl with the toothy grin and dirty nails.

I am filth.

I am *shlyukha*.

Minutes pass after the car is gone. Eventually, Maksim comes up behind me without me hearing him, and he gently guides me to the car.

"Come on," he says. "I'm already sick of this city."

He mercifully doesn't ask me what was said or what I'm feeling, and I don't ask him if he knew all along this would happen. He probably did. He probably knew I was a fool for this the same way he knew I was a fool for believing my engagement to James/Daniel was real.

I never had a real father.

My memories, once pure and soothing, come up like acid and make me wrap my arms around my stomach to quell physical pain.

He doesn't love me.

He never did.

Worse. A deeper fear. A fear I've never spoken aloud, a fear realized over and over again.

I'm not lovable.

The city fades in the rearview, and the roads Maksim takes become increasingly rural. He stops at a small grocery store and comes out with a bouquet of lavender flowers.

I turn my head from him, thinking he's trying to cheer me up or something, but he doesn't give them to me. Instead, he sets them in the back seat and pulls back onto the road.

"Where are we going?" I ask, breaking the silence. My voice doesn't even sound sad. It just sounds empty. Like my father took the last of me.

Maksim takes a long time to answer. "There's something I want to show you."

23

ELIRA

*T*he sun is setting by the time we reach our destination, and if I didn't trust Maksim, I would think he might be bringing me out here to kill me. It would be the perfect spot to hide a body.

We haven't seen a gas station, a house, a car, or any other sign of civilization in a while. Even the cornfields stopped at some point, leaving nothing but barren land.

Maksim slowly pulls the rental car onto a dirt driveway that vibrates the car so badly my teeth chatter.

I bite down and hold onto my seat while he eases the car down the driveway. There's an old farmhouse up ahead with weeds surrounding it so tall they whip the windows.

"Where are we?" I ask, my brow furrowed as I look over at Maksim, but I regret the question when I spot his white knuckles gripping the steering wheel.

His face is cold and blank, nothing I haven't seen before. I would miss the tension if it wasn't for that grip.

Without answering me, he parks in front of the house and shuts off the car. His gaze veers toward a barn that looks like it used to be red but is now faded with only paint chips to hint at its past. It's leaning slightly. A few good windstorms would blow it down.

I watch him watching the barn like there's something sinister inside. He isn't noting the paint or wear. He's remembering something.

I look around, trying to make sense of this place, like the ghosts Maksim is looking for will be there to answer questions I'm not so sure Maksim will.

The paper wrapped bouquet in the backseat ruffles, and I turn just in time to see Maksim throw open his door and carry them out of the car.

He doesn't wait for me or ask me to come with him, so I just watch as he walks up to the house, disappearing behind it.

I wait a minute, my teeth digging into my lip.

Am I really just going to sit here?

I look around again. The more time that passes, the creepier the place seems.

Letting go of my lip, I climb out of the car and jog after where Maksim disappeared, stopping when I spot him standing in front of a tree fifty metres behind the house.

My feet find something hard when I step beneath an arch, and I look down to see weeds popping from broken pieces of brick that go all the way to Maksim. It's hard to tell, but I think this used to be a garden. There are old pots sprouting long, green weeds, and when I look closely, I spot a piece of fencing fallen over and swallowed up by greenery.

I creep up behind Maksim, my head bowed with what I tell myself is respect but what may be fear. I feel so dead inside, but there must still be life because I couldn't take his anger right now. My chest tightens just thinking of it.

The flowers he brought are laid carefully at the base of the tree.

"This was Anya's mother's garden," Maksim says, making

my eyes dart to him with surprise. I hadn't expected him to speak.

He stares at the flowers instead of me.

"Elizabeth." His head tilts as he looks up. I follow his gaze to the ripened peaches dangling from branches. "I planted this tree. She said she had one when she was a child, and her mother used to make the best peach pie she'd ever had. It still hadn't produced by the time she died, but uh…" Maksim shrugs, blinking away a memory. "She liked it anyway."

I look around, trying to picture Maksim here, but it's hard. He said he wasn't free when he came here. It's impossible to picture Maksim as anything but in control.

"So this is where you grew up?" I ask, my voice low and soft, unsure if I should ask at all.

He turns with me to take in the house and nods. "Sort of. I came here when I was nine to work the farm. I stayed until I was eighteen." Tucking his hands in his pockets, he starts out of the garden with me beside him.

"My mother was a strong woman. Not kind, but not cruel." He rubs his chest. "Her face is foggy in my mind, but I tattooed her last words to me on my chest when I was eighteen so I'd never forget. *U stráha glazá velikí.* Fear has big eyes."

His chest is clothed, but I still find my eyes drifting to the covered tattoo. If I had known its hidden meaning, I wonder if I would have looked at it differently, looked at *him* differently the first time I saw it.

Fear has big eyes. It's like what he said to me before.

Your fear has eyes like bowls but does not see a crumb.

"My father was a very wealthy man who owned a chain of supercenters in Russia. I'm the youngest of his five sons, and unfortunately, he felt he only needed three."

"What?" I ask, stopping in my tracks. Maksim stops, but he doesn't turn to look at me. He stands rigid, his shoulders squared, carrying himself as if this is merely a story. A memory equal to the rest instead of a trauma that shaped every facet of his life.

"I don't know what happened to my older brother," Maksim goes on. "But I was sent here." He waves his hand toward the land.

"Your father sold you?" I ask, my stomach dropping. I inch toward him, wrapping my arms around myself so I won't risk reaching out. I'm too afraid he'd pull away.

He shrugs. "I don't know. I didn't ask. I think uh…" His eyes start to glaze. "I think it was an exchange for a favor or something. The owner of this farm had a powerful family in Russia. I wasn't the only kid here, so there had to be some leverage… But I've stopped thinking too hard about it."

No he hasn't. No one could stop thinking about that.

I hug myself tighter. "Maksim…"

"I would never call this place my home, but it gave me Anya, so I can't say I would trade it." He swallows while looking off, and I follow his gaze to the barn. I believe him, but I can tell it isn't easy. How could it be? The best thing in his life came from the worst thing he's ever experienced.

My eyes burn.

He starts walking again, his feet aimed toward the barn, and I walk with him. He's quiet now, but I don't press, don't ask anything. I'm too busy sorting through everything in my head, seeing the look of horror on my father's face.

I get why Maksim brought me here. Get what he's trying to say.

He's trying to say that he understands. He can empathize. He knows what being unloved feels like. What being unwanted feels like. Except much, much worse.

My father doesn't love me. Doesn't want me. And it *hurts*. It fucking *hurts*.

But … at least he didn't sell me. At least it was my own

actions that led to me losing my freedom and not my parents giving me away.

But I have my freedom back now, the same as Maksim. I glance over at him, noting his stern expression. I understand him so much better now. Respect him so much more.

A week ago, I wanted him to tell me what happened to him, and when he wouldn't, I thought he didn't trust me enough to open himself to me. Now that he has, I don't know what to do with it. This feels so significant. I don't feel worthy.

"Does Anya know you aren't blood related?" I ask, facing the barn as we approach.

"Yes. She believes I was an orphan her family took in. I haven't had to lie to her about much. She was only three when her parents died, so for a while, I just told her they were in heaven. Eventually, I told her they died in a home invasion, which is what the papers say if she ever decides to look. She assumes that the boys she saw around were paid to work the farm… She doesn't suspect anything nefarious, so she doesn't usually ask questions that I can't honestly answer."

"Did they really die in a home invasion?"

When Maksim tenses, I flinch.

"No," he says, stopping at the barn. "A boy named Kofi got free one night."

"Free?" I wring my hands, waiting for a response, but he just pulls the barn door open, his forearms flexing from the old wood that hasn't been moved in what must be years.

I squint into the barn while my eyes adjust to the dark and walk in after Maksim. Cages, like ones you put dogs in, line one side of the barn, some stacked on top of another. I stare at them but don't wonder what was kept inside.

My heart falls, and it snaps me back to the semi-truck, sitting in our own filth, being treated like animals.

He spent nine years of his life like this.

"I was asleep when it happened," he says, his tone no longer cold. Now his voice is pained and full of regret.

It wasn't your fault.

He knows it wasn't his fault, right?

I turn to him as his hand reaches to brush a rusted chain hanging from the ceiling. I don't ask what it was for, but I can guess.

"I can understand wanting to kill the old man. If I hadn't been such a coward, I probably would have years before Kofi did. But Elizabeth was as much of a prisoner as the rest of us." His voice sounds strained. I go to him, touching his arm gently. "He'd stabbed her three times in the abdomen by the time I reached them." He shakes his head. "It was too late. She bled out in my arms."

"It wasn't your fault, Maksim."

He doesn't say anything. I open my mouth to repeat myself, but I know it would do no good. It's been years, over a decade. In his mind, this woman's blood will forever be on his hands.

"Sometimes I have these vivid dreams..." He speaks so softly, I lean in to hear him. "I'm running toward the house, but my legs feel too heavy, and I can't get there fast enough. By the time I make it inside, Kofi is stabbing her, but as I get closer, it isn't Elizabeth. It's Anya." He closes his eyes and shakes his head. "I'm so fucking terrified all the time that I'm failing her, but I have no idea what to do. The more I try to control her, the more she hates me. But these guys she dates...."

"She's going to be fine." I take his hand and squeeze as my heart does. One by one, things click into place.

He's never had help with Anya. Never. But not only that, he's never seen the proper way to raise children, let alone teenagers.

He never dated. Had probably never seen a woman other than his surrogate mother through his pubescent years. That's what he meant when he said he hasn't had ideal experiences with women.

He was a slave. A slave who only knew how to be cold and detached.

No wonder he had no desire to own me. No wonder he was so desperate for me to help with Anya.

I'm here.

I squeeze his hand and hope he knows this. I'm here to stay. I don't have anywhere else to go, anyone left in this country to love me.

I wonder if that's how he feels.

"She loves you," I say in case he doesn't know it. "She's a teenage girl who pushes the envelope because it's her way of checking to make sure you'll still be there. My sister Asher is the same way."

Maksim has been staring at the chain, but now he looks at me curiously.

"You're all she has," I explain. "It wasn't their fault, but she may feel like her parents abandoned her. It must be terrifying for her to feel like she could lose the only person she has left, so her subconscious is constantly testing you. Asher feels abandoned by our father, so it's a similar thing."

Maksim nods slowly before leading me from the barn by my hand. Stars twinkle in the sky, brighter than I've seen since leaving Albania. He closes the barn door like he's afraid of letting out the ghosts, then he takes my hand and leads me to the bed of an old pickup that makes a loud creek when he lowers the tailgate.

He helps me onto it, then sits down beside me, both of us looking up at the stars.

"You've never mentioned your sister."

A chorus of crickets speak to each other in the field, and a frog groans. I close my eyes for a second and pretend to hear the call of the sheep telling me I'm home.

The mere mention of my sister makes me homesick, but I know I can't go back. More than that… I don't want to.

We had a good life, but it was impoverished. With me here, they will have an opportunity to feel financial security for the first time in their lives, maybe even taste abundance.

And me… I don't have it so bad either.

"Two sisters. Asher, fourteen, and Bora, eight. Both my father's, in case you were wondering. My mother only ever had children with one man."

A scumbag, no less.

And Mami doesn't even know it.

My throat feels like it's been punched. I'm going to have to tell my mother, aren't I?

"I wasn't wondering."

Pushing away my thoughts, I look over at Maksim.

In the moonlight, his blue eyes gleam at me, and he looks … kissable. Touchable.

Lovable.

"I'm not nearly as judgmental as you think I am."

I blink, barely remembering what we were talking about.

"I want to know about you, Elira," Maksim says, shifting to face me. "You know I would never hurt your family, don't you?"

I look down, not because I don't believe him but because I'm embarrassed.

He wants to know about me. About the world I come from. About my family.

I thought… I don't know what I thought. I guess that he would see me the way others do, the way James did. A poor girl from Albania. From a village too outdated to impress anyone. Living a life no one would see the beauty in, that would only be pitied.

I didn't want him to look at me like that. Look at my family like that. I don't know, I just… I just wanted to keep my home in my heart.

This place makes me change my mind.

"I know," I say at last. "I trust you."

We're quiet a long time, listening to the frogs croak while our fingers rest inches away on the tailgate.

"I'm sorry about your father," Maksim says.

My head lowers to my lap, but I feel less empty than I did earlier. "I'm sorry about yours."

He shrugs as if it doesn't matter.

It eats at me, the look on my father's face. There was no sign of remorse, no sign of *joy* at seeing his eldest child.

He does not love me.

I swallow and move my hands to my lap to pick at my nails. Maksim has been so open with me, so vulnerable. Summoning courage, I do the same.

"Do you think I'm lovable?"

Silence. Chest piercing silence.

"It's a stupid question, I know," I go on, my words rolling off my tongue. "But I just mean um…" I close my eyes. "My father doesn't love me. Daniel didn't love me. I'm apparently only good for being a whore, so… You spend more time around me than anyone else. Is there something wrong with me?"

"No." He says it too quickly. Like he didn't even consider the question.

"You can be honest. I won't get angry. I just want to know."

"Elira, there's nothing wrong with you."

He takes my hand, and my first thought is to pull away, but I don't. For once, I fight it. I face him when he urges and take in his sincere, blue eyes.

"Your father is a coward. He wanted a family in another

country, knowing he'd never be there for them. He never deserved you. And Daniel..." Maksim laughs, but there's nothing funny about it. "He was a trafficker. He was just doing his job. He wasn't really looking at you, so he couldn't see all you have to offer, but you are..." He looks over me. "Incredible. You're incredible. You're the strongest survivor I've ever known."

I nod, but I can feel my lips even out. "But that isn't the same as lovable."

"If I was a man capable of loving a woman, I would love you."

I freeze, taken aback.

Maksim looks so serious, so ... honest. Like he could possibly mean the words he's saying.

"But I'm your whore."

He looks up and sighs like I'm missing something, and when his gaze hits me again, he scoots closer, taking my jaw to make sure I'm paying attention.

"You are *no one's* whore."

I stare into his eyes, my nose itching like I'm going to do something as stupid as cry. I want to kiss him, but if I did, that would end this moment, take away this touch.

He doesn't know how badly I need this. Doesn't know how much I need those words, need this touch, need ... him.

"You *are* capable of love," I say, although I don't think he'll believe me. To me, it's obvious. I've seen the way he loves his 'sister,' the daughter of his captor. And the *wife* of his captor. He doesn't even see them that way, holds none of the man's crimes against them.

I thought I'd been lying to Anya, but I was wrong.

Maksim *is* a good man. With a *good* heart. And love that makes me envious.

"If I was a woman capable of loving a man who tried to

kill me ... I would love you," I whisper, another moment of vulnerability.

Except, it's a partial lie. I don't care that he tried to kill me. Not even a little.

I don't care what he does for a living. I don't care about anything that went on between us.

I think... I think I may already love him. Here, in this moment, a feeling deep inside me blooms, and I just pray it doesn't show on my face.

He stares at me, serious, unsmiling. I think he's going to pull away or tell me not to be an idiot or something, but he surprises me.

He leans forward, closing his eyes just before he kisses me, and although he's kissed me before, this time feels different. *He* feels different. I feel different. The world feels different.

The rough skin of his palm caresses my cheek as I lean into his kiss, my lips soft against his. My hands instinctively drift to his shirt to lightly grasp the blue cotton.

The crickets keep chirping, the frogs keep croaking, oblivious to the fire Maksim starts on the tailgate of the truck. I don't hear the imaginary sheep anymore, don't have to pretend I'm at home, because at this moment, I don't wish to escape. I want to be here, on this horrible farm, in this horrible country, with this horrible man.

Maksim's hands grasp my shoulders so he can ease me onto my back, never moving his mouth from mine. My legs spread without him asking, and he situates himself between them with ease.

He breaks away from me, pulling back to look me in my eyes while the backs of his fingers move up my inner thigh.

"I want you," I whisper, shivering at his touch. He stares at me another moment before drinking in the rest of my body. My nipples harden at his lingering eyes on my chest, and when he brushes his fingers beneath my shirt, I sit up to take it off.

He helps me pull it over my head before stuffing it under my body then doing the same with his own.

My eyes find his tattoo that no longer looks the same. No longer careless words scrawled on in a drunken fashion.

I touch the ink, feeling the hard muscle beneath, but my hand pulls away when he removes my bra and lays me back down.

I cry out when his mouth finds my nipple, sucking the bud hard between his lips. My hips lift as my core squeezes like it's begging to be next, and Maksim seems to understand because he unbuttons my shorts then snakes his hand inside.

My eyes go to close, but the night sky looks so beautiful filled with stars that I can't help but stare up at it, my lips parted, my spine arching as Maksim rubs me.

He moves to the other nipple, restarting the shooting, sweet pain that preludes ecstasy, and I bite down on my lip as another moan slides from my lungs.

His hand grows more eager, more anxious at the sound of my moan. Denim scrapes my legs with every movement until I shrug my shorts off my hips, my own eagerness growing.

I want him.

Really want him.

My whole life I had planned to wait for marriage and thought others' inability to do so was weakness. Now I understand. Now I feel weak. Feeble. Decrepit. Because I can't wait another day, another hour, another minute.

"Maksim, I want you," I whimper, angling my neck for him when he goes to kiss me there.

He peels my shorts and panties the rest of the way off, leaving me bare before working himself out of his pants.

He makes a bed beneath me with our clothes then lays me

down flat, lining up at my entrance and putting his lips to mine.

It's a warm night, and his body heats my skin until I'm breaking out in a sweat. I'm lost in his kiss, so when I feel the sharp pain of his intrusion, I'm caught off guard and freeze.

My eyes clench shut as my fingers dig into his sides.

I don't tell him. I'm *terrified* he'll stop if I do, so I just lie still and wait for the pain to pass like it seemed to with Daniel.

Maksim doesn't move, just stills himself inside me while planting kisses on my neck.

"You're perfect, Elira," he coos. His voice may as well have hands because it feels like it massages my tense muscles, relaxing me. "Don't ever let anyone make you feel differently."

I open my eyes at his words and stare at the haunted house for a moment before blinking softly and closing them again. The pain is no longer so intense when he starts to shift inside me.

My legs wrap around him in a tight embrace as tingles roll through my core, and I grasp onto his sides as hard as I did before but no longer due to pain.

His thrusts quicken as his breaths grow more labored, and I listen to them, naturally breathing in rhythm with him. The more worked up he gets, the more pleasure I feel. Or maybe it's the opposite. Maybe he loves the pleasure he brings me.

Maybe he loves me.

I am not *shlyukha.*

My mouth opens on a cry as I come around Maksim, my walls squeezing him. Tears leak from my eyes, but I don't swipe them away. They roll into my hair to hide, unnoticed.

His length pumps in and out of me at an even faster pace

while I run my heels over his back and tilt my chin toward the sky.

He groans with three hard thrusts as he spills into me, stilling with one hand grasping my knee.

My body feels full and empty at the same time when he nestles beside me, situating his arm under my head. I nuzzle into him and close my eyes for a moment while I try to capture this forever. I don't know if it can last. I don't even know if it's real.

But it's perfect. Right now, it's perfect.

MAKSIM

*H*ugh's deep roar fills my backyard as I turn shashlik skewers over on a grill I picked up for this occasion like a true suburban dad. It would be painful if Anya's shy laugh didn't follow Hugh's.

I peek over my shoulder at Elira and Anya sitting together with polite smiles on their faces as they listen to Hugh ramble. Both look uncomfortable, surrounded by five of my brothers, and it doesn't help that Altus and Fox are already showing signs of intoxication.

This, as I explained to Elira repeatedly, was a terrible idea.

Hugh, while my brother, has met Anya once, by chance, briefly. He doesn't come here. No one involved with the Bratva comes here just to hang out. The things they do and say aren't meant for a young girl's ears, so my two worlds have always been kept separate. I never wanted her to be a part of my Bratva family. I *vowed* to keep her out of it.

And yet, here they are, gathered in my backyard for a fucking barbeque because, apparently, isolating Anya from my world is a bad thing. *Apparently*, Anya feels I don't want her around. That she's a burden. That I wish she was gone so I could live my life with the people I really care about. And the list goes on.

Elira's solution? This.

This was a terrible idea. *Horrible*.

I close the grill hood and toss the tongs down with too much force, angry at myself for letting Elira work me so well. Make me so weak.

I grab a beer from an ice chest then amble over to the group.

"Because you're late everywhere you go," Hugh says to Fox.

It sounds like a lighthearted conversation I'm walking up to, but Fox isn't smiling.

He rolls his eyes while letting the cigarette dangling from his lips collect ash.

"He has a valid excuse," Zinovy cuts in. "His ride is slow as shit."

Fox shoots a glare at Zinovy. "You challenging me, asshole?"

Zinovy laughs. He's leaned back so far, the chair looks like it could tip at the slightest movement, and his heels rest comfortably on the tabletop like he's at home. "I could *outrun* your Suzuki."

"You could kiss my ass."

"You have a Suzuki?" Anya asks, perking up.

Fox pulls the cigarette out of his mouth, almost looking caught off guard by Anya's presence as he turns her way. He nods as he blows a puff of smoke from the side of his mouth.

"Cool. My boyfriend has a 1,340cc Hayabusa." She says this with pride, her chin lifting slightly while I shift my feet.

Did that piece of shit put her on a fucking *motorcycle*?

I open my mouth, ready to jump into the conversation but catch Elira's pointed stare. I can read her mind the same way she can read mine.

Bad idea, Maksim. Let it go.

Fox whistles. *"Damn.* That's a nice ass bike." His eyes search until they find me. "Your sister knows how to pick 'em, Mak."

No, she does not.

"Thanks, it's a 1999 he got from his uncle," Anya gushes before I can respond. "So not exactly new, but it could definitely murder a Harley."

"Mmm, no," Zinovy says. "Not mine."

"Yeah?" her head tilts. "What are you packing?"

What is he *packing*? What?

Laughter roars, and Zinovy pulls his heels off the table and thumps his chair back to level ground. He folds his arms on the tabletop then leans toward her. It's all playful, but I hate this. I watched Zinovy do a line of coke off a hooker's tits yesterday. He should not be chatting up the same little girl I fumbled through bedtime stories of princesses and frogs with once upon a time.

"A Sportster S, but it's tuned the fuck up, and I promise it could take you on, princess."

"That so?" She smiles as she arches her brow.

Zinovy nods.

Is this conversation really happening?

"Well, that's probably true since I'm not allowed to *ride* on motorcycles, let alone drive them." Her shoulders lift, and she falls back in her chair, her hands relaxed on the arm rests.

Her eyes find mine, and when she smiles, I find myself smiling back, my nerves calmed.

"I'll take you for a ride if you want," Zinovy offers. "Your brother trusts me."

I don't miss a beat. "No, I don't."

Another round of laughter, but when it quickly dies off, I follow the others' gazes to the back patio door.

Anthony Gruco, a capo for the Italian mafia and the only criminal I've let around Anya, steps onto my patio with his wife, Bailey, on his arm. Her growing bump peeks out from beneath a tray she carries, and when Anya sees her, she jumps from the chair and skips that way.

"Bailey!"

When she reaches them, she grabs the pan, shoves it at Anthony, then wraps her arms around the glowing mother-to-be.

My brothers are not nearly as happy to see them.

"Elira," I say, holding out my hand and ignoring the glares I'm thrown. "Come on, I want to introduce you."

She stands and takes my hand, letting me lead her to people who are the source of my never-ending string of punishments. And the reason Elira was forced upon me.

The other night when Elira and I were laying in the back of an old farm pickup in what used to be my living hell, I was struck with a feeling of contentment so strong, if I'd been standing, I would've doubled over.

I remember tensing and hoping she couldn't tell what was happening or the effects she had on me. I've felt love and the crippling weight of vulnerability it brings, but I'd never felt what she made me feel in the back of that truck. I let down walls I didn't realize had anything on the other side of them and felt things I didn't know I was capable of.

I laid there the entire night, thinking of what led to this and what life could have been if things went differently. Elira fell asleep after some time, but I knew I'd never be able to sleep on that farm. My mind was so wound in the morning, I didn't feel the exhaustion until well into the day. I just kept thinking.

What if Nikita hadn't gifted Elira to me? *Forced* me to take her?

Every time I thought of it, it made me sick. It made me hug her tighter, it flared protectiveness that was fresh and new.

I've asked myself hundreds of times if my relationship with Anthony Gruco was worth the trouble it caused. In truth, it only grew because Anya took to Bailey so intensely.

Now I know, without a doubt, it was worth it.

"Hey." Bailey smiles and spreads her arms for a hug when I approach.

I lightly wrap my arms around her and glimpse her bump when I pull away. "You're getting fat."

"So are you," she jokes dryly as she nods to Elira. "It looks like you've gained about a hundred and twenty pounds." Her face lights up as she holds out her hand. "I'm Bailey, nice to meet you."

Elira cups a hand over hers warmly. "Elira. And you look beautiful."

"Thanks." Bailey rubs her stomach. "I puked on your lawn, but other than that, I feel pretty great." She pats her husband's arm. "This is Anthony, the driver."

"Jesus Christ." He rolls his eyes, then smiles at Elira. "Pleasure to meet you, Elira. Maksim's told me a lot about you."

"He has?" she asks, not sounding convinced. Her eyes dip to the pan. "Oh, please, let me take that."

"They're cannolis." Bailey peeks over at the Russian criminals glaring at us and crosses her arms over her chest.

"Yay!" Anya claps and takes the pan from Elira before trotting away to set it on a table.

"Probably not a crowd pleaser here, but Anya's favorite." Bailey shrugs, timid all of a sudden.

"Ignore them," Anthony says before I get the chance to.

He takes his wife's hand and leads her to the others while Elira and I follow, ready to defuse the potential conflict.

It isn't that the Italians and Russians are enemies. Not officially.

But with a Pakhan like Nikita, it's hard for organizations to work together. For us, for *Nikita*, everyone is an enemy.

"Hi." Bailey gives a light wave before wiping her hand on her dress. "I'm Bailey. This is my husband, Anthony."

Fox leans forward to stub his cigarette out on his boot, the only movement among my brothers. "We know who you are."

I shoot daggers at Fox, but I don't know what to say to them. Their mouths being shut is as much as I know to ask for.

Have I mentioned yet that this was a bad idea?

Anya shuffles, clearly sensing the tension. Chewing her lip, she looks at Bailey. "Hey, did I show you the anniversary present Tanner got me?"

Anniversary present. I would roll my eyes if I wasn't concerned about other things.

Bailey blinks. "Uh, no."

"Come on." Anya takes her hands and graciously leads her away. Elira watches them like she's debating following, but she rubs her arms and stays put.

"It's hot." Zinovy stands, eyeing Anthony up before taking a step my way. "I'm gonna take off." He claps me on the shoulder as he walks by. "Good to see you, Elira."

"You as well," she meekly replies.

Fox stands as well, and the others follow, offering weak goodbyes. Hugh is the last, lingering behind the others.

"You too, huh?" I ask.

He stands in front of me and glances at Anthony before rolling his neck and walking to the ice chest. "Just getting a beer, brother."

He pulls two out and walks one to Anthony, his face serious as he hands off what can only be a silent peace offering. My lips lift at the corners.

"Thanks," Anthony says, nodding before taking a seat. He leans back like he's perfectly comfortable. "So... What's burning?"

My head turns to the grill. "Oh, fuck."

Hugh and Anthony both snicker as I jog to the grill and take care of the charred meat, a hopeless attempt at cooking for once. Even when Anya was little, we scavenged food somehow or ate freezer meals, but with Elira around, I'm getting accustomed to homemade shit. I'm getting accustomed to a lot of things. I'm getting accustomed to *her*.

I think... I think it's going to hurt when she leaves.

I don't think I want her to go.

She grins at me, amused when I walk in shame back to my seat beside her, but she pats my knee when I sit down. "It was a good try, *sobaka*."

I rear back and just stare at her.

Sobaka. *Dog.*

She presses her lips together to fight a grin. "I looked it up online. If I am your lislchka, your *little fox*, you are my hound."

"*Gonchaya*," I correct, although I don't know how much I like that either.

"*Gonchaya*," she repeats, then again until her pronunciation is right. She sounds cute with my native language on her lips, and there are a few other phrases I make a mental note to have her memorize for another time. Preferably when her mouth is full.

I clear my throat and look away before I get an erection that won't go down. Anthony and Hugh are talking, surprisingly. It's stiff, but it's effort, which is more than I could ask for. Maybe this wasn't such a terrible idea after all.

"I looked it up after speaking to my mom today," Elira says. There's nervousness in her voice that brings my attention back to her.

I study her face but can't tell what she's feeling. "How is she?"

Elira's lips part as she drops her eyes to my chest for a moment. "She's good. *Really* good, actually. She uh… She said when she checked her account today, there was a hundred grand in it."

Her face reddens as she stares at me expectantly, but I don't really know what to say. Discomfort settles in my chest, shrinking my lungs.

"Oh."

"I don't understand that, though, because obviously I didn't make fifty thousand dollars for you to match." She lets out a nervous laugh that dies as seriousness takes over her features. "And there's no way I could pay it back anytime soon. I'd have to work…" Her head shakes. "I don't know how long I'd have to work."

She looks so uncomfortable. So uncertain.

Should I not have done that? Does she feel like she owes me now?

"You don't have to pay it back." I open my mouth, then close it with a sigh, wishing I'd prepared for this. "It's payment," I lie and motion toward my house. "I'm matching your pay at the bakery, but you do so much more for my home. I just…"

Just what?

I care about you, Elira. I admire you. You came here for your family, to help support them, and I can't bear the thought of you progressing slower than you want on a baker's wage. I want to help you. I *need* to help you.

I love you.

The words squeeze so tightly, my eyes shut.

She's going to leave. Any day, she can go when she chooses. Now that her family has the money, she doesn't need the bakery job. She could go. Today. Now. The Bratva wouldn't follow. The trafficking organization has been paid off. Any day now, she'll realize she no longer needs me.

And it'll hurt. I'll survive, but it'll hurt. And I need to prepare for that pain.

"You just what?" she asks, lightly placing her hand on mine.

I swallow and stare into eyes I could look at forever. "I just want to make sure we're even before you leave… I owe you that."

I can't say for sure, but her body seems to shrink. Her eyes flicker with something that looks like disappointment for the briefest moment, but she smiles and nods. "Yeah, Maksim. We're even."

That was too casual. Forced.

Fuck.

I open my mouth, but Elira stands before words come out. "I'm gonna go to the bathroom. Do you need something from inside?"

My hand raking through my hair, I close my mouth and shake my head.

I try to join in on Anthony's and Hugh's conversation, but I'm too distracted by my conversation with Elira.

Minutes go by without her return.

My leg becomes restless, tapping away at the patio until I can't take it anymore, and I go after her.

I check my bedroom first but see no sign of her. "Elira?"

Someone clears their throat behind me, and I turn to see Alik, of all people, standing in my hallway.

My eyes narrow. "What the fuck are you doing here?"

He looks over his shoulder. "Looks like you're having a

little gathering I wasn't invited to. Is this a traitor's only thing?"

"You gonna run back to the boss, Alik? Tell him I have an Italian in my house?"

His lips thin. He doesn't like that.

"I have information I think you may want."

"What?" I snap.

It could be uncalled for, but lately, I'm seeing Alik as more of an opponent than an ally. Nikita seems to be using him more and more as his personal handyman, and I don't like how Alik knew to find me at Hugh's the night the trafficking organization came for Elira. It's possible it wasn't the first place he checked. That it was a lucky guess. But more likely, he knew I was there because I'm being tracked, something I already suspected. What I didn't suspect was that Alik was the one tracking me, and I don't know who I'm more pissed at, me or him.

"It's sensitive information." He looks over his shoulder at Anya's room like he can sense someone listening in on our conversation. He's probably right.

"Outside." I jut my chin and lead him through my house and out my front door. When we're free of eavesdroppers, he turns to me and tucks his hands in his pockets, about to drop news that holds zero importance for him.

"The wife of the trafficker you had me look over wired seven hundred and fifty thousand dollars to a Swiss bank account early this morning."

"Whose bank account?" I ask, knowing he has no answer.

She isn't wiring seven hundred and fifty thousand dollars to a Swiss cousin short on cash. She's paying for a service. An illegal service.

A hit. More likely three. And there happen to be three people living in my house.

He lifts a shoulder while I run a hand down my face and sigh. *Shit*.

"I can do some more digging into this, but I thought it would be best to get this to you as soon as possible."

"Just kill her," I say, dropping my hand to my side. "Find out who she hired to do the hit before you finish it."

"Of course, sir." He nods, expressionless. "Should I inform the Pakhan that you'll be staying at his residence for safety concerns?"

"Jesus, no," I spit. I would never put my sister nor Elira's lives in danger. But Nikita's house is not what I would call safety.

"We'll go to Hugh's. Set up a patrol. Two cars should be plenty."

"Yes, sir." He turns to walk away but hesitates.

"What?"

He spins to face me again. "I just want to point out a possible alternative. The wife mentioned her interest in your whore's family before. She could've placed the hit on them instead of you."

I roll my eyes. "They're in Albania, Alik."

"She isn't flying there herself. She's paying someone to do it."

I want to dismiss it as easily as I did the first time he brought this up, but my stomach flips.

I am a lieutenant in the Petrov Bratva. Killing me has consequences.

Killing a family in Albania... Not as many. If someone didn't know any better, they'd think there would be none.

Revenge is a powerful thing. People do all kinds of things for revenge.

But it's Elira she wants... Right?

I don't know anymore, but I shouldn't dismiss it so easily. They're her family. They're as important as Anya.

"Find someone in Albania to take the family to a secure location."

"Find someone in Albania?" His brow raises.

"I don't care how you do it, just *do it*."

I turn around and grip the door handle, but before I pull it open, a pair of caramel eyes hiding behind a bush steals my breath.

25

ELIRA

*T*he demon leaves before Maksim so much as blinks.

Our eyes are glued together while the rest of me is in a puddle of anxiety on the ground.

Hit. As in hitman. As in danger.

Asher. Bora. Mami.

They're all in danger.

When the demon peels away, in a hurry to obey Maksim's commands like the errand boy it's hard to believe he is, Maksim gives him one last look before going to me. His face has turned white, and when he reaches toward me, he's hesitant, like he thinks I might bite his hand.

"It's okay, you're safe," he assures me. "I promise, I'm not going to let anyone hurt you."

I don't take his hand. Don't move. I'm frozen in place behind this bush. I never meant to hide from Maksim, only jumped back here when I saw Alik pull up, but now I'm glad I did.

Would Maksim have told me the truth otherwise?

Danger.

Asher.

Bora.

Mami.

I have to get to Albania.

On this thought, my head moves toward Maksim's car, and I climb to my feet. Leaves and twigs scrape dirt off my dress as I shimmy between the bush and the house, but I make no other move to remove the rest. My mind is numb.

"What are you doing?" Maksim asks, his voice full of worry. And something else. Something… Guilt?

Hit.

Danger.

Wife.

Wife?

What had the demon said? How was it he'd known my family should be cautious?

The wife mentioned interest in your whore's family before.

Alik knew this?

I blink and stare at Maksim, searching my mind for surprise in his features when Alik told him this. It had been a cannonball to my abdomen, so I hadn't been paying attention, but I don't remember surprise.

He wasn't surprised.

"Did you know?" I ask, so quiet that he may not hear.

But he does hear it. He hears it because he was expecting it. The guilt in his voice is masked when he contorts his lips in a frown, a *lie*. "Know what?"

"Did you know my family was in danger?"

"Of course I didn't." He reaches out to me, but I pull away, taking a step back.

"Maksim," I whisper with so much disappointment, I can't muster saying any more.

He hangs onto his innocence for a moment, keeping the mask on, but when he closes and opens his eyes, the gut-wrenching guilt makes everything inside of me tear. I was wrong. Honesty makes nothing better.

"Weeks ago, before I paid off the organization and before your location was even discovered, Alik found out Daniel's wife was making the ridiculous request that your family be murdered. I knew it wasn't going to happen then, and it isn't going to happen now."

"You knew." A bitter, dry laugh bubbles up my throat. "Are you psychic?"

"They're in Albania." He says it without the conviction needed to offer any level of comfort. Because regardless of how confident he was then, he isn't so confident now.

"Then why are you sending someone to protect them?"

He opens his mouth but hesitates before speaking. "Because I don't want to risk it."

"*Now*," I say, not quite sneering. Not with nearly the amount of bite I wish I had. "Now that we're sleeping together, you don't want to risk it. Before, you had no trouble."

"There was no potential hit out before," he counters. As if reminded of the fact, his eyes scan the road before finding the house. "We need to go. We can talk about this later."

I give my head a slight shake before stepping toward the drive. I don't know how I'm possibly going to get to Albania, but I know for certain I won't stay here. "Be safe, Maksim."

"Where are you going?"

I don't answer.

"Elira, stop being proud and get back here."

When I make it to the drive, I start toward the road, pulling out my phone.

"*Lislchka*."

My chest squeezes hard enough that I put my hand over my heart, but I don't stop. Ringing is loud in my ear, but when my mother's voicemail plays, the world silences as panic slices me. I hang up and try again.

When I hear Maksim's heavy feet shuffling down the drive, I pick up my pace.

"You know I can't let you leave."

"I'm not your prisoner," I yell over the ringing.

Voicemail again.

"Then let's talk."

Hang up. Redial.

Voicemail.

"Elira."

"You want to *talk*, Maksim?" I yell, whipping around and stabbing at my phone in frustration to hang up on my mother's voicemail.

Talk.

As if this is something we can work through. As if there's anything to salvage.

A half hour ago, he was talking about me leaving this place. He's been putting measures in place, hinting at wanting me to go. When I first learned of him giving my family money, I thought it was... I thought it meant something different. It felt like love. Now it feels like he was paying to get rid of me.

And it's worked.

But I don't care about that anymore. I can't. The only thing that matters is getting to my family somehow. Getting a hold of them. Warning them.

"While you were putting my family in danger, I was mending yours." I take a step toward him and get the urge to slap him but keep my shaking hands at my sides, my phone tight in my grasp. Frustrated and scared tears blur his image.

"I cared for your sister from the day I met her. She's a

child. She…" I shake my head as my voice cracks. "Even when I hated you, even when I was ready to *kill* you, I never would've stood by while she was harmed. Never."

"I know," he says, pained. "I know that. If I could go back in time and make another decision, I would. I…" His throat works as he swallows. "Come to Hugh's with me, and the first thing we will do is search for an associate in Albania to help your family. As soon as it's safe, we'll get you a flight there. I promise. I'll even go with you, if you want."

"You have all the answers." My heart feels like it's coming up my throat. "But it's too late. I'm sorry."

I turn and start down the road, already feeling the ache of unrequited love. The fear of the unknown. The grief of loss.

I hold up my phone, ready to dial my mother again, terrified of what I'll do if I'm too late, but I gasp as I'm jerked backward.

Maksim throws me over his shoulders with strong arms that would never make for a fair match and ignores my protests when I yell out and beat my fists on his back.

"I'm sorry," he says, but he sounds sure of his decision. "You'll forgive me for this."

"Let me go!"

"I have to keep you safe. I'll never forgive myself if I don't."

"You don't even want me," I cry. "You're trying to buy your way out of my life."

His hand on my thigh squeezes. "That isn't true."

"It is true!" My body goes limp against him as I drop my phone in the grass and let out a loud, embarrassing groan against his back. This sight must be absurd, but it's hard to care.

Why? Why is my life so full of heartache?

How much can one person take?

Maksim stops on the porch and sets me on my feet, taking my shoulders to steady me. *"Lislchka…"*

"Stop," I snap, swatting his hands away and taking a step back. For a moment, he looks like he's trying to corner a wild animal, ready to pounce at me if I try to get away, but I don't run. We've done this dance before. I know he's faster. "Don't call me *lislchka* anymore. We're not a couple. We're not even friends."

His eyes narrow. "Stop being ridiculous."

"I'm not being *ridiculous*." My words sound over-the-top. Dramatic. Resembling Anya. They sound, well, ridiculous.

I don't have time for this.

I tuck my hair behind my ear while pretending to look away shamefully, while really searching for a weapon. If he won't let me leave willingly, I'll have to leave by force. He's stronger, faster, and more practiced. But I'm smarter, and he never ceases to underestimate me. Of all of Maksim's flaws, that's his biggest.

The clay flowerpot I'm hopelessly trying to grow oregano in sits on a bench by the door. There are others, bigger and sturdier, but my eyes choose it.

"I *love* you."

I freeze, my hand still at my ear, my heart stopping for a moment.

I couldn't have heard him right.

"I can't tell you how sorry I am for not taking the threat to your family seriously, but I still believe they're safe. I will do everything in my power to ensure it and will treat them as my own blood from this day forward, I swear on my life. You are…"

My eyes find him as he clears his throat. I don't know what to think. I want to be happy, but I'm in too much shock to process his words.

"You are not a prisoner, but you are my life. And I can't

bear the thought of losing you like this, so please," he gestures toward the door. "Let's get Anya and Hugh and get someplace safe."

"I'm just supposed to trust you now?" I ask, my voice small, swept up in his revelation. My heart begs me to proclaim my love, but I hate him and love him simultaneously for doing this now. Here. Like this. With so much going on. So much happening. "I'm just supposed to stand by while my family is in danger?"

"You *can* trust me." He steps forward and takes my hand. "I promise you—"

"Would you do it?"

His mouth closes. Lines form between his eyes as he waits for me to go on.

"If it were Anya in danger, and I promised you I had someone on their way to protect her, would you sit back with me and wait?"

His face hardens slightly, but I can tell he's trying to stay neutral. We both know the answer.

Of course he wouldn't.

I squeeze his hand and lean into him before he can lie. "I trust you… Just don't let me down."

He sighs, his shoulders sagging with what looks like relief at not having to answer my question. "I won't."

He turns to the door and opens it while I lean forward and busy myself brushing dirt off my legs. "Could you try calling Mami? I can't get through to her."

"Uh, yeah, sure." He pulls his phone from his pocket and unlocks it. "What's the number?"

While his eyes are aimed at the screen, I give him the number and grab the clay pot as I stand. In one graceful movement, I swing it across his head, shattering it to bits.

He topples in a giant heap of perfect muscle, and I dive to catch his head just in time.

Closing my eyes and letting out a long-held breath, I gently lower his head to rest on the ground.

Planting a kiss to his lips while snaking my hand in his pants to retrieve his wallet and keys, I ignore the pain in my chest.

"I love you too."

26

ELIRA

I don't know Vegas. I'm not familiar with 'the streets' or 'the bad sides of town.' But as I stare up at the dilapidated, red brick building with a corner of it tinged black like someone unsuccessfully tried to burn it down, I know I'm here.

I look down at the address written on my palm to ensure it's correct for a third time before wrapping my arms around myself, staying tucked inside the alley out of sight. Any moment it feels as though the Bratva will snatch me up. Maybe even hurt me for wounding one of their lieutenants.

Maksim's car is parked safely in a parking garage on 'the good side of town.' I borrowed a tarp from a kind, unaware owner of a very classic looking American model to keep it hidden and have gone on foot since then, walking with my head down to a nearby Internet cafe before ultimately hitch-hiking to this location. Still, it's only a matter of time before I'm caught.

For one thing, Odessa, my friend from the bakery, the one who told me how to get this address, knows where I am. And if she knows where I am, Maksim might. Worse than that, I still have my phone which he's no doubt tracking. I should've dumped it already, but it's still my lifeline to my mother, so the best I've managed is keeping it off for long stretches of time, only turning it on when I'm prepared to run to a secure location.

It burns the skin of my chest now as it's tucked beneath the strap of my bra, begging me to turn it on to check my calls, but I don't. I can't. Not until I leave here.

With a shaky breath, I step from the alley and head to the building. I was told the best chance of making it to Albania is to drive to Mexico before flying home, but I still need a fake ID. Mathew Smith—not a real name, I presume—in 4D is supposed to be able to help with that.

My skin crawls as I walk through the building, and any minute it feels like a Russian mobster will step from the shadows, gun in hand. Or even worse, a hitman.

I swallow and wrap my arms around myself. The truth is, if it were a hitman popping from the shadows, I might be relieved. If they're coming after me, maybe it means they aren't going after my family.

But the sick feeling in the pit of my stomach tells me I'm not that lucky. I can sense the danger lurking over them, feel the hopelessness of not being near. It makes my steps quicken and fingertips tingle. By the time I make it to Mathew Smith's door, I'm a nervous wreck, which must make me look less suspicious because his boyish face slumps with a frown.

It takes twenty minutes and everything in Maksim's wallet to make me Iris Kissinger—not a name that seemed fitting, but I didn't get to choose. Once I'm out of the building, new ID in hand, I force myself to wait until I've walked four blocks before I turn on my phone.

My plan is to allow myself thirty seconds. If Mami has called, I will listen to the message, then find another device to contact her if she's safe. If she isn't, I'll call her right away. If there are no messages, I'll turn the phone right back off, run two blocks, then catch a ride back to the parking garage.

My eyes are wide as I stare at the screen while tucked into an alleyway, praying my search party or killer isn't nearby.

It takes a minute for everything to load but only a second for my heart to fall. No calls from Mami. Twenty-six calls from Maksim. One from Anya.

What if I'm too late?

What if they're dead?

I let out a shaky breath and go to turn the phone off, but Maksim's contact appears as he tries to call, deepening the ache in my heart. My body longs to be wrapped in his arms, to give in to his comfort, to accept his support.

But his support isn't real. It isn't good enough. I decline his call but hesitate to turn off the phone.

Staring at my missed call from Anya, I try not to think about the fear she must be feeling. The confusion.

Does she understand why I left?

Does she... Does she know I didn't abandon her? Her brother will keep her safe. She has an army in front of her. She's *safe*. So much safer than Asher or Bora or Mami. She must know this.

Biting my lip, I go to my voicemail and listen to her message.

"Elira," she says, her voice strained like she's upset. "I'm with Tanner at his uncle's house right now, and umm..." The line goes quiet for a moment, the calm before a storm. Sobs erupt, making me press the phone against my ear. "Can you please come get me? You and Maksim were right. He isn't a good guy. I should've listened, but... Please don't tell Maksim. Just you." She sniffles. "I'll text you the address."

End of message.

Does she not know the danger we're in?

In a panic, I go to call her, but it goes straight to voicemail.

Damn it.

Damn it, damn it, damn it, Anya. What are you doing?

I bring up Maksim's contact, ready to text him where she is, but the hurt in her voice gives me pause.

It's her life at stake. He has to know.

And I have to leave.

If I call, he'll catch me.

If I don't, Anya is in danger. She already is.

If Maksim goes there... If he loses it—which he will—and hurts that stupid boy...

Anya would never forgive him.

But...

Asher.

Bora.

Mami.

They are the ones I'm supposed to be saving. Not Anya. Not the sister of the man who constantly betrays me.

But...

"Even when I hated you, even when I was ready to kill you, I never would've stood by while she was harmed. Never."

My own words. Were they a lie?

I think about it for a long time. Too long with the phone in my hand that was only supposed to be on for a minute.

My eyes close as I growl.

I make note of the address Anya sent, shut off the phone, then sprint three blocks before finding two young boys to give me a lift to Maksim's car. One pitstop to make before Mexico.

* * *

TANNER'S UNCLE'S house is bigger than I expected given the state of Tanner. And nicer. It's modern, sleek, and gray on the outskirts of Las Vegas, with a pond surrounding it that strikes me as abnormally large even with limited experience of American homes. The few neighboring houses are spread out between acres of shrubbery that allow privacy.

Bright orange fish swim around below my feet as I walk over a small bridge to the front door, my steps determined.

I pound my fist on the front door then use the knocker when no one answers after a few seconds. Heat radiates from my ears, my teeth grind, but if I'm honest, the anger is a welcome distraction from fear.

"Hello!" I bang again. "I'm here for Anya!"

Gradually, as a minute goes by without an answer, my anger begins to wane. I listen carefully for anything inside, and when I don't hear a peep, the fear returns.

Maksim was almost certain the hit wasn't placed on my family. That it was placed on us.

What if…?

I try the door and find it unlocked. Is that a bad sign or good?

"Anya?" I call, my voice much softer than before as I stick my head inside. I still don't get a response.

What if I got the address wrong?

I step back outside and look for evidence of Anya being here. Tanner's truck or that motorcycle she talked about. She said he got it from his uncle, and this could very well be a wealthy uncle's home.

Toeing inside, I scan the entryway, searching for her white purse with the chain strap she carries. Nowhere.

"Anya, I'm here!"

I listen carefully.

Nothing.

Goosebumps raise on my arms that I try to ignore but

can't. Something is telling me to walk out the door. Drive away.

But I can't. I could never do that to Anya.

I pull out my phone and turn it on, but when I try to call Maksim, there's no service. *Fuck.*

I should step outside. Find service. She called me from here, so this must just be a dead spot. This must be...

Something tiny and green catches my eye in the next room as I cautiously move that way, and when I spot it, I can't stop moving. More tiny green balls appear, scattered throughout this sitting area.

My subconscious knows what it is; it's the only explanation as to why my stomach balls into a knot then stuffs itself up into my throat. My brain, on the other hand, is slower to process, searching through memories until finally I see the band of beads that had been wrapped around Anya's wrist this afternoon.

My lips part with what would be a gasp if my lungs were working.

I hurry several steps that way but force myself to stop and look at the phone that still doesn't have service. It can't be a coincidence. Something—or someone—is blocking the reception.

"Anya!" I call despite my better judgment as I hurry into the hallway.

"Elira," Anya cries, snapping my head toward the kitchen.

I dart that way, letting the phone fall through my fingers. As soon as I pass through the doorway, I halt at the sight of Anya's trembling form tied to a kitchen chair with a woman pointing a gun at her head.

Tanner lies in a pool of blood at her feet, the chair he's tied to tipped over with him. His eyes are closed, but there's so much blood around his head that there must be a bullet in the back of it. He's dead.

"I'm so sorry," Anya cries, lowering her eyes as a sob overtakes her. "They made me do it."

They.

My attention turns to the last person in the room as she walks toward me, no weapon, no fear. She doesn't even wear a smirk on her Botoxed face. She looks like a woman out for revenge who's far too angry to enjoy it.

Her brown hair is swept over her shoulders and perfect while the woman with the gun has hers high in a ponytail. She wears black slacks and a white, loose-sleeved blouse, an outfit familiar to me. I threw out several just like it.

This is the woman from the photo. Daniel's wife.

The first thing I felt when I walked into this room, saw Anya in that chair with the gun pointed at her, was fear. The kind that swallows you whole. Makes you freeze. The kind that, frankly, I'm used to.

But now… Seeing this woman…

I can't help the way my shoulders square or the way my mind brings my attention to the ring suddenly too loose on my finger. A poor fit.

It's sick, but I find my eyes moving to her left hand. Her rock is so much bigger.

"Do you know who I am?" the woman asks like she's the godfather. When my eyes find hers, I imagine they're blazing, and I just hope Anya doesn't pay for my mistakes. But the thing is… I'm not afraid of the godfather. I've met worse. I damn sure am not going to cower for the woman trying to avenge a human trafficker.

"Daniel's wife."

She tips her chin in confirmation. "And do you know why you're here?"

I flex my fingers, my damn ring feeling as uncomfortable as ever. "So you can pretend he was a man worth killing for."

The first bit of emotion breaks out on her face in the

form of a smile cracking one side of her lips. "Because the man you viciously murdered was a husband and a brother." She waves to the woman holding the gun, but I don't take my eyes off her. Not even when the ponytailed one pulls a chef knife out and brings it to her. She takes it in her perfectly manicured hand, her ring shining.

That must've cost a fortune. More than Daniel ever led on to having. I bet her wedding dress did too. It made mine, *the dress*, look like a rag.

What the fuck did she do to deserve that?

"And today you're going to learn how it felt to be him," she goes on, tipping the knife at me suggestively, trying to intimidate me. "And you're also going to learn how it feels to be me."

I stare at her, unblinking, my chin lifting slightly. I think she's expecting me to ask what she means. Maybe even beg. But I'm not an idiot. Well, I am. I am for trusting Maksim. Or for not trusting Maksim, I'm not sure which at this point.

But I know what she wants to do. She wants to kill Anya. And my family. She wants me to feel her pain, and then she wants to stick that knife into me and watch me bleed out, all while begging her for mercy.

Remember how I said I didn't know what the men who took me wanted? This woman and I are two sides of the same coin. I don't need to guess when it comes to her. We live by the same principle.

Hurt my family, hurt me, and I will fucking destroy you.

Slowly, without breaking eye contact, I remove the imposter ring from my hand and toss it to the floor.

MAKSIM

"*Y*ou're driving too fast. We could pass her and not know it," Anthony says, gazing out the passenger window at the pedestrians on the sidewalk.

My foot feels heavy as a brick on the gas pedal, but I ease up, knowing he's right. It feels hopeless. I'm not even sure which *her* he's referring to, but if either Anya or Elira were stupid enough to walk along the sidewalk when they believed a hitman was coming to get them, I might kill them myself.

Still, my search shows just how reckless they both are. Anger tightens my grip on the steering wheel, bulges the vein in my neck. The lump on the back of my head feels hot and swollen.

Fear came and went hours ago. About two hours after I came to, Alik confirmed that the hit was put on Elira's family. He was able to find a contact in Albania who went to Elira's childhood home to find it torn apart, as if someone was either looking for something or putting up a struggle. My whole body had frozen listening to that piece of news, and I held my breath for the next half hour until he called to tell me the family was found hiding in a nearby root cellar.

The hit was on them. I am... I have so much making up to do. But with them safe, my anger at both Elira and Anya is barely contained.

They fucking ran. Both of them, like stubborn sheep desperate to be eaten by wolves. Bailey said she went outside while Anya claimed to be right behind her, but Anya must've slipped away because she was gone before I woke up and could warn her of danger. It doesn't get her off the hook. Her free reign with piece of shit men ends today.

And Elira...

I have men at the airport. The bus station. Men speeding up and down the highways searching for my car and staking out every hotel in the city.

She has no ID. No passport. No means of leaving the country. Her fucking phone isn't even on. If she would've just stayed with me, we could be finding Anya together and on a private plane to meet her family tonight.

Stubborn, stubborn fucking sheep.

Or she hates me so much she'd rather die than be near me.

Pushing away that thought, I look at the people on the sidewalk even though I don't expect to see either of them there. Anya's phone is off, and no one even remotely connected to Tanner knows where he is, so they obviously don't want to be found.

My phone rings, and I snatch it from my cupholder. No part of me thinks it will be Elira or Anya, but my heart quickens anyway.

"Yes?"

"Still looking for the hitman's ID," Alik tells me. "Shouldn't be much longer. I'm tracking the financials to an organization. Doesn't look freelance."

My teeth grit as I turn a corner. I'm running out of places to drive.

What if she isn't in Vegas?

Where else would she go?

"You called to tell me no news? Why are you not getting all this out of the wife?"

"Lev went to Bakersfield, but she wasn't home. She's at her mother's home in New York, according to a neighbor. The Koslov Bratva is looking for her for us."

"I told *you* to find her," I growl, although I don't know why I care. I'm just angry. Especially at Alik for being right and knowing it.

"In the middle of the day? I'm more memorable than Lev, boss. Easier to pick out of a lineup. But uh, sorry. Did you want me to go to New York myself, or do you want me to track the payment? I can't do that on my phone."

"Just shut the fuck up, Alik." I lean forward to look down an alleyway when I see someone, but it isn't Elira.

He starts to say something else, but I hang up, my heart hammering as I slow the car to a crawl and look around.

Anya will turn up. She always does.

But Elira…

I may have lost her.

"You all right?" Anthony asks.

I don't answer. Don't know how. It's been too many hours without any sign of her. She could be long gone by now.

And if she is… What am I going to do about it?

Nothing.

She isn't in danger. The hitman is in Albania, and he'll be taken care of soon enough. The wife is in New York. The organization is paid off. She's … free.

I pull over to the side of the road, my face hard even while my insides turn. After putting the car in park, I just stare out the windshield, unable to look Anthony in the eye. "I think it's time to call off the search."

It's quiet for a full minute while he waits for me to change my mind. But I won't.

I meant it when I said that I loved her. That she wasn't my prisoner.

But… But what?

Anthony makes the call to send his own men home, and I shoot Hugh a text to do the same. I'll keep looking for Anya, all night if I have to. But I'd rather do it by myself.

"I'm sorry, man," he says, letting that hang in the air for too long. "Just give her some time. She'll be back."

What he's saying could apply to either Anya or Elira, but I don't have to guess who he's talking about.

I shake my head. "I wouldn't come back. Would you?"

"No. *Fuck* no. But she loves you, so… Love will do shit to you, you know?"

I laugh dryly. "She doesn't love me."

"She *said* that she loved you."

My eyes narrow as I turn to look at him.

He gives me a nervous, lopsided grin. "You're about to be really pissed at me."

"What the hell are you talking about?"

He rubs the back of his neck and sucks in a breath through his teeth. "So, Bailey didn't really go back outside. She and Anya heard you and Freaky-eye and went to spy on your conversation through the window. You know how Bailey is."

I just stare at him.

"Anyway, after Elira knocked you over the head, I guess she, like, kissed you and told you she loved you. Either fucked-up or cute, I'm not sure which."

My face doesn't crinkle, doesn't soften. As far as I'm aware, I show no signs of being affected by what he just said.

But inside…

This changes everything.

I clear my throat. "So Anya…"

He flinches. "Heard everything… Sorry."

A sigh blows out my mouth while I close my eyes and lay my head back.

Well, that better explains why she's hiding.

"Just wait for them to turn their phones back on. They will at some point."

I huff and don't open my eyes. They're both clever enough to figure out that's how I can track them. Phones are a convenient means of tracking someone but too obvious and have their limitations.

Alik standing in Hugh's backyard comes into my mind.

My eyes shoot open.

He wasn't tracking me by my phone.

He was tracking me by my car.

I hurry to put the car in drive then peel back onto the road.

"Woah." Anthony grabs the center console. "Did you think of a place they might be?"

"No." I step on it to get through a yellow light, Alik's apartment my destination. "But I know how to find Elira."

* * *

MY FIST POUNDS on the chipped door to Alik's apartment, startling the woman across from him trying to get into her own. "Open the fucking door!"

The woman fumbles with her key in her lock while I ignore her gasp, and a few moments later, her door opens and shuts. I can feel her watching me through the peephole.

How does a Bratva enforcer manage to live in a shitty

apartment building on the Westside? Does the kid need a fucking raise?

The door swings open, revealing an expressionless Alik, neither surprised nor bothered by my presence. "Hello."

I shove past him into a living room with old, brown carpet that might've been white once and catch sight of the tiny, depressing kitchen table with one chair. There are three holes in the walls beside the front door that I linger on for a half second before snapping to him as he waves my way.

"Please, come in," he deadpans, shutting the door.

I grab him by his shirt and throw him up against the wall, caving the drywall in farther where one of the holes is. "I should fucking kill you."

His jaw clenches, but he merely raises his chin. "For?"

"You let me unleash a search party on Elira when you knew how to find her this whole goddamn time."

"I don't know what you're talking about, but I would never go against a lieutenant's orders. You think I would *stop* your search?"

"Shut up!" I lift him before slamming him back into the wall, making his nostrils flare. "You *know* she has my car. Have you known where she was this entire time? You little shit."

"No," he says through his teeth. "If I knew where your whore was, I would tell you."

My grip on his shirt tightens. "*Don't* call her that."

"Just trying to be consistent, *sir*. That's what you've been calling her."

The smug look that crosses his normally expressionless features pushes me over the edge, and I rear my fist back before landing a blow to his jaw.

His head whips to the side, and there's a split second of shock before anger starts to emanate from him. I remember this. This lack of control, always answering to someone else, taking someone's shit. It's how you pay your dues. Alik will never move past a smug soldier.

I pull him away from the wall to shove him in the direction of the computer desk occupying a corner of his living room. Three monitors all play the same colorful display of ribbons forming as the computer sleeps.

"Find her. Now."

He saunters that way, his shoulders straight even as he mouths off. "How exactly am I supposed to do that?"

"*Do not* play stupid with me," I bark, stomping to the computer with him. "Just do it."

He sits down at the computer and jiggles the mouse to wake it up. A spreadsheet of numbers appears, and he minimizes the page.

"You know, I liked you for a minute there," he says. "You had me convinced you had more character than … others."

Others. As in Nikita.

"Yeah? You had me convinced you weren't a conniving cunt."

He brings up a program then types in his credentials. "I'm not sure what you're talking about."

"This entire time Nikita has been punishing me, I figured he had some rat following my every move, watching to check up on my loyalty. That was you, Alik. For months, you've been tracking me and running to Daddy every time you find something you deem interesting. I've been loyal to the Bratva my entire adult life. Go fuck yourself." I shake away the betrayal. "Just find the car."

"But you're not loyal to the Pakhan."

My spine stiffens as I glare at Alik's head. He stops typing to turn to me, his expression serious.

"I'm not sure what it is you want me to do, Mr. Sokolov."

"Find the car."

"I am not Nikita's pet," he says as if he can read my mind.

"I am *no one's* pet. I follow orders. His, yours, Roman's... You think you're the only one being watched? *Everyone* is being watched. I found the same bug on my car that I put on yours, Roman's, and every other lieutenant's. It isn't personal. It's Petrov paranoia."

Petrov paranoia.

I can see Nikita doing this, and hearing Alik say it calms the anger I've had for him.

He's right. I'm not loyal to Nikita. I try. I try to follow his orders, respect his wishes, but... Leadership like Nikita's isn't sustainable. We've already been to war. One day, the Petrov Bratva will fall. Nikita's paranoia isn't paranoia, it's intuition.

After a few seconds, I look away, Alik's intense gaze unsettling.

"Are *you* loyal to the Pakhan, Alik?"

He takes his time responding, as he should. I asked him a dangerous question.

"When Nikita gave you that girl, he had me follow you. I know you took her to the desert, and I know what you planned to do. I wasn't close enough to see, but I know something happened there, and I know you wound up pawning his gift to you off on Hugh. I know a lot of things."

"What's your point?"

"I reported none of this. I've never reported anything that would result in me being given the order to put a bullet in your head, and do you know why?"

I stare at him and wait for him to continue.

"Because I'm stingy with my loyalty, and I've respected you since the day I joined the brotherhood. Does that answer your question, dickhead?"

Silence.

It's possible I've been an asshole.

My jaw ticing, I nod. When my eyes get the urge to

wander, I find the computer screen. Guilt is an uncomfortable thing.

A red dot flashes on the screen, and I lean in to take a look.

"Looks like she's just outside of Vegas," Alik says. "Your car stopped fifteen minutes ago."

"Where the hell is that?" I squint at the area surrounding the dot.

"Residential area, it appears."

Whose house would Elira have gone to?

"Here." Alik grabs a pen and scribbles the address on a scrap of paper before handing it to me.

I glance at the paper before tucking it in my pocket. "Thanks," I mutter and start toward the door but stop when I remember I drove here in Anthony's car. I need to do this alone.

"One last thing," I spin to face him. "I need to borrow your car."

He's already standing as he reaches into his pocket, pulls out his keys, and tosses them to me before heading for the door. "Good. You drive."

"What?" My face pinches.

He looks at me like he's the one who should be confused. "You could need backup."

"The hitman is in Albania."

"Sure, but—"

"Alik, you're not coming with me," I interrupt, suddenly anxious to get out of here. "Watch the monitor and tell me if she moves. I'll bring your car back in one piece. I promise."

Alik doesn't say another word as I leave, my anxiousness growing with every step.

I don't know what I'm going to say to Elira. All I know is I need to convince her to stay.

28

ELIRA

*H*enrietta taps my nose with the tip of the knife while standing over me like the authority she believes she is.

I wish I could say I put up a fight. That she has scratches up and down her face, that her skin is beneath my nails.

But the gun pointed at Anya's head left me little choice. I had to cooperate.

"You have no idea how much I'm going to enjoy this," Henrietta says with a sick amount of satisfaction as she caresses the knife down my neck and over my chest. Anya whimpers beside me.

She's going to die because of me. Because of my need for revenge. My eyes remain dry, my stare firmly pointed at Henrietta, but self-hatred turns my stomach. "You'll enjoy it as much as I enjoyed killing your useless, pig of a husband."

I'm sorry, Anya. I'm so sorry.

The satisfaction melts from Henrietta's expression, and she retaliates by digging the knife just below my collarbone. I cringe and clamp my mouth shut, trying not to cry out, but a groan escapes me anyway.

"No," Anya sobs for me. "Don't hurt her."

Henrietta's head jerks toward Anya. "Don't hurt her? She's the reason you're in this mess."

"No." Henrietta holds up a hold to correct herself. "Sorry, your *scumbag brother* is the reason you're in this mess. Elira doesn't get all the credit."

"He isn't a scumbag," Anya snaps. For the first time in a while, I'm able to drag my gaze off my enemy to look at Anya. She glares instead of cowers like she's truly offended for her brother.

Henrietta lowers the knife, slowly, resentfully, and takes a step toward Anya to get in her face. I work at the rope around my wrist tying me to the chair, but all it does is rub me raw.

"Do you have any idea who your brother even *is*? What he's done?"

Anya leans her head forward. If she could, she'd be knocking her forehead against Henrietta's. "I know exactly who he is. No matter what he's done."

Henrietta leans in even more and smirks. "Do you know who *you* are?"

Oh no.

I squirm in my chair. "Could we get back to the reason we're here? Daniel isn't worth all this buildup. We both know he never showed us the same courtesy."

She raises her chin with an obnoxious laugh. "He took your virginity, you dumb slut. We laughed about you as soon as he got home." She turns to Daniel's sister, Caroline, and nods to me. "Shut her up."

Caroline stomps to me and slaps me across the face, leaving a sting that doesn't come close to being as painful as Henrietta's words. When she points the gun at my head, Henrietta turns back to Anya.

"I asked you a question."

Anya shakes her head. "I don't know what you're talking about."

"I know. That's what makes you pathetic."

"Just stop it," I growl, eliciting Caroline to grab a handful of my hair and pull. I grind my teeth while straining to rise from the chair.

Anya looks between me and Henrietta, her lips pouted.

Henrietta stands straight and clasps her hands behind her back. "Did you know that Maksim is not your brother?"

Anya's wide, puzzled eyes, narrow in a glare. "Shut the *fuck* up. We may not be blood related, but he's my brother."

"How is he your brother?"

"My parents adopted him."

Henrietta smiles, wide and cruel. She struck me as calm and collected when I arrived, but I'm starting to see that she's only beginning to unleash the wickedness locked behind all that makeup and Botox.

"What?" Anya asks, a sudden hesitancy in her voice. She turns her head to me. "Elira, what is she getting at?"

I want to lie. Of course I want to lie.

But how can I?

I bite my lip and feel my face pinch with pity.

"He was a slave," Henrietta answers for me. "One of many. Your father took foreign, cheap labor to an extreme. He farmed out dozens of boys when they were young and raised them like the crop he forced them to harvest."

Anya's lips part as her shoulders hunch. "What?"

"Maksim killed your parents and took you as revenge."

My eyes widen, and I shoot up. "That isn't true!"

Henrietta smirks. "You're not his sister, Anya. You're his *revenge*. His means of controlling the people who controlled him. He took away your childhood the same way they took away his."

"Shut up!" I sneer, the legs of my chair rocking as I jerk.

"Just shut the fuck up. That isn't true, and you know it." I look at Anya and soften my features. "Maksim loves you. He has *always* loved you, from the day you were born. You were his sister then, and you're his sister now. Your mother claimed him as her son, and he would *never* have hurt her."

Tears slide down her cheeks while she stares at me in disbelief. "What about my dad?"

I take too long to answer. I hesitate. And in that hesitation, she sees the truth. She turns her head to stare at her lap and says nothing.

"He didn't hurt your dad. I swear to you, he didn't."

"Whether he did or didn't," Henrietta pipes in, "it's safe to say you were as much a burden to him then as you are now."

"That—" Caroline yanks my hair again to shut me up and slaps me for good measure.

That isn't true.

"Imagine an eighteen-year-old with no citizenship or knowledge of the country they'd been a slave in their entire adolescence, trying to make it on their own. Now imagined them with a *toddler* weighing them down. Honestly, I'd be impressed if I didn't hate him so much. I don't know if he'll feel pain at your death or relief. Maybe I'm doing him a favor."

Anya's lip trembles.

"You're a monster," I say, feeling my strength drain as Anya's pain grows.

Henrietta walks to me, her eyes fiery as she brings the knife from behind her back. "Are you just now getting that?"

I expect her to stab me. My eyes clench shut, and I brace for the pain, but the sharp slice along my shoulder pulls a groan from my throat and shoots my eyes to the knife. A thick line of blood forms before drops run down my arm.

She moves the knife to my other arm and slices along my bicep.

"Ahh!" I cry, throwing my head back.

"Stop it!" Anya screams, then sobs. "Please, stop."

Henrietta moves the knife to my stomach and makes a slow, curved cut up my torso. My pride shreds as I scream at the top of my lungs.

It's hard to think. Hard to breathe. Hard to register anything but pain.

But still, I understand what she's doing.

She isn't going to kill me by stabbing me. That would be letting me get off too easily.

She wants me to die a cliché. Death by a thousand cuts.

"Beg," she spits in my ear before cutting my side with a quick jerk of her hand.

No.

It will not make it better. Only worse.

Still the words are on my tongue.

Please stop.

No more.

"I'll end your misery," she assures me, but it's a lie. She may end Anya's, but she won't end mine. I won't allow my words to be what puts a bullet in Anya's head.

"Elira, please," Anya sobs, her voice so clear it's like she's in my ear.

I sob with her.

Regrets, about a million, slap me in the face one by one, harder than either of these women ever could.

We're here because of me. Because of my anger. My need for revenge. My family will be dead because of it. Any minute, Henrietta assures me the call will come to confirm that it's done.

Bora.

Asher.

Mami.

Anya.

All dead. All because of me.

I can't hold it in anymore. My anguish bubbles to the surface, but it doesn't come out as a useless plea.

"I'm sorry," I sob around the pain of the knife in my knee. "I'm so sorry."

Henrietta gets in my face. "Sorry for *what*? Say it."

Say it.

She thinks I'm sorry for Daniel.

I'm not talking to her.

"I never should've done it," I say, knowing Anya is listening. "He deserved it. He destroyed more women than I'll ever know, but if I would've known it'd cost your life, I would've found another way… I'm so sorry."

"My life?" Henrietta laughs. "Daniel was my *world*."

"It's okay," Anya says, her voice soft. "I forgive you."

I close my eyes and allow myself to tremble with remorse.

Above me, Henrietta's rage brews as the room quiets. When I open my eyes, she stares at me with so much malice, that I think she'll end this early. Her plan to keep me alive long enough to confirm my family's death, to watch Anya die, doesn't seem as worth it to her.

I know her plans for Maksim. She wants him to find us, the way he found me before. Only now it'll be my corpse brutally shredded. She can't kill a made man, but she believes she can kill his whore.

She'll pay for this too. It'll be a cycle of revenge until there's no one left.

Maybe if we were still yelling and crying, we wouldn't have heard it. Maybe things would be different.

But in the quiet of the room, everyone's head moves to the entryway as the front door opens.

29

MAKSIM

*M*y finger hooks over the trigger of my gun as I push the door to the secluded home open, my eyes roaming the entryway. The safety is off. The hairs on the back of my neck are standing.

It's safe to say that something is wrong.

My car is parked in the driveway with the keys still in it. In plain sight. All evening I've been searching for Elira, and now she decides to leave my car in plain sight? It isn't even that she has the cover of night or a property outside the city. She wouldn't be this careless, not when she's still hiding from me with her phone off.

I step inside, swinging the gun behind the door in case someone's waiting for me there, and when I see the empty corner, I face forward and creep into the living room.

Her name is perched on my tongue, but I don't yell it out. Not yet.

A sound comes from a room to my left, and I turn to move that way, my gun steady in front of me. A few more steps, and it happens again, more coherent this time.

A whimper.

Elira.

Resisting the urge to run that way, I creep past her phone on the ground toward the room the sound came from and prepare myself to fire at whatever is causing her to make that sound.

With a quick stride, I swing myself into the kitchen, gun first and point it at a woman holding a knife to Elira's throat. Tape covers her mouth.

When my eyes find Anya, I stiffen.

It was her whimper.

My gaze moving to the woman with the knife, I barely keep my finger from squeezing the trigger. That knife is lined up right against Elira's carotid, the same cut that ended Daniel's life. One move of this woman's hand and Elira is dead.

Even if I hadn't seen a photo of the woman, I wouldn't need to guess who this is.

"Drop it," I snarl, taking another step into the room.

Anya's whimpering gets loud, and I don't have time to wonder about it before a barrel presses between my shoulder blades.

"You first," a feminine voice says, sounding unworried.

Not a chance.

"You have no idea the trouble you've just caused yourself, Henrietta," I say, struggling to keep my voice even. Elira is covered in blood. It seeps through gashes throughout her body, and it's all I can do not to home in on it, not to show its effect on me. If Henrietta had any idea what I would do if I got my hands on her, her partner would shoot me in the head immediately. "Your husband isn't worth the things the Petrov Bratva will do to you if you don't put that knife down right this second."

"How about you put your gun down before I blow your fucking brains out." The woman behind me sounds angry now. She jabs the back of my neck with the barrel, making my jaw clench.

"You shoot me, I shoot Henrietta, she slices Elira's neck. Congratulations, you're a lone survivor."

"Sounds like a good deal to me," she says, sounding deadly serious.

I feel my own brows pinch, but the look of surprise on Henrietta's face is unmatchable. She recovers, blinking away the betrayal, and opens her mouth to speak, but the other woman interrupts.

"You're kind of right, though. It does mess up my plan to make you suffer." The gun leaves my neck, and I feel her take a step back. "How about I shoot Anya first?"

Anya's eyes widen with fear, mirroring the horror-stricken expression that's surely on my own face, and I quickly raise my hands, my gun pointing to the ceiling.

"Good boy," the woman coos. "Empty the clip and toss it."

Swallowing, I obey the command, my emptied gun thumping across the room.

She taps my back with the barrel. "On your knees, handsome."

"Let them go." I flinch as Henrietta rips the tape off Elira's mouth and finally allow myself to take in her injuries.

My legs fold as I lower to my knees while inspecting Anya. She looks uninjured. Tanner... He's a corpse that they've dragged off to the side of the room, as if proving what they're capable of.

"Why the hell would I do that after all the trouble it took to get you all here?" Henrietta asks, matter-of-fact.

"Why would *we* do that?" the woman with the gun corrects.

Henrietta looks like she wants to roll her eyes, but she's hesitant. She looks back at me. "We weren't expecting to have you, Maksim. I was hoping you would have found them here, mutilated beyond recognition, and blamed it on the boy you seemed to hate so much. I went through all the trouble to secure a solid alibi and everything."

"You put a hit on Elira's family, you bitch. I was already looking for you."

Her eyebrows raise. She looks between me and Elira.

She had no idea how much Elira means to me.

I may have just fucked up. Not that things could get much worse.

"Are you in love with your *whore*?" The woman behind me laughs.

Henrietta smiles. "That's … sweet." Her eyes move to Anya. "Is it because you know what it's like to be a whore, Maksim? Were you Anya's mother's whore? She looks an awful lot like you. Maybe I was wrong. Maybe you *are* blood related, just not brother and sister."

My hands tremble with rage before I clench them into fists. I don't know who I'm angrier for, Anya or Elizabeth. "*Shut up.*"

"Tell your sister the truth," Henrietta snaps. "Tell her who she is to you."

"She knows who she is to me."

"Liar," the woman behind me sneers. She presses the barrel up against the back of my head and bends to hiss in my ear. "Tell her what her parents did to you."

I'm quiet for a moment while I stare at an anguished, scared Anya. This is nothing but a cruel game to these women. Nothing but a show. This doesn't even have to do with Elira. Isn't even a punishment for me.

They're demanding I unlock secrets I've kept Anya's entire life to protect her, all so she can suffer before they put a bullet in her head to get on to the main event.

I'm going to kill them for this. I don't know how I'll do it yet, but I'll do it.

In the meantime... I have to keep them talking.

"You really want to know?"

Anya cringes like I've raised a fist to her, and after letting out a muffled cry, she nods.

"Your parents gave me you. That's what they did to me. That's all that matters. I wouldn't change it for anything."

The woman growls, unhappy with my response. "You wouldn't change it for *anything?*"

I don't hesitate. "No."

"Let's test that," Henrietta says, her face brightening. She nods at Anya. "Choose who dies first. Your sister or your love."

"Go fuck yourself."

"Sister it is." The gun leaves my head, and I turn to watch it point at Anya.

"Stop." I reach for it, but the woman yanks it back.

"Choose."

I face forward, my heart hammering in my chest. My brain doesn't even consider this a choice. Instead, it works to find a weapon, a solution, *something* to stop this.

I have to stop this.

"Who's it going to be, Maksim?" Henrietta asks, the knife firm against Elira's throat.

Neither.

Neither.

Neither.

I can't say. I *won't* say.

Weapon?

Solution?

Help?

Panic morphs into fear which morphs into sorrow as I lock eyes with Anya. The fear I feel is magnified on her face.

My little sister.

The girl who hid behind my legs when strangers

approached. Who fell asleep on my chest while watching cartoons. Who sought safety in my arms for months after her parents died, plagued by nightmares.

I am this girl's protector.

And Elira.

When I look at her, it's a new kind of heartbreak. She doesn't look at me with fear, but with a stern, brave expression that is a kick to the gut.

When I look at her, I see things I didn't know I should be looking for. I see a life together. A home to share, secrets I no longer have to keep. I see love. I see *her*. I see something remarkably irreplaceable and a mark on my heart that could never be erased.

"I love you," I tell her, a tear slipping from my eye for the first time since my mother told me the words scrolled across my chest.

She closes her eyes as her own tears fall. "I know. It's okay. Just do it."

"*Now*," the woman behind me growls.

I wait. I keep waiting. It isn't until the gun points at Anya again that my answer, the one I will hate myself forever for, is ripped from my throat.

"Elira."

No one is surprised. The two women are pleased. Even so, it feels like a silence takes over the room for a moment. Things feel sluggish.

I watch the knife in shame, waiting for Henrietta to move, not allowing myself the mercy of looking away.

She doesn't slice Elira's carotid. Her lips spread in a pleased smile as she moves the knife to Elira's collarbone and slices.

I narrow my eyes, but it takes me only a moment to react.

She must not realize it. She must believe she's already won, must've gotten too cocky.

Because with the knife no longer at Elira's throat and the gun on me, they just lost their leverage.

I jerk my head to the side while snatching the gun at the same time and twisting it in the woman's hand. It fires over Elira's cry just to the right of my head, but once it's in my control, I don't even take the time to scan for injuries. I point at Henrietta and fire.

She ducks behind Elira's chair, using her as a shield, but by the scream she lets out, I can tell I hit her.

The other woman growls and jumps at me, but all it takes is an elbow to her jaw to send her flying to the floor. I glance to see her out cold before I walk to Henrietta.

She whimpers and scoots away from Elira's chair, knife shaking in her grasp as she weakly points it at me while using her other hand to cover the bullet wound in her stomach.

I want to take my time with her. Wrap my hands around her neck. Use her own knife on her. I want to be as sick as she is, make her feel the pain she's made Elira feel.

But Anya and Elira need me. And sometimes you just have to finish the job.

I point the gun at Henrietta's head and pull the trigger, allowing myself only a moment to stare at her dead eyes before grabbing the knife and going to Elira.

"Anya first," she says when I go to cut her bindings.

I look down at the blood covering her, and if it weren't for the silence, I would think I'd been shot in the chest.

"It's okay," she says, her voice low. "The cuts aren't deep."

I swallow as I look at her, caressing her jaw and planting a quick kiss to her forehead before going to Anya.

I cut the rope around Anya's wrists first then go around to cut her ankles free, but she rips the tape off her mouth and pulls me against her.

I wrap my arms around her and shut my eyes as she cries

onto my shoulder, unleashing more heartache than one person should ever feel. More heartache than I ever thought I'd allow her to feel.

"You're safe," I say, hugging her close.

"I swear, I'll never leave again. I'm so sorry."

She's sorry?

"Anya…" I sigh, ready to correct her, but Elira's gasp runs my train of thought off its track.

"Maksim!"

Before I can pull back, a gun goes off and someone falls on top of me.

My arms around Anya flex as I look over my shoulder at Henrietta's partner on my back. I buck her off before turning around and facing Alik standing in the entryway, gun in hand.

He gestures to the knife on the floor at my feet that must've fallen out of the bitch's grasp when he shot her.

"Good thing you had backup," he says, emotionless.

I close my eyes and sigh before nodding my thanks.

Why is the little shit always right?

One side of his lips lifts in a smirk as he walks to retrieve the knife, then he goes to help Elira. I finish with Anya's ankles before taking his place.

"You're going to be okay," I say to her, inspecting the cuts as I lay her on the carpet. She winces but doesn't protest.

When she looks away from me, it's like a fresh wave of pain comes over her. "The hit was on my family."

I busy myself studying her wounds to avoid her eyes. "I know. But they're safe. They were hiding in a root cellar when our guys found them."

I feel her gaze shoot to me, but it's still hard to look.

I'm sorry.

I'm so sorry.

This is all my fault.

"We found the hitman," Alik pipes in. "He's been handled. Your family is safe."

She lets out a long sigh that ends on a sob, and *now* I have no choice but to look at her.

"I'm so sorry," I whisper, rightfully ashamed. "Elira, I never would have intentionally put your family in danger."

She nods like she understands, and when she looks at Anya, guilt crosses her expression. "I'm sorry too."

I follow her gaze. Anya is staring at Tanner, but when she feels us looking at her, she comes to us and drops to her knees. Elira sits up and puts her arm around her, painful as it may be, and I do the same.

We lock eyes, each of us exchanging the guilt we feel.

In the end, it doesn't matter. We're alive, all of us. We're going to be okay.

I love you, she mouths to me, then smiles like my expression amuses her.

I love you too.

We sit for a few more minutes before loading up in the back of Alik's car and driving far away from the house Henrietta rented for the occasion.

* * *

WHEN WE'RE BACK HOME and Elira is stitched up—courtesy of Zinovy—I sit down next to her on my bed, my heart in my throat. After everything, I didn't know I was capable of more fear.

"Tomorrow, I will get you your plane to Albania," I say to Elira, taking her hand. "If you can wait until then."

She stares up at the ceiling like she's lost in her head. "I've been thinking about that."

I clear my throat. "Oh?"

"I'm anxious to see my family and prefer not to wait another day."

I nod my understanding and start to get up to make the call, my anxiety about her never coming back a fist in my chest.

"And before you offer, I don't want you to come with me. You'll be far too busy here."

I pause, my gut roiling as I sit back down and stare at her. "I'm not too busy to go with you."

"Yes, you are."

"Busy with what?"

Finally, she looks at me. "You need to convince the rest of your brothers to embrace Anthony. Albanian weddings are a big deal, and I'm not letting some petty feud gain more attention than my *very expensive* dress."

I don't realize my eyes are narrowed until they soften, and my mouth opens.

Her lips quirk.

"What?" I ask because I'm at a loss for words.

Her face starts to fall, but before it can, I open my mouth again.

"I mean, I… Are you saying you want to get married?"

She shrugs shyly. "We've been fake married for a while now. I just thought… I mean…"

"Elira Martin."

She closes her mouth as I take her hand.

This isn't how I would've done this. I would've bought a ring. I would've reserved the nicest table at the finest restaurant in Vegas. I would've done … more.

But somehow, this is better. If we waited another day, it would never be the same.

"Will you marry me?"

She bites her lip as if she's trying to fight a smile when she nods, and then she reaches over to the nightstand and pulls a diamond ring from the drawer. It isn't the same one as before. This one is...

Jesus Christ.

"We already have a ring," she offers with an amused grin.

I take it and chuck it across the room, then shake my head while slowly inching my lips closer to hers. "You're a fucking lunatic."

Her teeth shine with a smile as her eyes close. "But you love it."

Yeah. Yeah, I kind of do.

EPILOGUE

ELIRA

"*I* guess he's already paid the dowry," Asher mutters, her jaw working as she gazes around the back room of the banquet hall in disapproval. Her arms are crossed over her chest, and her thin brows are nearly touching.

She's referring to the money Maksim deposited into Mami's account a month ago, before we were even engaged.

I turn back to the mirror with a smile. "We're not that traditional."

"Oh, so should we give it back, then?"

My nose crinkles as I snicker, smoothing an imaginary stray hair back into the updo that took an hour and a half to perfect.

"What's so funny?" She cocks her hip out like the drama queen she is.

When I meet her eyes in the mirror, a surge of joy overtakes me.

Back home, back *before*, there were times I thought I could kill her. We fought like crazy, but having her here these past few weeks… I don't know if it'll ever get old. And I don't think I can ever go back to the way things used to be. When I look at her, I see a gift I'll never take for granted another day in my life.

"Maksim is family now, *zemra*. Give the man a chance."

Her lips purse as she swings her head away, freshly-curled, brunette locks swaying. "Maybe him. *Maybe*. But not the sister. She's tactless."

"Yeah?" I shrug and apply powder to a brush before dabbing my face. "She said you're a *fucking cunt*."

Asher's jaw drops in shock as her head swings back my way, and I laugh while dipping the brush in more powder.

"See what I mean?" She throws out her arms. "Mami would scrub my tongue with soap if I said such a thing."

"I know, I can still taste it."

"Then how can you condone it?" she demands like it's a criminal offense. If she knew about the criminal offenses I *do* condone, she'd really freak.

But that isn't what this is about. She was always going to find something wrong with my new family. She just needs time.

"Maksim doesn't parent that way."

"He doesn't *parent* at all."

"Then you two should get along well." I turn to her and wink, but she doesn't react to it.

Her pretty brown eyes glisten as she looks at me seriously. "Are you happy here?"

My smile falls slowly, and I turn toward her before nodding. "Of course, I am." I gesture to my dress, one far superior to the one I came to America in. The engagement ring on my hand is fit for a queen, and despite me insisting we had a perfectly good ring already, this one wasn't stolen. It was chosen, just for me. Not earned, just gifted. Maksim doesn't make me feel like I have to earn anything. Maksim makes me feel like I've already completed everything in the world I set out to do. Maksim makes me feel whole.

"Look at me. Don't I look happy?" I ask, unsure what she sees.

Tears well in her eyes, and her lips twist to one side as she looks away and nods. Seeing the hurt on her face, I understand. She just misses me. She misses me the way I miss her, only she isn't the one who left.

I open my mouth, ready to say more, but she comes to me and throws her arms around my waist, hugging me so tightly, my lips part with surprise. My eyes close with a sigh as I lay my cheek on her head and hug her back.

When she pulls away, she looks at a scar on my chest that I worked hopelessly to cover up. Her fingers run over it before she looks me in the eyes.

"You look beautiful."

* * *

"*You look beautiful.*"

I shiver as Maksim's warm breath kisses my neck, his fingers entwining with mine as we come together for our first dance.

"You're a sight for sore eyes yourself." I whisper back to him as the music starts to play. It's a song Mami picked out, one she and my father used to listen to with me when I was a little girl. I never plan on telling them the truth about him. He isn't worth the heartache. He isn't even worth spoiling a song over.

So now, with my feet moving with my husband's and all our loved ones watching, I let the music sweep me away.

Something brushes my back, and I lift my head up as money starts to rain over us, a wedding tradition I neglected to tell Maksim about.

I glance at the guests doing the tossing then look at Maksim with a smile. "How the hell did you—"

"Mami," he interrupts, reading my mind.

I laugh under my breath. "We don't need the money."

He shrugs. "Neither do they. Tradition is tradition."

Without warning, he twirls me, making me let out a tiny gasp before I recover, and cheers ring out. When he rolls me into him, he whispers in my ear. "Do you think I'm not going to get my turn? I have traditions of my own, *lislchka*."

"Oh, do you now?"

"Mm-hmm."

"And I suppose these are wedding night traditions?"

His hand subtly curves over my waist. "*Mm-hmm.*"

We move together, my neck craning to look at him as I smirk. "Tradition is tradition."

When his lips spread into a stupid grin, my heart floods. He's a liar. A deceptive, manipulative, dangerous man.

But fuck, he is mine.

"I love you," I say to him in case my vows didn't cut it.

His grin falls as his gaze drops to my lips. "I love you too, *lislchka*."

* * *

THANK you so much for your interest in *Maksim*! I'm thrilled to have introduced you to the world of the Petrov Bratva, and I hope you're ready for more.

The next book up is ALIK, a twisted dark romance between Alik and his neighbor across the hall. He moved next door to her six months ago because she's the daughter of a DEA agent the Bratva wants to keep an eye on. Little does he know when he's ordered to kill her that she's been stalking him for months, but when he learns of her obsession, well … things get a whole lot more complicated.

If you like strange characters who might be a bit loony, this one's for you!

"PUT THE KNIFE DOWN, OLIVE."

She lowers her eyes to the blade, then gives me a challenging stare. "Why?"

When I don't answer, she laughs. "Am I scaring you, baby?"

Get it here.

THANK YOU

What a wonderful way to kick off the series! *Maksim* was so much fun to write. I absolutely loved the fire between Maksim and Elira, and although it included such dark subject matter, I found myself cracking up while writing them.

Even more fun than writing this story was plotting it. Getting to know the characters is often my favorite part of the process, but for this book, my enjoyment went even deeper. Learning about Albanians, their interesting history along with their culture, their traditions, their *food* was a treat I'll never forget. I even learned how to make a few recipes, including tavë cosi, the national dish which I would recommend to everyone I know. Elira inspired me, and I hope her strength inspired you too.

If you enjoyed *Maksim*, please consider leaving a review or shooting me an email. I love hearing what readers have to say <3

After that, sign up for my newsletter at nicolecypher.com for my FREE bully romance, Vicious Knight, as well as exclusive bonus chapters and updates on upcoming novels and giveaways.

    With love, always,

    Nicole

FREE NEWSLETTER EXCLUSIVE

Vicious Knight

Everyone has secrets...

What do you do to the person who learns yours?

I'll tell you what I did. I went after her.

I **wrecked** her credibility.

I **destroyed** her friendships.

I **ruined** her reputation.

And she responded in the most foolish way possible. She fought back.

My last name might be Knight, but she's the furthest thing from being rescued.

This book contains scenes and situations that may be triggering for some. Reader discretion is advised.

ALSO BY NICOLE CYPHER

This list was compiled at the time of publishing. For a comprehensive list, check out Nicole's website

Gruco Crime Family Series:

HIS PROMISE

HIS PET

HIS PRIZE

HIS PUPPET

HIS PROPERTY

HIS PASSEROTTA

Las Vegas Petrov Bratva:

MAKSIM

ALIK

VITALY

LUKA

ARSENI

NIKITA

Liberating Deceit:

CAGING LIBERTY

TAMING LIBERTY

CLAIMING LIBERTY

The Darker Places Series:

DESIRED

DEPLORABLE

DETHRONED

DEMOLISHED

JULIUS

Soulless Kings MC:

FENDER

JOKER

Standalone Novels:

UNHINGED

VICIOUS KNIGHT - Newsletter exclusive

ABOUT THE AUTHOR

Nicole Cypher is a hopeless romantic who enjoys reading gruesome thrillers but usually finds herself rooting for the villain. When you combine these traits, you get a dark romance author with a knack for writing plot twists, serial killers, mafia men, troubled heroes, and villains who still manage to win her over in the end.

For access to bonus chapters as well as her free, newsletter-exclusive bully romance, *Vicious Knight*, be sure to sign up for her newsletter at nicolecypher.com. While you're there, browse her full catalogue of books, check out her lists, and shoot her a message via her contact page. She'd love to hear from you.

Milton Keynes UK
Ingram Content Group UK Ltd.
UKHW011912120724
445574UK00004B/209